A TOUCH OF THE SUN

"Can you do that for me?" Jed asks, handing Molly the sunscreen. "I've got the wheel."

She reaches for his knees; they seem the safest place to start. She runs her fingers down each leg, working the cream in. His thighs are pink; they must not burn. She does his arms, too.

"Put some on the back of my neck," he says. "Please."

Molly slips behind him. The warm smell of his body mingles with the smell of coconut. She squeezes cream across her palms.

They are all alone at sea. The horizon sits before them, the sea wide all around them; the boat glides far away from land. Her hands touch his neck, run across his shoulders, flow down his back. The sun is warm.

Later, tacking back toward the island, she still stands behind him, her hands on his shoulders. The sky is beginning to darken. She sees the white lighthouse ahead, looking like a wise old woman rising out of the sea. This island has a secret. She whispers to Jed, "What is it you call this island?"

"We call it paradise."

The word resonates in her head. Paradise. She puts her arms around Jed, kisses him lightly, ruffles his hair. "I think I know why," she says.

IT'S NEVER TOO LATE FOR LOVE AND ROMANCE

JUST IN TIME (4188, $4.50/$5.50)
by Peggy Roberts

Constantly taking care of everyone around her has earned Remy Dupre the affectionate nickname "Ma." Then, with Remy's husband gone and oil discovered on her Louisiana farm, her sons and their wives decide it's time to take care of her. But Remy knows how to take care of herself. She starts by checking into a beauty spa, buying some classy new clothes and shoes, discovering an antique vase, and moving on to a fine plantation. Next, not one, but two men attempt to sweep her off her well-shod feet. The right man offers her the opportunity to love again.

LOVE AT LAST (4158, $4.50/$5.50)
by Garda Parker

Fifty, slim, and attractive, Gail Bricker still hadn't found the love of her life. Friends convince her to take an Adventure Tour during the summer vacation she enjoyes as an English teacher. At a Cheyenne Indian school in need of teachers, Gail finds her calling. In rancher Slater Kincaid, she finds her match. Gail discovers that it's never too late to fall in love . . . for the very first time.

LOVE LESSONS (3959, $4.50/$5.50)
by Marian Oaks

After almost forty years of marriage, Carolyn Ames certainly hadn't been looking for a divorce. But the ink is barely dry, and here she is already living an exhilarating life as a single woman. First, she lands an exciting and challenging job. Now Jason, the handsome architect, offers her a fairy-tale romance. Carolyn doesn't care that her ultra-conservative neighbors gossip about her and Jason, but she is afraid to give up her independent life-style. She struggles with the balance while she learns to love again.

A KISS TO REMEMBER (4129, $4.50/$5.50)
by Helen Playfair

For the past ten years Lucia Morgan hasn't had time for love or romance. Since her husband's death, she has been raising her two sons, working at a dead-end office job, and designing boutique clothes to make ends meet. Then one night, Mitch Colton comes looking for his daughter, out late with one of her sons. The look in Mitch's eye brings back a host of long-forgotten feelings. When the kids come home and spoil the enchantment, Lucia wonders if she will get the chance to love again.

COME HOME TO LOVE (3930, $4.50/$5.50)
by Jane Bierce

Julia Delaine says good-bye to her skirt-chasing husband Phillip and hello to a whole new life. Julia capably rises to the challenges of her reawakened sexuality, the young man who comes courting, and her new position as the head of her local television station. Her new independence teaches Julia that maybe her time-tested values were right all along and maybe Phillip does belong in her life, with her new terms.

Available wherever paperbacks are sold, or order direct from the Publisher. Send cover price plus 50¢ per copy for mailing and handling to Penguin USA, P.O. Box 999, c/o Dept. 17109, Bergenfield, NJ 07621. Residents of New York and Tennessee must include sales tax. DO NOT SEND CASH.

CALL IT PARADISE

MARY JANE LLOYD

ZEBRA BOOKS
KENSINGTON PUBLISHING CORP.

One

Molly tucks her thumb under the strap of the Coach bag on her shoulder. The bright sun and warm breeze propel her down Madison Avenue. The street swings like a party: smiling couples arm in arm, coats unbuttoned. Winter is yesterday. Molly wishes she could shed her life like winter and start again or back up fifteen years.

She wishes he would call. The man at the window. She saw him only minutes, maybe five; they talked. His image sits inside her head, wakes her in the morning and lingers as she goes to sleep. She glances at the men walking toward her down the street. Will she react to one of them the way she did to him?

She swings her arms and swerves around the talking couples blocking the flow of strollers. The traffic light has changed; she zips before the coming cars. He stood before her desk, one hand in his pocket, a pleading semigrin across his face. They exchanged information—that was all.

She scans the shops along the avenue and stops. Her hand goes to her head, her fingers through her hair. She laughs: the restaurant is behind her, a half a block away. Molly threads her way back between the window-shoppers and pulls the handle of the door. Inside, the chatter is like coins on glass.

"Good morning, Olga." Her hand touches the woman's arm. "Is my sister here?"

A grin sweeps across the woman's flat, broad face. "Good to see you again. She's at the table beside the wall."

Molly follows Olga's glance across the bobbing people, across the yellows, pinks, and greens: a spring surprise in New York City. She sees Grace wrapped in pink and waving. Molly pulls her bag from side to front and steps hips first between the tables. Grace is waiting, birdlike, chin up, one hand outstretched.

"That pink looks great on you. Perfect with your chocolate hair."

"Chocolate hair?" Grace takes a strand and twists it.

"What's new? Is Harlan grinding away at the office?"

"He's grinding away at home. I can't go to the museum today. How's Porter?"

Molly spreads the napkin on her lap. "He's fine, I guess."

"Haven't you seen him? How about tonight?"

"Probably." She watches the waiter fill the water glasses. "We had dinner Wednesday."

The waiter interrupts and asks about drinks, white wine, would they like borscht, as usual.

"Is it still the best borscht west of Kiev?" Molly asks.

"Best borscht anywhere." His eyes grin above his bushy mustache.

"I'll have it and a glass of chardonnay. You, Grace?"

"That's fine." Grace picks up her water glass. "Did Porter say anything?"

"About what?"

"I think he's going to propose."

Molly crosses her legs and leans forward. "Propose? What are you talking about? He's been married once."

"I want you to marry him."

"That would be good for you and Harlan, my marrying a partner in his law firm."

"It's good for you. Molly, you don't want to be single forever. It's now or never."

Molly sips the wine. "You hate to see your older sister free and reckless."

"I hate to see my older sister unhappy. Porter would be perfect."

"That's what you think."

"That's what I know. We've saved you before. Shall I mention Jacques. He was going to heal your wounds when you lost the job at Hopper/Wang/McGrath. Did he set you up in a new business the way Harlan did?"

"I didn't lose that job. I quit."

"You wouldn't quit. You loved that job. It was your dream since you were ten."

Molly pulls her jacket off and drops it on the chair beside her. She runs her fingers across the moisture on the water glass.

"Molly, listen to me. Porter is a sensible, responsible, adult man. Not like Jacques. He divorced his wife. Not like Jacques. He is—"

"Stop it. I know the litany, Porter is rich, Porter is perfect, Porter is—"

"The man you should marry." Grace leans across the table. "Or are you still looking for the scruffy artist without a penny, the farmer boy who rolls you in the hayloft."

"Are you referring to Rudy? That was years ago."

"I hated going to Grandpa's house with you. You would run off with Rudy and I would—"

"You were a baby. I adored Rudy."

"This is serious. You are in love with Porter and you know it."

"I am?"

"You're sleeping with him, aren't you?"

"We're friends and yes, we sleep together."

"Sounds like marriage to me."

Molly glances around the room. She watches Grace eating. She sighs. "I don't know. I want a man that gets me in the gut."

"What does that mean?"

"You know. A guy who walks into the room and . . ."

"How about having a child? Being a mother?"

"I think it's too late for that."

"It isn't but you need to hurry. I'll get pregnant, too. We'll have little girls who will be best friends."

Molly scoops the soup. Her eyes sting. She breaks off a piece of the black bread and stuffs it in her mouth.

Grace wrinkles her forehead. "I have it all planned.

We'll share a summerhouse, our children will play together. I know Porter will be a super uncle . . ."

Molly follows a woman walking through the tables hand in hand with a little girl. She looks at Grace. "That would be nice." She pushes away the empty bowl. "Do you really think Porter will propose?"

"The rumor is he's hooked on a large apartment on the upper East Side."

"For himself?"

"That's what I assume. Porter won't stay single."

"No, he won't."

"You could quit working and paint again."

Molly drains the wineglass. "I could. I hate the job I am doing, no challenge left."

"Drop some hints."

"I can't do that."

"Give him an ultimatum, marriage or you break up."

"Mom told me to marry a tall man."

"Do we have a deal?"

"A deal? What do you mean?"

"Shall I speak to him?"

"You do and I'll kill you."

"Start looking for the gun."

Molly picks up her jacket. "I didn't tell you. I have a new guy."

"If you have a new guy, I'll look for a gun." Grace takes the check. "Listen to me. Porter Drummond will become a senior partner in Harlan's firm. I want you to be his wife."

"Thanks, Grace. Give me the check. The lunch is on me."

*   *   *

Back on the street, Molly holds her jacket by a finger, letting it flop against her back. She crosses Madison Avenue and takes a side street toward Fifth. She lingers, surveying the town houses behind the iron fences and boxed hedges: pale stone houses, curved windows. Marriage could feel good, good to have a proper home. She could sell her business and paint again and maybe even have a child. Women her age do, nowadays.

She stops and cranes her neck to see beyond the tied-back curtains on the long windows. The ceilings must be edged with eggs and darts like pictures in an English country magazine. The beds, large and carved and covered all in linen. She tugs her arms into her jacket sleeves.

Her mother would like Porter. He is not unlike the boy her mother made her date. "He's so polite," her mother said of Ryan. "He doesn't honk his horn, or drape his arm around your shoulder. He doesn't drive too fast. Ask Ryan to the party, not Tommy."

Tommy was the one who pushed himself against her when they danced, chewed her ear, drove baseballs to the outfield, and recited poetry. Tommy talked of climbing mountains, riding horses, and love, and Tommy cried the day he left to move out West. His leaving freed her of her guilt. It's easier to like the ones your family likes. With Tommy, guilt was always there and family seemed so far away.

She pushes back her hair and races for the corner

and the light; she sees again the face that watched her through the window and feels again the guilt she felt with Tommy.

The museum's steps are hidden by a mass of sprawling bodies, their faces lifted to the sun. She smiles at the banners, like giant wrinkled bed sheets hanging down above the entrance, red, bright yellow, pale sky blue. Her feet step carefully, finding spaces in the puzzle made by arms, legs, bodies, backpacks, books, and hot dog wrappers.

Inside, she blinks and stops and holds her breath. The great hall feels cold and cavernous and voices echo. She gazes at the ceiling domes, the skylights, and across the huge expense of space. The Metropolitan Museum of Art has always felt like home, but not today. There is an emptiness like the emptiness she feels inside.

She pays and hesitates before the stairs and then turns right and walks along the slick, hard floor. She wants a place to sit and think and be alone. She goes through galleries of mummies, huge figures of Egyptian men and women, stone walls etched with hieroglyphics. The sign is on the wall: Temple of Dendur. The room is like a place for giant birds, domed with glass and open like a plastic cave. Molly feels like a bug emerging from beneath a rock or Alice in a Wonderland. Her heels lift off the floor in silence; she tiptoes, finding the perfect place to sit.

Mother knew that she was dying. "Your father's gone. It's time for me. I'd like to see you marry, see your children. I'd like to be around to see your ads on television and in magazines. It will not happen.

Be friends with Grace and have your children close together."

They were having lunch right here at the Met. Molly assumed that she would marry soon, like Grace. She loved her job. The bad part hadn't started. Grace is wrong: Jacques had saved her, welcomed her, loved her. She never knew he had a wife.

She never knew her mother's death would be so painful. She hadn't lived with her for years, and yet it left her with a need for constancy, something solid in her life. Grace is all she has. Grace and Harlan. Maybe Grace is right and she should marry Porter.

The stillness of the room is nice. She follows sun spots patterned on the floor. The tiny temple exudes strength, survival, toughness. She is tough. A dam broke over her when Jacques said he was going back to France. She misses him, the fire in her gut, the sense of who she was.

The last four years have been all gray, the color of the coals when all the heat is gone. What would her mother say? Marry Porter, be a woman with a home and husband? Her mother had that life . . . or did she? There had been another husband before Molly's father, the one who died, a traffic accident. Her mother told her, the night before Grace married. "Jack rode a motorcycle, rode it fast sometimes. I rode on back but not this time. He swerved around a truck, they said he never saw the curve. He flew like he had wings. That's how he was, a man with wings." Molly thinks about her mother's face, the pinkness of it as she spoke. It is hard to see her mother on a motorcycle, with another husband not Molly's father, a man who rode a motorcycle, a man with wings.

Outside again, she notices most people on the steps are gone. The sun is down behind the massive building. The air is cool. Molly walks uptown. The buses, taxicabs, the hundred-year-old sycamores, the old stone wall, Central Park. At Eighty-sixth, she crosses Fifth and starts the long walk east to her apartment. Porter will have called.

She checks again the faces of the men. His name was Jed. It's on the card that sticks out of her wallet every time she opens it. He said he'd call; he needed someone soon.

Her desk was by the plate glass window on Forty-second Street, not like a bank but like a clothing store. People stopped and watched. She never cared, hardly noticed, except the time that Jed was there. She felt his look before she raised her head and smiled. Before he smiled. Before she blushed and looked back at the screen of her computer. She felt him leave and stood and stretched her neck and looked both ways along the street. She put a Tic Tac in her mouth and then she felt his presence in the room, beside her desk.

"I saw you from outside and wondered—"

"How did you get in?"

"I found the door. I was watching you."

"I know."

"You're working on a Mac?"

"Yes. Doing a newsletter."

"Using PageMaker?"

"Yes."

"Do you work here at the bank full-time?"

"Why do you ask . . . ?"

"I need someone who knows PageMaker. Someone part-time."

"Oh?"

"I'll give you my card. Do you do other jobs?"

"I free-lance. This is one of many clients."

"How do I find you?"

"I have a card."

"Do you have time . . . soon?"

"Not really . . . but . . ."

"I need something done in the next few weeks."

"Are you a—"

"Advertising. I have my own agency. It's fun, you'll like it."

Molly stares at the faces walking toward her. He hasn't called. Perhaps he lost her card.

She walks faster. She wants to be inside, back inside her studio apartment, the place her mother wanted her to live. "Move to Grace's. It's safer than the Village." Grace was getting married. She sees the building, big and white and hard: a corporate kind of building, like Grace.

The doorman holds the door. "Lovely day, Miss Mitchell." She gets her mail and shuffles through it in the elevator, a tiny space redolent of lingering gardenias. Smells of curry fill the hallway. She struggles with the locks and flips the light switch just inside the door and glances at the phone machine. Four calls. She fills a glass with ice and

water, stirs it with her finger, pushes down her leggings, steps out of them. The light blinks four; one
is Porter, maybe two. One Grace. But four . . .

Two

Molly stands on one foot watching the message tape rewind. Four calls.

"Jed Saunders calling. Remember me?" She slumps against the wall. "We met through the window of the bank. I need you next week, if possible. My number's 638-9040. That's area code 718."

She slurps the water in the glass, splashing it down her shirt.

"Fun lunch." It's Grace's business voice. "Work on Porter. Do it tonight. Call if anything happens."

Molly rubs her arm across the wetness and reaches for the rewind button.

"Jed Saunders again. Did I leave my number? 718-638-9040. Office phone is 884-9898. That's in Manhattan. Get back to me this weekend if possible."

She searches for a pencil.

"Porter. I'm at the office. What about tonight?"

Molly flops on the couch and picks at the plant on the coffee table. He hasn't lost her card. She crumples a dead leaf, springs from the couch, and goes to the windows. Next week—impossible. She bounds back across the room to the machine, presses rewind, and pushes up the volume

Jed's voice bounces from the walls. She grabs the pillow from the couch, hugs it, throws it, kicks it. He needs her—next week. She swings open the closet door and looks in the full-length mirror tacked on the back. Her legs are bare and long and white. She tugs the edge of her underpants high above her hip, pulling the fabric tight, taut against her pubic bone. His name is Jed. She goes back to the phone machine; she needs to hear his voice again.

"Remember me?" It's the window at the bank, his face, his smile. "We met through the window." She sprawls on the couch. "I need you." She'll find a way.

The phone rings; she leaps. "Molly, where have you been? What about tonight?"

"Porter, I—"

"Did you get my message? I thought you'd call."

"I just got in. I had lunch with Grace and went to the Met. How are you?"

"It's after six."

"I know."

"Shall I come up for supper?"

"Here?"

"Or my place, if you prefer."

"I have no food."

"I'll stop for Chinese. See you in thirty minutes."

Thirty minutes: no time to think, no time for Jed, no time to call him back or think of what to do. She opens the refrigerator and scans the shelves: two cans of beer, no wine. Underneath the sink she finds a bottle and puts it in the freezer, then takes the pillow from the floor and sets it on the couch, drops the blinds and lights the lamp with the pink shade. The room feels intimate and cozy. She glances at her portrait on the wall, done by her in college. Her hair was long.

She runs the shower and twists the head to make the water come in spurts. Jed. What made him stop and watch her through the window? What made her blush? Perhaps he's just a weirdo; she never thought of that, just handed him her card. Perhaps she shouldn't call back. Grace would not approve. The soap is lemon cream; the lather covers up nerves that jump like blinking Christmas lights. It's good she's seeing Porter, good to have distraction; she needs a man. The message on the phone was Jed. "I need you soon," he said.

She pushes off the shower and rubs the towel roughly on her skin. Monday's job is at Pace Lewiston; it will take a week. She rubs the towel on her hair. She could work Monday night, arrive at noon, and see Jed Monday morning. That's it: Monday morning, do it right away and get it over with.

She stands before the mirror, drops the towel, and sees her body, toe to head, her slimness, small breasts, white skin. A flash of anger catches in her throat. It's quick and wrapped in sadness and carries with it images of Hopper/Wang/McGrath.

She wraps the towel back around her body. She must call Jed. The number's on the phone machine but where's the pencil? The tape whirrs as papers tumble to the floor. She dials. The ringing's like a screw winding up her heart, two, three, four. "Jed Saunders here. Do it at the beep."

"Molly Mitchell returning your call." The receiver feels like lead. She should have said, "Call me tomorrow," or "I'll call tomorrow," or "I'll come by Monday morning." She goes into her closet and pulls the hangers across the bar. She knows he'll call tonight when Porter's here.

She bites the edges of her nail and finds her cherry-colored jumpsuit, her lavender and lace bikinis and brushes midnight blue along her lashes. Her stomach whirls with butterflies; she feels the way she felt when Jacques came into the studio. She glances toward the phone machine, smiles at it.

The buzzer rings. "Mr. Drummond's coming up." Standing by the open door, she listens for the elevator. It stops. She hears it open, sees Porter emerge and walk toward her down the hall, a briefcase in one hand, flowers in the other. He is attractive in a legal sort of way, a look that reads as smart.

"I stopped at Chin Chow." He hands her tulips wrapped in tissue paper. "They are going to deliver."

He leans his briefcase up against the wall, takes off his jacket, pulls off his tie.

"Working hard?" She smells the flowers.

"The SEC is getting out of hand. You think you've got it right and then they change their minds." He reaches in the closet, takes a hanger, and puts his jacket on it. "The client wants it done by Friday. The SEC makes that impossible." He drapes his tie around the jacket. "Might try going to Washington on Monday. How are you?"

His lips kiss hers; he pats her arm above her elbow. The kiss feels like a butterfly that drops and flies away again. He sinks onto the couch and sighs and lifts his leg as if it were an iron bar, and lays it on his knee.

Molly puts the tulips in a vase. "Want some wine?"

"Got scotch? With a tad of water."

Molly searches in the closet. "Will vodka do or shall I call?"

"Vodka's fine. Keep it neat, one ice cube."

Molly pours the vodka in a glass. She hands the glass to him across the sofa back. Her fingers linger on his neck, on the edges of his close-cut hair.

He pulls away. "Your hand is cold. How's Grace?"

"She's okay." She steps backward to the counter and screws the top back on the vodka.

"We should see them soon—all go to the theater." He sips from his glass. "What could we see?"

"I'll talk to Grace." She looks from Porter to the vodka bottle, shrugs, then works the top back off and fills a glass and reaches in the freezer for the ice. The cubes slosh as she walks back to the couch.

"This vodka is exactly what I need," Porter says.

The buzzer rings. Chin Chow.

"I'll get it." Porter hauls his body, six feet three, off the couch and gets his wallet from his jacket in the closet. Molly watches, tasting vodka in her mouth. Porter hands dollars to the man and takes the two brown paper bags. She pulls her knees up toward her chin, sinking in the cushions that feel like giant marshmallows. Her arms and chest tingle and her face feels flushed.

"I'll have another drink, mind?" He stands by the counter.

"No." Her mother would like Porter; he's polite. She holds the vodka in her mouth, savoring the stinging on her tongue.

Porter relaxes on the couch beside her. She reaches for his hand. He squeezes it and lets it go. "My folks are coming into town. I want you to spend some time with them."

"When?"

"In two weeks."

"I've never been to Minneapolis."

"You'll like it. I'll take you someday soon."

Molly pictures the mantel in his co-op with the silver-framed photograph: the house is red brick, three-storied with a sloping green lawn. His parents stand in front of it. Molly untangles the foot she sits on and topples onto Porter. "Oops." She straightens up. "Should we have dinner?"

"Not yet."

She tucks her foot back under her and runs her hand along his arm. "You should get tickets to a show, maybe an opera for your parents. What would they like?" The cotton of his shirt is smooth, like silk, his forearm hard beneath the silkiness.

"They like a lot of things. They like being in New York. I'll talk to them." He drinks and watches her above the glass. "You're very kittenish tonight."

"Kittenish? That's a funny word." She rises from the couch, stands, and looks at him. Her arms reach to the ceiling, like wings lifted from her body, her elbows straining higher than her head. The jumpsuit tightens across her lengthened torso meeting her nipples in a caress of silk on skin. She bends her body over his and puts her lips against the smoothness of his forehead.

"I'm not a kitten," she says, and flops down at the far end of the couch, her back against the arm, her legs across the cushions, making a bridge to Porter. Her toes reach for his thigh; she lies back, aware her nipples make buttons in the fabric.

Porter adjusts his body, turning slightly to face her and stretching his arm along the sofa back. "You're not like Grace, are you?"

"No, I'm not like Grace. Why?"

"No reason I guess."

"Grace says she's the good one, I'm the bad."

"She's the small one, you're the tall one." He laughs and rubs his neck.

"Your wife, how tall was she?"

"Like Grace, I guess." He stands. "We better eat." He walks around the couch.

"Am I too tall for you?"

He bends and kisses her. "You're fine." He laughs again and goes to the refrigerator.

"There's wine in the freezer. Have you ever had a girlfriend tall like me?"

"I don't think so."

"In high school?"

"I didn't have a girlfriend in high school."

"No girlfriend? Were you a nerd?" She leaves the couch and goes and stands behind him.

"I guess."

Her arms wrap around his waist. "I always liked boys like you. The smart ones. You were one of those?" Her fingers trace his backbone.

"I guess I was." He pours the wine in green-stemmed glasses and turns around.

"First in your class?"

"Second."

"You dummy." She looks into his eyes. "I was, too." Her body nestles close to his, she feels his breath against her cheek. She feels her breasts, the silk, his shirt, his chest.

He pulls away, turning to the counter and the brown paper bag and white containers which he takes from the bag and places on the plastic surface.

Molly reaches in the cabinet for two plates and hands the one with yellow cows to Porter. She smells garlic, soy sauce, and orange. He scoops shiny pork and pea pods onto his plate and hands the cardboard box to her. She pushes sticky rice stuck on the spoon, then licks it from her fingers. Sitting at the table with the tulips, she sips the wine and waits for Porter. They eat with chopsticks and talk about the weather and the SEC.

She takes fortune cookies from a tiny paper bag and puts them on the table. "Choose one. If you like the fortune, eat the cookie."

Molly reads her strip of paper: Love will soon unfold—Be Ready. She rolls the paper in a ball, hides it in her hand. "What's yours?"

"Fortune is for those who wait."

"Is that true?"

"Who knows. What about yours?"

"Something about love."

She eats the cookie and takes the dishes to the sink. It's automatic: scraping dishes, running water. Porter moves beside her, dumping cartons and the empty bottle in the garbage. She feels his touch against her back and like a flash of heat she wants his arms; she wants to kiss. She runs her tongue along her lower lip and turns. He's gone. She sees him close the bathroom door. She takes his cookie from the counter and puts it in her mouth.

Down the apartment hallway she carries the brown bags of garbage and dumps them in the chute and puts the empty bottle on the floor. When she returns she finds Porter lying on the couch, shoeless. His eyes are closed.

She goes into the bathroom and runs the comb hard through her hair. The plastic teeth feel good against her scalp. She fills a glass with water and drinks it to the bottom, wishing now she hadn't drunk the vodka.

She sits along the cold hard bathtub edge. Porter's in the living room, lying on the couch. Jed is on the phone machine. She folds her hands and squeezes them together. Grace says she's in love with Porter. In love? In love was Jacques, her teacher, art professor, mentor. Even now, she thinks of him and feels a flush. She posed for him without her clothes. She loved to watch him paint. He taught her how to see, how to draw, how to kiss, how to wallow under the strokes of a man. Making love, he told her, feeds the soul. She rubs her hand across her face.

Porter's in the living room. "You've been sleeping with him for a year," Grace said. She'd known him for months before she did. He'd never asked; she volunteered. Grace told her gossip: Porter's wife had left him for a woman, a fellow lawyer. Grace laughed. Molly winced; she ached for Porter. She yearned to be his ally, his friend, the one to make him feel all right again, a woman he could know and trust. That night she told him she would stay with him, at his house, if he'd like. He held her and trembled and led her to the bedroom and her passion was aroused and ready and she was pleased.

The bathtub rim is hard. She stands, stretches, and pushes the eyelet curtain across the shower bar. She looks in the mirror, combs her hair again, and undoes three top buttons to expose her skin, show her breasts between the open vee. Jacques said never let a man be careless with your body. Sex is sacred, an act that must be honored—a man should treat a woman as he does a holy image. It is she who gives man the entrance to his soul. Be careful and honor the man who gives you pleasure.

The living room is still except for Porter's breathing, heavy, slow. She sits and watches. His face is calm, smooth, with barely any trace of beard. His nose is straight. She'd like to put some putty on his chin. His eyelids flick, then flick again. His fingers, laced, rest on his chest. His feet below his trouser cuffs look warm and woolly in his socks. She might as well be there alone. She looks down at her feet. They're bare. Porter sleeps.

She puts the buttons back inside the buttonholes

then stands and walks around the chair and gazes at the poppy on the wall, red like her, alone like her. She lifts a pair of blinds. The dark is broken by the lights from neighboring apartments. She goes out on the terrace. The tiles shock her feet and soot, like sand, grinds in between her toes. The air is full of smells of cars and dampness from the river. The breeze is cool. Figures walk the entranceway, couples, pairs of people, together in the night.

A horn, a taxi door, echoes in the courtyard. Purple lights shine and blink behind the windows. She sees a person in a chair, the television on, another person stand and walk across the room—silent scenes embedded in the white brick wall. She hears the door. Porter stands beside her.

"I wondered where you were," he says.

"You were sleeping."

"You must be cold." He puts his arm around her waist.

"I was." She snuggles close against his warmth.

"Sorry I fell asleep. I guess I should leave."

She takes his hand and pulls it tight around herself. She feels his lips press on her temple, along the edges of her hair.

"Let's go inside," he says.

He moves directly to the couch and piles all the cushions in a stack against the wall. She watches from the terrace door. He moves the table to the side and pulls the handle, yanking out the hidden bed. He reaches underneath the shade that's on the lamp and clicks it off. The only light comes from the street. She sees him in the shadows. He pulls each pant leg down and lines the creases to each other and drapes them on the straight-back chair. She yearns to feel his body's warmth.

"Take off your clothes," he says as he unbuttons his. Jacques, she thinks, would do it for her. Jacques said making love's a drama, each button is a line of speech.

She waits and watches Porter take the pillows from the closet and pull the pink sheet back. She starts her buttons. He turns his back and puts his thumbs inside the waistband of his shorts. His naked body slips beneath the sheets.

"Molly," he calls.

She drops her clothes and flings herself across the room and in the bed beside him. It's warm. He feels so warm. His skin feels good against her skin. He rolls his body up on top of hers. She feels his knee against her leg, his hand a saucer on her breast. The nipple strains and reaches for the warmth. She wraps her arms around his back and pulls him down. She wants his lips, his mouth on hers. He kisses and her eyes close with the kiss. His legs push in between her legs. She spreads them to accommodate his body, to make his body fit with hers.

He breaks the kiss, and lifts his head. The bottom of his torso sways. Up and down, up and down. She sees his neck, his veins; he moves on his own. She strains her arms to pull him back, to have his mouth again. The only touch is far away, somewhere down below her waist. She feels abandoned, left alone, left out of what he's doing. His movement speeds.

Up, down, up, down. Faster, faster. Stop, she screams inside her head. Stop.

She hears the phone—a ring—another ring. Porter's breath is in her ear, she feels it on her chest. Another ring—a gasping breath—a ring—a groan—a voice speaking in the distance—her voice. She braces. Porter pushes into her. A cry—a groan—the recording of her voice. She pushes with her hips against the heaviness and hears the beep. His body drops upon her, a blanket full of lead. Silence. "I'd like to talk to you." It's Jed.

Porter rolls away. She leaves the bed and wraps a robe around her naked body. She plays with dishes in the sink, and runs a sponge beneath the toaster. Porter's up and getting dressed.

She washes all the glasses, drying each one with a paper towel, liking how the smooth hard surface feels. She puts water in a glass with ice and slowly pours it in her mouth, the coldness numbs, the liquid satisfies a small amount of thirst. She feels his hand pat on her buttocks, his mouth brush on her hair.

"We'll talk sometime next week. Maybe dinner Wednesday." She trails him to the door.

"Good night." He walks away, down the hall. She watches. The briefcase bounces by his side.

Three

Molly watches Porter disappear into the elevator. She listens for the thumping metal door, the groaning motor. Hovering by the door she waits, hesitant to turn around, to see the open bed, the rumpled sheets.

She starts toward the sink, stops, turns, lurches to the bed and grabs the pillow. She shakes it, then waits and listens, looking at the pinkness of the linen case. The refrigerator hums. Her fingers squeeze, tightening on the three-inch hem. The slamming starts. She swings the sack of feathers. She whacks the mattress, whacks the sofa, whacks the other pillow on the bed. She flogs, whips, listens—no sound but humming. A horn outside. The bed's a mass of wrinkled pink, a blur. She tugs the sheets together and rolls them in a ball.

She goes back to the terrace. The wind is cold, her skin is wet. The sky looks dark and far away. She wants to fly, to disappear. Her hands reach up as if to grab the moon.

Porter doesn't mean to hurt; he doesn't understand. She tiptoes back, past the bed and to the bathroom. Water fills the tub, gushing from the faucet hard and fast. She watches as it climbs the hard white shiny sides. She fills a plastic spoon with apple foaming gel and shakes it on the steamy water. One, two, another. She feels the moisture on her face and sees it cloud the mirror.

She puts one foot inside the hot, green water, then the other foot, and bends and slips her body underneath the froth. The heat creeps up her legs, her hips and waist, covering up her breasts. The bubbles make a blanket. She rests her head, her eyelids close. She feels the warmth and smells the apple, baking pie.

It's Grandpa's clapboard house and fields of hay. She's in a tractor at the wheel, thirteen years old and driving on the pasture land. She's milking cows with Rudy and licking sticky fingers. There are plates of sliced tomatoes, newly picked and warm, chewing corn right from the cob out in the field, hiding in the corn, rolling in the corn rows, Rudy there and rolling in the fields with Rudy and sun and summer. Her body drifts. Her toes flick; hot water drips around them. Salty drips run down her cheeks and off her chin.

It's early Monday morning and the phone is ringing. Molly reaches for it from the bed.

"After you left last night, we decided you shouldn't take the job. Don't even go."

Molly rubs her eyes, "What's that, Grace?"

"The whole thing sounds phony. A man you don't even know, barging into the bank and luring you downtown. It worries us. There are too many crazy people in New York."

Molly pushes back the covers, stands, and yawns. "I'll find out, I guess."

"I'm serious. You don't know him. It's not like a referral. Please, Molly, don't go."

"I'm just checking it out; I told you that." Molly pulls the phone cord to the kitchen sink.

"Harlan can run a check."

"It's easier to go myself. Chances are I'll hate it." She spoons coffee in the paper filter and puts water on the stove to boil. "I'll be back at Pace by noon." Molly moves back to the bed.

"Can't you wait a couple days?"

"No, I can't. Thanks for dinner last night. Got to go."

"Wait. Harlan wonders why you need this job at all."

Molly fluffs the duvet.

"He can get you clients, anytime. No need to pick them up on the street."

"Thanks for your concern, but I'm late."

"You never listen."

Through the shower water, Molly hears the phone again. Grace's voice recording. "Where are you? Harlan wants to speak. He says men like this are dangerous."

Molly soaps her hair and faintly catches Harlan on the speaker, "It's not smart, Molly. I can have a report in one or two days. Better safe than sorry."

Water runs through Molly's hair. Grace is there

again. "We care, Molly. Do what Harlan says. I know you're listening."

Molly takes two black skirts, holds up one and then the other, checking them against her body in the mirror. The longer one she hangs back up and finds the shirt with jungle prints in shades of green. She pulls on dark gray stockings, peels them off, and chooses mossy green instead.

She stuffs the paper with the address in her pocket and leaves. After pressing the button for the elevator, she turns around, walks back down the hall, unlocks the door, goes inside, and takes the boiling water from the stove.

As she stands on the subway, fear starts in her fingertips and runs along her arms. Maybe Harlan's right and Jed is just some nut, barging into her office. He said he was in advertising. Advertising what? Advertising is the one job she's avoided. It comes with too much pain, regret, resentment. She once quit the tennis team in high school until her mother told her failure had a creepy way of causing paranoia or paranoia had a creepy way of causing failure but both were things that should be dumped. "Losing is just a way of learning," her mother said. If she had been alive . . .

The train swerves and screeches, bends. Molly grabs the silver pole: Forty-second Street. She stretches on her toes to let the people pass with elbows in her back and feet kicking at her feet. She changes hands. Advertising was her love; is her love. Since Hopper she hardly watches television, at least the stations with the ads. The train smells stuffy, sour stuffy. The doors slide closed; papers open. The car lurches and her hand grabs tighter to the pole. She yearns to be inside an advertising office once again, to get the rush she always gets, the smell of innovation. Jed Saunders's may be nothing but a tiny space, a place that handles sales promotions.

Fear is in her legs. He was looking in the window watching her, a pervert luring her to who knows what. He sounded normal on the phone. "That's great. See you Monday A.M." The train slows, glides, stops: Fourteenth Street. She pushes past the paper readers. The swarm of exiters is single-minded, climbing up the stairs to reach the open air. She loves this part of city life, going with the crowd, people front and back and on all sides, moving all together like a flock of flying birds. The crowd splits on the street, like water splashed. She stops and looks, her vision arcing left to right to find which way is north or south, which way is east or west.

She reads the crumpled paper from her pocket, 147 Fifth at Twentieth. She crosses west, then north, and climbs the two wide steps into Union Square park. The trees are old, big giant oaks in bud and beds of hyacinths in purples, whites, and yellows. There are people everywhere: walking, sitting, sleeping, gazing into space. She glances at her watch, then at a statue of a soldier and a horse.

Walking helps her nerves. Ahead the building looks like Rome, green-roofed and long and low, a public place with tables. She crosses by it to the curb, out of the park, and then across the street. Jacques had loved this part of town: the buildings made by architects who thought that they were sculptors. He's right. Each building is a decorated piece of art. She glances up and looks at buttresses and cornices with scrolls and loopy edges. Ahead's a building striped in green and copper, with columns halfway up, and huge red bricks and windows in a dozen different shapes.

Her eyes dart, drinking in the shapes and colors, hungry to absorb the smorgasbord of detail, like the first time she saw London. This is the old New York, the street built when Otis made the elevator and the city began spreading up as well as north.

She sees herself reflected in a window full of books, a tall woman in a raincoat. She pulls the raincoat off and drapes it on her arm and squints to find the numbers on the building. A body bumps against her side.

"Hey, baby." The voice is deep and slurred.

She moves the raincoat like a shield and spots a deli on the corner. She'll go inside. The door before the deli has a number: 147, the number on the paper. A buzzer and phone hang on the wall. She buzzes, says her name, and pushes on the door. The voice says use the stairs. "It's one flight up."

The room she enters stretches long and narrow and is bathed in light. It's like a picture in a glossy magazine. She smells ink and paint, the greeting of old friends. Green metal-shaded lamps hang by narrow wires projecting white, clean circles on the honey-colored wooden tables. Molly holds her breath. She has entered into whiteness, freedom, an

open space, a studio. There are dabs of hunter green
and lemon yellow, all like poster paint and simple.

Sunshine spreads like theater lighting through the
long, wide windows that stretch the total distance
of the room. Where are the desks, the neat parti-
tions? She sees tables, stools, lights, and giant posters on the walls.

She runs her hand across a tabletop and watches
two young men who sit at drafting tables underneath
a poster of a train with mountains and large letters:
See Norway, Your Way. Her hand goes to her heart.
She waits, afraid to break the spell, absorbing the
feeling she has just come home.

One man gets up and walks half the distance to
her. "Molly?" he calls. He wears a T-shirt with the
letters B A M across the front.

"Yes, I'm Molly Mitchell."

"Jed's in his office. Go on in." He motions to a
door across the floor.

Molly doesn't move.

"It's okay, he's on the phone. If you don't barge
in, he'll never get off."

She walks toward the oak door with the rippled
glass on top. Her hand goes up to knock. She hesitates, then grabs the knob and pushes, walks inside,
and drops her coat and briefcase on the couch beside
the door. She does not look at Jed. He's at his desk
and on the phone. He talks and laughs; she smooths
her hair and looks straight out the windows, long
windows, a match to those she saw before. Her heart
feels weighted in her chest. She feels his gaze, feels
it down her arms.

She sinks into the couch and turns toward him. He smiles. She freezes like a child in a game. The walls, the floor, the chairs around the desk lose focus. She's a person in a body not her own, sitting on a couch, smiling at a person at a desk who is talking on the phone. The skin on her forearms feels stiff. He drops his gaze to his pencil and writes.

The couch is old, the leather crinkled, the arms are oak and worn. Her legs, longer than the space between the seat and floor, slant to one side. She tugs the bottom of her skirt and feels his staring eyes. His grin attracts, pulls her in the way a prancing puppy might. She makes a survey of the room: It's oak and white and warm with wooden floors with grooves. She combs her fingers through her hair and listens.

"We are talking to *Travel & Leisure*. I have someone working on a piece about the North Cape, the Lofoten Wall, those great fishing villages, kind of like *Babette's Feast*. Yeh, that was Denmark, but it looks the same. Great film. Those places do exist, Svolvaer, the fjords slicing into barren cliffs."

Molly scrutinizes the poster on the wall, a boat, a village, the tag: See Norway, Your Way. It looks like *Babette's Feast,* a movie she remembers, a movie that she liked.

Jed turns his head, he's looking out the window. His profile has a hard-edged look, carved jawline, square chin, unruly hair, chestnut; not thin and blond like Porter's but long, running down his neck. She follows the pencil in his hand; he taps it, chews it, writes.

"This piece will have the reader picking up the phone. *T & L* loves Norway, high-latitude regions. They're crazy about Candace, too, the writer." He leans back in his chair, points to her, then to himself. She smiles and looks down at the floor.

"I know they'll run it, January, February, when people plan their summer travel."

She likes the room, the long oak table for a desk, the hanging lamps. She likes the chairs with slatted backs and leather seats. She moves her feet and slants her legs the other way.

"We need to support the story with a good-size ad, a page perhaps, four color, run it three times." She puts her hands together, taps her fingers on each other, and grins and pulls the bottom of her skirt from underneath her.

His hand goes up, one finger points; a signal for one minute. She points around the room and makes a thumbs-up sign. He does the same and points to her. She looks back at the windows and feels a twinge from neck down to her legs. Her heart feels full of liquid, a feeling that her life, this very moment, is just right. A slice of sun, ruler-shaped, lies across the floor. She traces it and runs her hand across the leather on the seat. The cracks and roughness scratch her palm. He finishes the call.

"You're here." His fingers lace behind his head. He leans back in his chair.

"I'm here."

"I'm glad you're here." He picks up papers from his desk and slides a chair in front of where she sits.

"Things are getting crazy. We're taking off. Up to now, I've been a one-man band but that's about to change. We use contractors except for those two guys out front. Joe is still at Pratt. I need to get an art director. I'm a word person. I'm fussy. The person's got to be just right. You'll be a great help. What do you think?" He gestures with his arm around the room.

"This office is wonderful." She slopes her knees the other way. "I like it."

"Me too. I've worked in that bank building kind of place. It's no fun. Smells funny."

"You're right." She laughs. "It does."

"We can smell funny when the guys downstairs cook curried chicken."

"How long have you been here?"

"Almost a year." His T-shirt's muted plum.

"Where were you before?"

"I was at Dane Hollenbeck."

"This is quite a change."

"You know them?"

"Of course."

"I'm not a big agency person." He puts his jeans-clad leg across his knee and rubs his hand along his sock. "I like being in charge. Choosing creative people to work with. Getting clients who take chances and no bigwigs screaming about billings. It's great. You must feel the same way, being your own boss?"

"Yes." She notices the light brown hair between his sock and cuff. "I couldn't have come otherwise. Especially on short notice."

Jed taps his fingers on his shoe. "I know you went out of your way to come today. You know what it's like to run your own shop."

"Yes." She folds her hands around her knees. "You did sound desperate on the phone."

"I am."

The line of sun seems longer on the floor. Their glances meet. "How big is the job?"

"I'm not sure." He flips the papers that he holds. "I've got a great setup for you. Bought you everything you need. The latest there is and, if there's something missing, the store is a block away. Come, let's take a look."

They go through the room she entered. The BAM T-shirt calls out, "Phone call, Jed."

Jed starts toward the desk, then stops. "Take a message."

She follows Jed along the wall of windows, by an elevator, and through another door of oak and crinkled glass.

Inside the room, Molly stops and gasps. Two walls are all windows, curving at the corner. Large windows letting in the panorama of the world outside. "This room is wrapped in city. It's wonderful."

"Here's the Mac, a laser printer, software, the works." Jed goes to a table in the corner.

Molly stays by the door looking at the buses, taxis, buildings. "I'm usually shut up in a cubicle. This is amazing."

"Nice, isn't it?" He stands by her. "I love coming here."

"I can't believe this view." She turns and looks at him. His eyes look back and do not move away. She pushes hair behind her ear. "I guess you'd better show me what to do."

Jed puts the papers on the long oak table in the middle of the room and hooks his thumbs inside his belt. "It's a presentation, a proposal, a new client. Really an old friend with a new product. I want to get some things on paper to talk about, make a plan. I think it should look good."

"Looking good makes a difference." Molly goes to the table and lifts a paper from the stack.

"I've written down ideas from time to time. It's a collection, a mess." He laughs. "I was hoping you could sort it out."

"I probably can. Give me some background."

He points her to a chair and leans against the table. "Bill's an engineer and a biologist, brilliant guy. It's biodegradable plastic, new idea, not that other stuff. The polymer comes from potatoes, not petroleum. He's partners with his wife. I love that."

Jed walks across the floor. "It's perfect. Having a smart wife you can work with. I've seen too many guys get closer to the woman they work with rather than the woman they sleep with and then they wind up sleeping . . . You know what I mean, don't you?"

Molly nods her head. "I do."

"Neo-Plastics has a lot of backing. We're the image makers. We're developing a strategy. That's what this is all about."

"I get it. Let me look it over."

"You're smart, right?" He folds his arms and half sits on the window ledge.

"Right." She laughs. "Leave me with it and we'll talk. Give me an hour."

"Anything you don't understand, barge in."

"I will."

He leaves and pulls the door behind him, then opens it again. "Do you want coffee? We get it downstairs."

"No, I'm fine."

Molly takes the chair beside the table. Her eyes move back and forth between the papers in her hand and the buildings lining Fifth. In her mind she thinks of Jed, the office, the excitement that she feels, the warmth she felt when he smiled, the way he knew that she was smart.

She spreads the papers on the table. They are a mess: full of circled notes and doodles, some typed, others ink or pencil with drawings in the corners and along the edges of the paper: footprints of his thinking. She smiles. He's like a playful little boy. She reads and circles and makes question marks. His ideas trigger ideas of her own bubbling up from places in her brain that she'd repressed. Adrenaline begins to pump. She takes a pad, and writes and scratches out and writes again.

She walks around the room, chews a finger and sits along the window ledge staring at the people walking by. Her pulse is pushing blood fast through her veins and dreams are forming, advertising dreams: he needs an art director. She checks her watch: ten to twelve. She glances at the software, the Macintosh and printer, then takes the papers back to Jed.

He's at a drafting table.

"What's the deadline? When do you need this?" she asks.

"By three o'clock?" He straightens up and turns around and laughs. "You'll do it then?"

"You really need me. These are impossible." She holds the papers up.

"Impossible for someone else." He walks across the floor. "Not you."

She swallows. It's recognition. She knows she can untangle his ideas; he does, too. "I'll have to work around my other clients. When?"

"You tell me."

"I'll be here the end of the week and then one day on the weekend. Is that a problem?"

"Is Sunday okay? I'll be here with you." He marks the calendar on his desk.

"Sunday's great. I'll be back Thursday afternoon. I'll start things going at home." She gets her raincoat from the couch.

"Thanks, Molly." He reaches out his hand. "Welcome to Saunders and Associates."

She takes his hand; his touch shoots up her arm. "It looks like fun." She struggles with the latches on her briefcase. "Do you have copies?"

"I do."

She walks to the door, then turns around. "I'll see you Thursday."

"I'll be here."

She crosses the room to the stairway. Her right hand holds the handle of her briefcase. She feels the leather. She also feels the inside of Jed's hand.

Four

Back at Pace Lewiston, Molly sits inside a metal-walled cubicle, her own private space, six-by-eight, cold, steely, impersonal, with no window and no view and constant sounds of ringing phones and muffled voices. She bites the eraser on a pencil and stares at the empty gray computer screen. Thursday is a million days away. She bends back, slides the chair across the floor, and looks at the ceiling studded with fluorescent lights. She flings the pencil on the desk. The phone rings.

"So what happened?"

"Not much, Grace."

"Good. You didn't take the job."

"I did. It's a little job. I couldn't refuse."

"How about this Jed guy? What's he like?"

"Worked for Dane Hollenbeck. I like him. He's okay, really."

"What did he do there?"

"I don't know."

"You should have asked."

"It doesn't matter. I—"

"Wait a sec."

Molly hears Grace's muffled voice. She imagines

her in her new office at Rockefeller Center with a
window and a sliver view of the Hudson River.

"Better go. Let's get together this weekend. Sunday brunch, you and Porter?"

"Can't. I'm working."

"What?"

"How about Saturday night?" Molly says.

"What's this working on Sunday?"

"It's the job I took today. It's the only way I can
do it."

"You're going there on Sunday? You're crazy."

"Listen, got to go."

"Wait, who else will be there?"

"I don't know."

"You won't be in an office all alone?"

"Jed's coming in."

"The two of you together, no one else?"

"Grace, work calls. Maybe Saturday night."

"I'll have Harlan talk to Porter."

Molly flips the switch on the computer. Her teeth
bite her lip and her mind walks through Jed's of-
fices, into his, into the corner room, through the
center room. It was like her studio at school, a place
that swelled with life, where air had magic powers
and those inside knew more and felt more keenly.
She will be there Thursday, Friday, Sunday. So will
Jed. He was like a spinning bullet, bottled-up energy, popping, intriguing.

She bends and reaches into her briefcase, rummages for Tic Tacs. She sees the papers, Jed's scrawl
with doodles and drawings. He slid his chair across

the room and sat before the couch and crossed his leg and fingered the edges of his sock.

Molly works until seven, then races home, stopping for a salad at the deli. She takes Jed's papers from her briefcase, clears the table, and spreads them out. It's like the days back at Hopper. She finds a large sheet of paper and a pad of Post-its; it's her way to sort and organize. Words and pictures go on the sticky papers. She lines them up and marches them around. She reads, writes, draws, paces, combs her hair, and fills glasses with water and ice. A Beatles' tape plays. She sings and hums and swings her hips and taps the pencil.

She looks at the digital clock radio: 11:18. Impossible. She dabs a Red Zinger tea bag up and down in boiling water and sprawls across the couch. She doesn't feel like sleep; her mind is on fast-forward. She's back inside the advertising world. Her head lies on the pillow looking at the wall, following the strips of streetlight sneaking through the blinds. What happened to her dream? It hurts to think about it, like remembering a favorite ring left lying on the public restroom sink. She holds the warm cup up against her cheek. Four years she's wasted, working at a job that has no soul. Advertising was her love. Why did she abandon it?

Harold Huntington Hatcher. She looks across the room and sees the chair in which he sat. She thinks about the night and the terror that she felt and disgust and the anger and the sinking feeling of disappointment. She puts the tea cup on the table.

Harold Huntington Hatcher, vice president of Better Bakers, a major client of Hopper/Wang/McGrath.

He'd been her mentor, her booster; he said he liked her work. She'd been promoted and become a major person on a major account in a major agency. Her design is still on cookie boxes: a classic look, simplicity. She fought for it, demanded it, rebelled against the current use of "lite." The box would say it all. It was a fight and Hatcher stood behind her.

She liked Gloria, his wife, the dinners that they had together, the theater and ballet. Gloria came to New York from Michigan twice a year and updated Molly on what sports their sons were winning and what grades their sons were getting and complained how Harold made her marry instead of going to college.

Harold was a father bear, a person who could run for office or head the local golf club. One night she dined with him alone. It was the day she'd won the battle over "lite." They ate at Raphael's, a table in the tiny room in back, near the garden. He took her there to celebrate. They talked about the office, Better Bakers, and his sons.

"My son in college shares a room with a girl. Gloria won't talk about it. What do you think?"

"I don't know. Why not?"

"We didn't do that in my day. How about you?"

"Some did, some didn't."

"Did you?"

"Did I what? Tell me about your tennis game, I haven't played in years."

"Forget the tennis. I want to talk about college.

Did you have boys in your room for the night? Was it okay to do that?"

"It was okay. I didn't."

"Good. That's what I like. Bravo for virtue."

"Virtue? What if I told you I posed for my art professor."

"Nude?"

"Of course."

"For the whole class or just the professor?"

"I was an artist's model. What's your son's major?"

"Where are the paintings?"

"I don't know. I'm tired. I'd like to leave. I don't want dessert."

"I have some art. I'd like to see these paintings. Where are they?"

"I don't know."

"You're quite a woman, Molly—posing nude. I'd have taken that class."

"I really have to leave. Thanks for dinner. It was delicious."

"You're great, I really think you are. You stick to your guns. You're account exec material. I'll talk to McGrath, talk him into it."

After that night, she felt a difference in the way he treated her: his hands would touch her back or arm and linger or he'd look at her for minutes without stopping until she wanted just to punch his face. Sometimes she thought she just imagined it and other times she knew his hand was left on hers on purpose. Once she noticed that his eyes were glassy, far away and scary. She dropped the playful way she always worked with him.

Then the fateful night. She was in the bathtub soaking, tired from a hectic day. The buzzer from the doorman rang but Hatcher hadn't waited; he was knocking at her door. She dived for her bathrobe. He brought her flowers, roses wrapped in cellophane.

She gave him scotch although she sensed that he'd been drinking. At first she thought he'd come to warn her of bad news, perhaps the client changing agencies.

"Why the visit, the flowers?"

"I have something to tell you. It makes me nervous."

"I'll understand."

"I knew you would. You're great and so darned pretty."

"Wait until I dress. You caught me in the tub."

"Don't go. I have to say it now. Sit."

"Okay. Out with the bad news."

"It's about the way I feel. I mean . . . I'm crazy about you. I'm obsessed. I think I—" He was by her chair and he lunged and grabbed her arms and pulled at them and fell against her, yanking at her robe until it opened. "Oh God, I can't stop thinking of you." His hands mauled her body, squeezing her flesh, her breasts, grabbing at the flat skin across her abdomen. She dug her hands into his arms and pushed and found she had no strength and watched his one hand work its way between her thighs. "I must have you."

"Stop. Harold, this isn't—"

"You're beautiful, so goddamn beautiful." His

body pressed on hers and one hand fumbled with his fly and reached into his pants and then his naked part was sliding on her belly and his mouth was gnawing on her neck.

She strained and found his ear and bit until she tasted blood and bit some more until she felt the drops of blood. He was like a spring uncoiled, jerking and grabbing at his ear and crying out. She escaped. She was in the bathroom with the lock turned, crumpled on the floor, shaking and listening and hoping he would not be violent with the door. She could hear him, walking back and forth, running water, opening the refrigerator, slamming ice trays in the sink. She sat a long time, hoping for the outside door to open and to close. Her fear began to wane; her anger grew. She found underwear and put it on beneath the robe and tied the belt around her waist and turned the lock. She looked into the living room. He was sitting in the chair.

"I'd like you to leave my apartment."

"Are you all right? I'm truly sorry. I guess I lost control."

"If you just get out, I'll be all right."

"Let me apologize. Please sit down."

"Leave. That's enough apology."

"I never did this before."

"Get out of my apartment."

"I'm a good husband, a good father, believe me."

"I believe you. Go."

"Don't tell Gloria."

"Never."

"Will you give me another chance?"

"No."

"I've never been unfaithful to Gloria. It's you. I want you, Molly."

"No, Harold."

"I thought you liked me."

"I did, too."

"You led me on. It's not fair."

"Put on your coat and go."

"I've waited too long dreaming of this moment. Please take off your robe before I go."

"I thought you were my friend."

"I'm your professor. Treat me like you treated him and model for me. That's all I ask. You know how."

"Go or I'll call someone."

"No, you won't. I'm not a stranger. We are friends, like college. Come on. I'll stay in the chair. I promise."

"You're crazy. I don't believe—"

"Damn it, you owe me this. You hurt me. You owe me."

"This is my apartment. You can't do this."

"I got you the promotion. You like that. Admit it, you like being an account executive."

"I—"

"Do it. Damn you. Drop that robe. This is payment time." He stands and stalks toward her.

"Stop. Don't ever touch me again. Don't ever put your hand on any part of me."

"I just want to see you. Let me touch you with my eyes."

"Get your coat and leave."

He takes his coat and puts an arm through each sleeve. He goes back to the chair and sits. "I will leave after you model. I'm the art professor and this is class."

"I am not a model."

"You are my model. I paid for you. I gave you your job."

"I didn't know—"

"You know what you've been doing—teasing me for months."

"Harold, please."

"Model. It's not too much to ask. It's a compromise after all."

"You're crazy."

"Do it. I'm sitting and waiting. Untie that robe."

"You want me naked?"

"Yes. Naked. I made your dream. You make mine."

"I don't like this."

"Think of art class. Didn't you casually drop your robe for your professor? Now I'm the professor."

Molly picks up the cup of Red Zinger tea. She remembers feeling red all over like a lobster dropped in hot water. She remembers untying the belt and letting the robe part and hearing Harold gasp.

"Off with the robe. Off, account executive."

She stood draped in the open robe. "Don't say any words to me. Don't open your mouth. Don't move from that chair or I will scream so loud that everyone from three blocks away will come running."

He rubbed his hands on the cloth of his trousers

on his thighs. She waited. He was silent, as she commanded him to be.

She put her hands on the shoulders of the robe and flung it off and watched him. His hands kept rubbing. "I can scream fire and everyone will come and I will tell Gloria."

She placed her fingers on the clasp of the bra between her breasts and waited. She snapped it and felt the air on her breasts and let the straps fall down and she raised her arms to the ceiling and he stood.

"I can stop. I can pick up the phone and call Gloria."

He sat down and touched himself. "Behave yourself. You are the professor. He would never be crude. This is an art show."

She turned her back to him and slid the elastic of her panties down her legs. She looked over her back. His hands grasped the arms of the chair. She turned around. She stood, feeling her nakedness, feeling the patch that cried for cover, feeling deviant, knowing his need, seeing it, showing him, and laughing at his crudeness. "You can go now, you bastard. I will count to ten and then I will scream. One, two—"

He didn't move. She picked up the robe, pulled the sleeve right side out, and put it on one arm, "Five, six." She flung the robe, raged, and flung the robe. "Get out, get out before I kill you."

He crept around her swinging arm. He ducked and grabbed the handle of the door. He never said a word.

She lasted three months at Hopper/Wang/McGrath.

Slowly, people replaced her on the account. McGrath told her the client was dissatisfied with her work. She heard gossip in the office. Hatcher called once late at night and said he thought she was unstable, she should find another job. He would send her money if she liked. He hoped she never thought of telling Gloria—she would not believe it anyway.

Molly had headaches and could not sleep. She took a leave of absence for a month. She went to Massachusetts and found Jacques and moved in with him. She resigned from Hopper. Her apartment in New York stayed empty. She paid the rent with money left by her mother. She painted and cooked and doted on Jacques. For four years she lived only for him. One day she found him in their bed with a student. She forgave him. Months later, there was another student. One day his wife called from France.

Harlan and Grace came and got her. Harlan told her about a company called Aldus. They made Page-Maker software for desktop publishing, a new field for computers. She went to a week-long workshop and bought a computer. Harlan introduced her to Pace Lewiston.

Molly pours the Red Zinger down the sink. Four years of desktop publishing. Four years with Jacques. Eight wasted years.

Five

Racing to be done by Thursday, Molly works two twelve-hour days at Pace Lewiston. At night she plays with Jed's papers. On Wednesday night she tries to sleep; instead, she tosses and turns and looks at the lights out the window and the shadows on the ceiling. Lying on her back, she traces the line where the ceiling meets the wall. Something is missing in Jed's proposal: it lacks sizzle. Her mind wanders back to Hopper days. "What's the story?" McGrath would bellow. "Where's the human interest, where are the people?" Molly sits straight up in bed. That's it: there are no people.

By noon on Thursday she's on the subway. She practices what she will say to Jed. She stops on Seventeenth Street to buy lunch: a salad of artichokes and beans and one chocolate cookie. She romps up Fifth Avenue, climbs the stairs, and turns into the corner room. The panorama out the window hits her like a giant painting at the Met. Goodbye metal cubicle.

She sheds her coat and drops it across a chair. Humming to herself, she pulls the papers from her briefcase and unfolds the big plan on the table. After pulling a brush through her hair and smoothing her skirt, she goes into the center room. Joe is working at a drafting table. A woman she doesn't know is on the telephone. Jed's door is closed.

"Jed here?" Molly asks.

"Who are you?" The woman says, cupping her hand over the mouthpiece.

"Molly Mitchell. I need to see Jed."

"Join the crowd."

"He's not here?"

"He's never here."

"I'll be in the corner office. Would you tell him I'm here?"

"If he comes before I leave, I'll try to remember."

"Thanks." She waves to Joe and retreats to her office, where she nibbles on the string beans and stares out the window and wonders why she feels as if she got the date wrong for a party. She eats half the cookie, then returns to the center room and the woman who is leafing through a magazine.

"Do you know if he'll be in this afternoon?"

"I expected him a half hour ago." The woman walks across the floor, opens Jed's door, and goes inside.

Molly stands, staring at the door closing behind her. She pulls her hair behind an ear, glances past the tables to the posters, to the drafting tables. She takes a breath and goes back to the office. She pulls the table from the wall, turns it around, and starts hooking up the computer. The cables, boxes, software packages, and shrink-wrap fly in all directions. She becomes totally absorbed.

A voice shocks her from her concentration. "Everything okay in here?"

She looks up to his eyes, his knitted brow. "I hate this part of the job."

"Need some help?"

"I don't need help, just praise."

"Looks like you're doing a swell job—best I have ever seen."

"Thanks. Do you have time for a meeting? I have some comments on your papers."

"Can it wait?"

"Sure."

"Maybe four-thirty or so."

"Is that called quarter to five?"

"Something like that. I'll come by." He leaves.

She checks her watch, scoops the salad into her mouth, and follows the traffic on Fifth Avenue. Munching the cookie, she thinks about her speech to Jed. He seems busy, in a hurry. She might call Porter and make a date for dinner. An hour later, she's done with the computer setup and goes across the hall to wash her hands. Passing Jed's open door she sees the woman on the couch and Jed in the chair the way he sat with her. An icy chill runs down her back. Jed signals to her.

"Molly, come meet Candace Long. She's doing a piece on Norway. Candace, this is Molly Mitchell."

Molly steps into the office. "We talked earlier."

"Molly's the new typist?" Candace says.

"She's a PageMaker expert. I found her in a window on Forty-second Street."

"You're a Peeping Tom as well as other things, Jed?" Candace laughs.

Molly backs out the door. "It was nice to meet you." She smiles at Jed.

"I'll be by later," he says.

Back in her office, Molly dials Porter. He's in a meeting. She doesn't leave a message. She puts the software on the hard disk, checks the dates and drives and drivers, checks the printer. She starts to enter data. It's four-fifteen. She watches the door, bites her lip, pats her hair, thinks about the things she'll say to Jed. By four-thirty the rays of sun are spread across the floor. She takes the only other chair and props her feet. She listens for the voices in the other room. It's Jed or maybe Joe. She hears a woman's voice and straightens the papers on the table.

The door opens. She sees his hand on the knob. "You guys have a great night." He comes into the room and slumps against the table. "I'm all yours. Tell me what you think?"

She pushes the extra chair toward him and pulls her chair to the table. "There are places I'm not sure about. Your writing, I guess." She leafs through the papers.

"My writing for sure." He laughs.

She finds the places; he reads the words. She re-writes them and comments on his drawings.

"There must be more than this. You sounded like you had something big to say—something about the proposal, perhaps an idea you didn't understand."

"That's not quite it."

He puts his foot on the table and leans back in the chair. "You hate the whole proposal. You want to quit."

"No, no, no."

"You think I'm crazy and I don't know what I'm doing."

"No."

"Then what?"

"The product is plastic bags, right?" she says.

"For now—right—plastic bags."

"Biodegradable bags?"

"That's the key."

"Are we educating the public. Is that our job?"

"Definitely a big part of it."

"That's not clear."

"It's there."

"But it doesn't jump at me. You tell me nothing. Where's the human interest? Where's the story that is going to make me listen?"

Jed takes his foot from the table. "You tell me. What's the story?"

"It's about potatoes."

"Okay. Make it exciting."

"It's about potatoes turning into plastic bags." Molly stands. "It's morphing, like Michael Jackson turning into a tiger on that video."

"Interesting idea."

"Who's Bill, the inventor? Was he a potato farmer? Or his father?"

"Have you been to the Old Town Bar?"

"What's that got to do with—"

"They've got mean home fries and ice-cold beer."

He springs from the chair and jiggles his hand in his pocket. "Close down that computer and let's get out of here."

She looks at the watch, at the computer.

"Have you other plans?" he asks. "We need to talk."

"I haven't finished telling you—"

"I know. This meeting might take hours."

Fifth Avenue is full of people, honking horns, and wheezing buses. Jed takes her arm and leads her left on Eighteenth Street and across Broadway to a street lined with ancient factory buildings. Midblock, he guides her through a glass-top mahogany door and into a bar that looks the way it must have looked a hundred years ago.

"We are in luck," he says, motioning to a booth that's being vacated. "I'll get the beer, light or dark?"

"Your choice."

Molly maneuvers around the couple leaving and slides across the green leather seat. The seats are high and topped with beveled mirrors. Etched glass lamps hang on the corners. The table is dark wood, pitted and carved.

Jed brings two bottles of Anchor Steam Beer. "Want a glass?"

Molly shakes her head. "Anchor Steam? What's this?"

"You'll like it." He lifts the bottle. "To a long, creative friendship."

Molly shivers. She's been abducted by a Martian and been cast back in time. "This place is amazing."

She notices the tiles on the floor, tiny tiles designed like her cookie box.

"I like it, don't you," Jed says.

"I really do." She looks down the bar, stretching the length of the room, packed with people and noisy. She lifts the bottle to her mouth and drinks. It's cold and slightly bitter.

"Let's talk about potatoes. Let's make a story." He grins. She notices the shadow of his beard.

"So Bill lived on a farm?" She peels the edges of the paper on the bottle.

"In Idaho."

"You made that up?" She takes a pencil from her bag.

"Boy Scout's honor. Idaho."

She doodles on the napkin. "He was raised on a potato farm in Idaho? When did he get into plastics?"

"College a little—he used to talk about it. But graduate school really did it."

Molly darkens the drawing on the napkin. She notices Jed reach into his pocket. "Do you want a pencil?"

She pulls sheets of lineless yellow paper from her briefcase and puts them on the table with a bunch of pencils. "How about his wife? Farm, too?" She continues to draw.

"City girl." Jed makes an oval on the paper, puts black marks inside.

"What are those marks?"

"Eyes, potato eyes. Ellen has an MBA. She worked for a greeting card company for a while."

The paper fills with ovals and circles. Molly draws people eyes and eyeglasses, hair and lips. Jed adds legs and arms. They draw on the same paper. Molly draws a grocery bag.

Jed makes a balloon and writes, "I feel attached to my bag."

"Attached?" Molly laughs. "He is the bag." She draws a mustache.

Jed makes clown shoes, a sloppy hat. She makes a space helmet with feathers. They touch bottles. They drink. They watch each other drink. They watch each other's pencil. They swap turns drawing, making pictures on top of pictures. They laugh.

"The story." Jed holds the paper up against the wall. "Here's the story."

"A masterpiece. Ta-daa . . ."

"Our masterpiece. Let's get some food."

"Potatoes?"

"With burgers on the side." He flags the waitress and orders: french fries, potato salad, and two burgers.

"What about the farm?" she asks.

"What farm?"

"Bill's farm. Have you been there?"

"No."

"Is it still in his family?"

"I think so. Want to go?"

"Sure." Molly reaches for her bottle of beer, rubs her thumb around the top. "You're not so bad with a pencil."

"I've always drawn. Cartoons. I was born drawing, but I love words."

"I laughed a lot at your drawings on the papers." The booth is dark. The lamp glows on the table. Molly feels warmth in her chest.

The hamburgers arrive and two big plates of skinny fries and one of potato salad. "No mashed?" Molly asks.

"We don't have mashed," the waitress says.

"We can find them another night," Jed says. "We'll try different restaurants."

"We'll do a survey. I'll put it in the proposal."

"Under public relations?"

"Under research." Molly picks up a fry.

"Ketchup?" Jed asks.

"No, thanks."

"I hate it, too. It ruins the flavor."

"I really like potatoes."

"I do too."

Eating becomes a game. She takes a fry and so does he. She stabs the salad and he follows. They order beer, one bottle, and take turns. She watches as he drinks, his lips around the bottle rim. She grabs it from his hand and puts her lips where his have been. They lean into the table. She wants to touch his face, his hair. Her fingers on the table make rivers out of puddles from the beer.

"Coffee?" he asks. "With whipped cream?"

"Definitely whipped cream."

The coffee comes. It's in a glass. Jed gets two straws. They drink.

"I feel I'm in a movie," Molly says.

"You are. What's the rating?"

"Four and a half stars."

Six

Friday morning, eight-twenty, Molly is back at Saunders and Associates. All night she tossed, potatoes popping in and out of her dreams. She looks for Jed; his office is empty. She works like a robot, shaping graphics, typing, marking places for questions and additional material. Her eyes follow the text on the computer screen; her body awaits a click, a door opening, a grin.

She runs the printer, stretches, and wanders through the office. She goes to the deli for coffee. Bubbles rumble in her stomach. The coffee makes them worse. Back in her office, she stands by the window and looks down at the sidewalk, to the entrance of the building. She stacks the papers and walks to the center room. "Has Jed come in?" she calls.

"Expect him after lunch, maybe two," Angelo calls back.

Annoyance grips her. He could have told her he'd be late. But why? She needs to work and finish—get it done: formatted, printed, and ready for discussion Sunday. She works, she checks her watch, she follows buses out the window, she gets a Coke, she walks, she works, she doodles on a pad and thinks about last night. The door clicks.

"What's new with potatoes?"

She smiles, presses her feet against the floor, and makes her chair scrape backward. Jed props himself against the table.

"They're at a new high," she laughs.

His glance circles the room and reaches her. Tiny gasps rise and hide inside her throat. She blinks.

"How's it going? Any problems, comments?"

"No problems, lots of comments." She runs a pencil through her hair. "Last night was fun."

"Did you get home okay?"

"Of course. How about you?"

"Singing spud songs all the way. Are we still on for Sunday?"

"I hope so. I've got some new ideas to hash out."

"Hash out, did you say?"

"I didn't mean it." She laughs "Mash out. What time, Sunday?"

"I'll be here by eleven-thirty. You come when you can." He stands, checks his watch. "I'll be leaving soon. Is there anything you need?"

"No." She hesitates. "I'm fine."

"Good. I'll catch you later."

He's gone. Molly looks around the space. It's hollow, emptied out. She sits on the windowsill. The buses move slowly. She hears Jed's voice and Angelo's. She hits her hand against her fist. The buses blur. She takes her jacket and bounds down the stairs, pushing her arms inside the jacket sleeves.

In the deli she takes a plastic box and walks

around the canopied-lit counter crammed with containers of rice concoctions, raw vegetables, salads, square-cut fruit. She picks up the tuna salad spoon, holds it, puts it down. She takes five black olives and a scoop of grated carrot. Using tongs, she lifts a square of tofu.

Back in the office, she eats the olives with her fingers and calls Grace.

"Where are you?" Grace asks.

"On Twentieth Street. Almost literally. You wouldn't believe this office."

"My friend Pamela and her husband are coming Saturday night. We may go to Brooklyn."

"Brooklyn? My sister going to Brooklyn?"

"The River Cafe. It's really good. Pamela lives in Brooklyn."

"You'll never get reservations."

"Pam knows the chef. She's a cookbook editor. Seeing Porter tonight?"

"I don't know."

"Give him a ring. Didn't you see him this week?"

"I was too busy."

"Too busy? Call him right away. He'd like that."

"You think so?"

"Men like to be called. They're basically shy."

"Not Harlan." Molly breaks the tofu and puts a piece in her mouth.

"He's the exception, born making deals. Tomorrow night will be fun."

"I hope."

"Got to go, meeting in three minutes. Call Porter."

Molly looks at the phone, at the computer, at the

place where Jed sat against the table. When he came in, her skin crawled, like it did with Jacques, the day after making love. It's a feeling she'd forgotten. She drags the menu down the screen and highlights fonts. He was only here a minute. Sunday they'll be here for hours.

She goes into the center room and fills a cup with water. "Anybody working Sunday?" she calls to Angelo.

"Not this guy," Angelo says.

"Just wondered. I'm coming in."

"Does Jed know? You'll need a key."

"He knows."

She sits on the windowsill waiting for the printer to finish, listening to the clacking. The sky is gray, bleak.

She dials Porter. "Are you working tonight?"

"You want to meet for supper? Sweets at six o'clock?"

"I'll see you there." She collects the printed papers, makes changes, darkens the lines around the boxes, adds copy, and hums.

At six-twenty Molly arrives at Fulton Street. Porter sits at a table, his hand around a glass. He stands, squeezes her hand, and brushes his lips on hers. She tastes the scotch.

"Hope I'm not late," she says.

He holds the chair. "I walked over. Left early. What are you drinking?"

"How about a Cape Cod, it matches the scenery."

"Do you know what it is?"

"Vodka and cranberry juice. Vitamins and booze." Molly laughs and looks around the half-full room, plain tables, simple chairs, a high tin ceiling.

"Did you have a busy week?" Porter says.

Molly smiles and feels the fatigue that comes at the end of a race. "I worked until midnight every night," she says.

"That's not necessary. You should plan your days better."

"I know." She presses back into her chair and feels the soothing who-cares from the vodka. The room is like Jed's office: long windows, wooden floors, old New York. "Busy week for you?" she asks. Porter looks untouched by work, as if he had just showered: pin-striped suit, rounded collar clipped with a silver pin, maroon tie with tiny white dots.

"No more than usual."

"Have you talked to Harlan about tomorrow night?"

"Grace has it all set."

"I talked to her. She said a woman from her office and her husband plan to come. We're going to the River Cafe in Brooklyn."

"I know. Have you been there?"

"No, have you?"

"Once, a couple years ago. First-rate—I think you'll like it."

Molly drains the glass and chews a piece of ice. She pulls her foot out of her shoe.

Porter signals the waiter and taps his glass. "How long have I known you?"

Molly's attention wanders to a table filled with Asian businessmen. She looks back at Porter. "When did we meet? It was March, I think."

"Yes, a year ago March—the Allied Truck merger. Harlan worked on it and invited me to dinner. You were there."

Molly remembers Grace's call: "An important partner is coming for dinner. Harlan wants you to come. He says he's very smart, well connected, and just divorced. Wear your great-looking black dress."

"I remember. We had poached salmon. I wore a black dress," Molly says.

"I don't remember what we ate. It was the first time I met Grace and I couldn't believe you were sisters. At first I thought you were Harlan's wife."

"Oh, please, I like Harlan, but he's not my type."

"Am I?"

Her chin snaps up; she studies him: the smoothness of his forehead, the earnestness around his eyes. She tips the glass to get the last remaining bit of ice. He drinks and dabs the napkin on his lips.

"Had you worked with Harlan before the truck merger?"

"Just little things. He impressed me. He's smart. He'll make partner in June."

"Does he know?"

"Not yet and don't tell. Shall we order? Would you like wine?"

"Sure." The smell of seaweed and engine oil

comes through an open window. Porter studies the list of wines. She watches him. She notices his hand, his square-trimmed nails, the way his eyes move back and forth through the tiny glasses perched low on his nose. She listens to him talking to the waiter, asking questions, nodding.

He puts the glasses in his pocket. "I was impressed that first night."

"Oh?"

"Two sisters who are good friends. I liked that."

"It's not always perfect, but we are friends, or we try to be. She's all I have."

"Did you fight as kids?"

"All the time. She hated me."

"I don't believe that."

"It's true, but it doesn't mean anything. We are different. You said that yourself the other night."

"I did? Grace will be a good mother."

"Yes. She's very traditional. I think she'll have kids soon."

"How about you? Are you traditional too?"

"Sometimes."

"How do you feel about children?"

"I don't know. I guess every woman thinks of having kids. It's biological. How about you?"

"It's not biological for men but I'd like to have a family. My parents want grandchildren, I know. I suppose I've let them down. Over forty may be too late." He pulls at the knot on his tie. "I've been too busy being a lawyer."

"Over forty isn't too late for Dad. It is for Mom."

"Not today. You could do it. Maybe squeeze in two. I bet you want children."

"I don't know. I had buried the thought. I'm working on something new and it has me excited—a company that makes plastic from potatoes."

"That's not new. It's been tried before and didn't work. I think Cornell was involved."

"This is different from that. It's a better idea."

"Sounds like another environmental nut's idea."

"I don't think so. This guy knows potatoes and has all the degrees and lots of backing."

"There are a lot of screwy ideas out there."

"I don't think this is one of them."

Porter leans across the table. His voice drops. "Shall we go to my place when we finish?"

Molly tugs the edges of her napkin taut and doesn't answer.

"Is something wrong? I haven't seen you all week."

"I know. I'm sorry." Regret and guilt mix with a need to be alone. "Sure, let's go to your place."

In the taxi, Molly leans her head on Porter's shoulder. He takes her hand and surrounds it with his. She thinks about his massive bed. It will be warm and comforting. She'll do the things that Jacques said all men like. There are places she has never touched, that Jacques said lovers should explore.

"Penny for your thoughts?" he asks.

"My thoughts are worth five dollars."

"Good thoughts?"

"They might be good, time will tell."

The taxi turns by Gramercy Park. Molly spies Porter's building, the three-story yellow house. He owns the second floor. It's perfect. That's what Grace said, the time they were invited there for drinks. "This definitely is first-class," she whispered, sitting on the matching love seats, soft blue leather flanking the fireplace, the walnut mantel surrounded by a wall of books and stereo equipment.

The taxi pulls to the curb and Porter pays the driver. Inside he takes her coat and flicks a switch that makes the mantel and the bookcase glow. "Would you like a Drambuie?"

"No thanks." Molly steps from her shoes and picks up the *Atlantic Monthly*. She watches Porter fill a tiny glass with amber liquor and click on CNN. She browses through the magazine, then retreats into the bathroom. The red toothbrush is hers; Porter put it there.

"Take a shower if you want," he calls.

The water washes down her back, warm soothing water that she stands under with closed eyes concentrating on the heat, the massage, the pleasure of the flow and steam. She yearns for his bed with its thick mattress and large down-filled pillows.

She hears a knock.

"I'm leaving a pajama top for you. It's on the doorknob."

"Thanks." Porter is a caring man. She turns the shower off and reaches for the beige towel, so thick it blots the moisture from her skin with a single touch. The blue pajama top falls on her body like a tent. She rolls the sleeves and does the large white buttons and notices that even with the yards of fabric its length is short and barely covers her, ending an inch before her legs begin.

She returns to the living room and Porter, her hands pulling on the garment.

"How's my pajama top?"

"It's funny." She stands in the glow of the television, her hands in front of her, conscious of her long bare legs, of his glance, and the stirrings in the part she covers with her hands.

She curls herself beside him on the couch and puts her head against his shoulder, lays her hand against his thigh. The screen is in the distance, a flashing light among the books. The channels change from talking heads to roaming lions. Her eyes close; she thinks of Jed.

"Why don't you go to bed?" She feels a kiss against her hair. "I'll be in soon."

The ironed sheets are smooth against her skin, the blankets heavy. She stretches out her legs and rubs her cheek against the pillowcase. The pillow's plumper than her own; she wraps her arms around it and lets her head sink in the down and lets the images of Jed roam in her head. She's in the booth and drinking beer and sipping coffee through a straw and feeling wrapped in bliss and liquid and strings pull inside her legs and her arms tighten on the down and her head nestles in the pillow.

A heavy weight is on the bed, a hand on her shoulder, and fingers sliding on her neck. "Are you awake?"

Her arms loosen around the pillow and her neck stretches, yielding flesh to his kneading fingers.

"Molly?"

She rolls and cuddles next to him. His hand moves to her breast, she feels it through the cloth. The room is hushed and dark and Porter smells of peppermint and Yardley soap.

"I'm glad you're here," he says.

She feels his lips against her cheek and now on top of hers. His kiss is gentle, lips on lips. She takes his hand and lays it on the large white buttons. "Undo these," she says.

He struggles with one hand, then braces on an elbow and works the buttons through the holes. She waits, anxious for his touch. Her skin has come alive. She reaches for his buttons on the top he wears like hers. Her fingers have no trouble; she wants to feel his skin and touch his chest and do the things she thought about while riding in the taxi.

"It's hard to see," he says.

Later, when she dreams, she's on a beach with houses that are missing walls and roofs. She climbs through doors and windows and meets distorted faces of people she does not know. She stumbles up and down the sand dunes and through the surf. Jed is there, in the water, bobbing in the waves. She swims. She struggles out to where he is. He disappears beneath a wave. She dives beneath the surface. He's there. It isn't Jed. It's Porter.

A hand is on her forearm, shaking it. "Molly, I'm

going to the office. You have to get dressed now and leave."

Molly rolls over on her back. She's in the dream, swimming. "Later," she says. "Leave me, I'll go later."

"You've slept long enough. It's after eight. I don't want to leave you in the apartment; I'd rather you left with me."

Molly rubs her eyes. "I won't stay long, I promise. Let me get up slowly."

"I'll make coffee. You get dressed like a good girl and I'll help you find a taxi." He walks out of the bedroom.

Good girl. He said good girl. She leaps from the bed and storms into the kitchen.

"What's this good girl? I will leave when I want."

Porter pours water in the coffee machine. She sees his profile and his clenched teeth.

"And I don't need help with a taxi," Molly says.

"Get dressed, Molly." He measures coffee grounds into the filter.

"Why can't I leave after you?"

Porter turns; faces her. His voice sounds robot-like. "Because I asked you not to. It's that simple."

Molly takes a breath. "When you ask me to leave, I feel like a two-bit whore."

"That's ridiculous. Get dressed."

"I don't understand you, you never leave me alone in the apartment. You bring me home, fuck me, and throw me out." Her voice shakes.

He spins around. "I think it's called making love

and I did not throw you out. We slept all night in the same bed. Watch your language."

"Fuck, fuck, fuck." Molly stamps around the kitchen. "That's what you did." Her hands make fists.

Porter grabs her arm. "Get dressed, Molly, before we both regret this morning."

She feels his strength. His eyes look full of fear. She yanks her arm away. In the bedroom, she pulls the pajama over her head and, standing naked, turns and sees him in the doorway.

"What are you doing?" he asks.

She freezes and stares. He's a figure in a jacket, fully dressed. She's a woman without clothes. Redness colors his neck and face. He steps backward. "Mrs. O'Shea is coming. Get dressed. Leave by nine-fifteen. There's coffee for you in the kitchen."

He turns his back to her and takes his wallet from the dresser. She puts on her blouse. The front door slams.

She stands at the bathroom sink and checks her skin, pulls floss between her teeth, combs her hair. Her head hurts. It's like a clock alarm that won't go off. Beside the dresser, beside the picture in the silver frame, Molly pulls on stockings. It's Porter and his parents and a woman in a yellow dress. Porter has more hair than he does now. He frowns into the sun. The mother smiles, the father's hand is in his jacket pocket. Elizabeth is looking to the left, looking at a tree perhaps.

Molly puts the picture back and straightens out the part that stands it up. She opens up the dresser drawer and closes it again. It was an impulse. It shocks her that she did it. She finds her skirt and puts it on. Her glances move around the room searching for her shoes. She finds them right beside the place where she's been standing.

Molly looks back at the photograph, the girl, the man beside her who is Porter fifteen years ago. She combs her hair and gets her coat. Before she leaves, she turns the coffeemaker off.

The air chills; the sky is overcast. She walks west, unaware of other walkers, unaware of dogs. She thinks of Porter in the kitchen, in the bed last night. She thinks of Porter's wife, who is living with a woman.

She boards a bus and sits beside the window. The bouncing churns the jumble in her stomach. Tonight she'll be with Porter and her sister and her sister's friend. She'll feel awkward seeing Porter: she had acted in a way he never saw before. She was angry. She doesn't feel it now, just empty once again, with a sadness that she can't explain.

She pulls her jacket close around her body and watches the blur of buildings, and people in the street. At Forty-second Street the traffic piles up; the bus stops in the intersection. She looks toward First, the bank, the place she first met Jed. He's just a guy, someone who's fun to work with.

At Fifty-ninth, she leaves the bus and walks to Bloomingdale's. She wanders up and down between the counters, gray and glass and black. She sniffs perfume and checks the banks of eye makeup. On one eye, she puts green, brown on the other. In the bakery near the street she buys one cookie, oatmeal chocolate chip.

She heads uptown. She'll take a nap and take a bath before tonight.

Seven

Molly rides a taxi to Grace's apartment. She planned to walk the fourteen blocks, but the waiting taxi at the curb tempted her. Walking would have eased the knot she's feeling in her stomach. She has to think what to do if Porter proposes. Grace sounded so insistent on the phone. "Porter is going for this apartment. Are you sure he hasn't hinted about marriage or anything?"

He did talk about family, his parents wanting grandchildren. Molly hunts through her purse for the five-dollar bill she slipped inside. Elizabeth never had a child. Porter is getting older, worried that the time will pass. Grace wants babies soon. Molly picks at her fingernail. Being pregnant isn't something she has thought about.

The taxi bumps and brakes. She grabs the strap. The green she's wearing is too bright; she wishes she'd worn the black. Damn. She always does what Grace suggests: "Wear that green tunic. It does great things to your eyes."

The taxi slows and stops. The doorman springs to the curb and opens the door. Molly settles the change in her purse before unbending onto the street. She follows the doorman into the lobby and waits at the desk for the call upstairs. She is alone in the elevator. As the door slides closed and the car ascends a huge thirst fills her, a yearning, a hollowness. Pictures of Jed crowd her mind. The door opens.

She emerges from the elevator and looks down the long hallway patterned with closed doors. Grace's door opens, spilling light into the dark tunnel. She sees Harlan framed in the doorway.

"My favorite sister-in-law wearing my favorite seductive color."

"I didn't think green was a seductive color." She kisses Harlan somewhere near his mouth.

"Grace thinks so, and maybe frogs and toads."

Molly looks toward the bedroom for Grace and hears humming that sounds like Mendelssohn's "Wedding March." She shrugs at Harlan. "Stop that, Grace. No one here is getting married."

"That's what you think." Grace comes from the bedroom. She is garbed in chocolate brown silk.

"Nice outfit. Yummy," Grace says. "You look good enough to eat."

"That's my line." Harlan winks.

"That green on you is fabulous," Grace says. "Have you noticed Harlan?"

Molly assesses Harlan. His hair is slicked back and shiny. He wears a dark shirt buttoned to his neck. "Where's the preppy?" she asks.

"What do you think?" Grace says.

"Sinister."

"I like that," Harlan says, cuffing Molly on the

arm. "I like looking sinister." He hands Molly a sheet of paper. "Here's the data on your guy, Saunders."

Molly scans the page: President, Jed Saunders, Vice President, Siri Peterson.

"Who's Peterson?" Harlan asks.

"I don't know."

"Have you met her?"

"I don't know who she is." Molly feels a panic in her stomach. It's a fear that she missed something, didn't listen carefully, mistook a lie for truth.

"She must be someone special. Wife perhaps?"

Molly swallows. "It doesn't matter. How's the rest of the report?"

"Not bad. The financials look strong. Nice first year."

Grace stands by the door. "Let's go, everybody. The car awaits and so does Porter."

The Lincoln Town Car smells like spearmint. Molly feels jammed between Grace and Harlan. She glances at the name Siri Peterson on the paper, folds it, and stuffs it into her pocketbook.

"Grace says you're working tomorrow, just you and the boss. Isn't that risky?" Harlan stretches his arm across the back of the seat.

"What's risky about it?"

"A guy and a gal alone in an office?"

"Are you implying I'm Suzy Innocence and Jed is Jack the Rapist?"

"I'm implying two people attracted to each other, alone in an office on a Sunday afternoon, can create a pretty tempting situation."

Molly crosses her legs. "The attraction is the job."

"I see." Harlan cracks his knuckles. "What's new with you and Porter?"

"Nothing."

Grace fills the silence with patter about the River Cafe, about Pamela and the cookbook she's editing and Keith her husband, the techno-wiz. Molly pretends she's listening but her thoughts are on the paper in her purse. *Who is Siri Peterson? Harlan said wife. Impossible or . . .* She feels her neck get warm behind her ears and the funny feeling in her gut which comes when one discovers an assumption is not so, being the fool. Gramercy Park is out the window. Porter's park. She needs to be alone and sort through the conversations she has had with Jed. Right now she doesn't want a party or to be with Porter or Grace or anybody.

The car slows. Porter waits by the curb. Grace nudges her. Porter waves. He wears a corduroy jacket and his hand is in his pocket, like his father in the picture. Molly hears her mother's voice. "Find someone tall. You'll make a handsome couple."

Porter opens the front door of the car and sits beside the driver. "How's everyone tonight? It's nice to see you, Grace." He sits sideways, the angle of his gaze on Grace.

"We're all fine," Grace says. "Harlan played squash today at the Yale Club."

"Anyone I know?" He shifts in his seat and looks at Harlan.

"Doubt it. I'm working on getting some business from him."

Molly looks from Harlan to Porter. She pictures Harlan at the Yale Club, the place where Grace and Harlan met. Grace loves to talk about the Yale Club, to say that Harlan went to Yale. The night they met she said that he would be her husband; in six months he was. Molly recalls her mother's comment. "I don't care about Yale. I care about Grace and there is something about Harlan I don't trust."

"This guy I played with is a great squash player, aggressive as hell. Does bonds. Works downtown. I'm sure I can get him to come with us."

"I hear you've got something going in California?" Porter says.

"Yep. Guys in the movie business."

"I'd be careful of the movie business."

"No problem. I know the L.A. type. Went to high school there once."

"High school in L.A.?" Molly asks. "Since when?"

Harlan pats Molly's knee. "There are secrets about me not even you know." He laughs.

The car pulls in front of the River Cafe. The undersides of the Brooklyn Bridge are overhead. The driver jumps out and opens the door. Porter gets out and Harlan writes on the chit attached to a clipboard. Molly smells the water from the East River. The New York skyline rises like dark stalks of overgrown concrete building blocks dotted with lights. She feels she is in a foreign port gazing at the New York harbor: Liberty and her lamp in the distance,

the underbelly of the bridge and lower Manhattan
pasted on the horizon with the twin towers as guard
posts to the city she loves.

Harlan grabs her arm. It startles her. "Come on,
Molly. Cheer up. Things can't be as bad as you
look."

Molly wraps her arm around Harlan's. "I'm pon-
dering my favorite place in the world."

"It's a crazy place." He ushers her through the
entrance and points to Grace and Porter at a table
by the window shaking hands with Grace's friends.
She follows the maître d' through the maze of tables, never taking her gaze from the water and the
bridge and the sparkles from the bridge framed now
by wide-striped awnings on the windows. Grace introduces Keith and Pamela and Pamela suggests the
seating.

Molly takes the chair between Harlan and Keith.
Porter is across the table between Grace and Pam.

"What's your business, Keith?" Harlan leans
around Molly.

"Laser disks."

"You mean CDs?"

"Big CDs if you like. We produce them."

"Are you a private company?"

"We're private." Keith turns to Molly. "Quite a
view, don't you think?"

"I love it. I love New York. We forget it's a big
harbor, once a huge port."

"Have you thought of going public?" Harlan interrupts. "You could make a lot of money and become millionaires overnight."

"I like things the way they are."

"Sure, I know, control. People like control. But money can be control too. If you're interested, talk to me. We know the big guns in investment banking. Porter does a lot of public offerings."

Porter turns his head. "What's this you're saying?"

"I'm suggesting Keith's company go public."

Porter smiles. "Being a public company is not for everybody."

Molly surveys the three across the table. The women bend toward Porter, listening, asking questions. Porter is like a college professor, nodding to one then the other. She hears words: Washington, the Smithsonian, panda bear.

Keith turns to Molly. "Are you and Porter . . . ?"

"Friends. He was married once."

"And you?"

"Me?" Molly laughs. "Nothing."

"I was married before I married Pamela. Divorced men make great husbands. Ask Pam."

"Really?"

"The breakup is hard at first, but you learn a lot about yourself. Victoria was a great person; we just couldn't live together—too opposite. She's very scheduled, plan, plan, plan. I live spontaneously. How about you?"

"Spontaneous or planned? I don't know. I never thought about it." Molly hears Porter laugh.

"What do you do?"

"Desktop publishing. I free-lance."

"Then you must be the scheduled type."

"Scheduled?" She watches Grace wrap her hair around her finger. "I'm not sure."

"Do you plan everything? Victoria planned every day of the week: Thursday, the movies; Friday, pizza; Sunday, Chinese restaurant. Drove me nuts."

"Grace does that—not me. I like surprises."

"Me too, and a bit of chaos."

"Opposites should never marry—is that what you think?"

"Just don't marry someone who bugs you. Pamela accepts who I am, calls me 'pandemonium.' We have a good time."

"Tell me more about being spontaneous."

"I don't know. I guess I drop my clothes on the floor. Stuff like that. Eat standing up. Put my finger in the peanut butter jar."

"What else? This is fun."

"Well, sex. I like to let it happen when it happens, any time, any place, any way."

Molly looks across at Porter. Her glance moves to Pamela. She feels a twinge of jealousy she doesn't understand. "So how do you work?" Molly asks.

"How do I work? I like it when a zillion things are going on at the same time. Sounds crazy, but it energizes me."

"I know what you mean." Molly thinks of Hopper days, the bedlam in the art department, the wow she felt. "I'm like that. Ideas flying around. Projects every which way. Grace doesn't understand."

"It's the mess theory: out of chaos comes creativity and eventually order. I may be in the minority but I'm glad I'm me. Life is fun."

Harlan stands, his glass in hand. She turns her head and feels a wave of pleasure, satisfaction. *Spontaneous,* she thinks, *that's me.* Keith is right. It's fun. It's fun to be spontaneous.

"To friendship, good wine, and rock and roll," Harlan toasts.

"Isn't it sex, drugs, and rock and roll?" Keith whispers.

"Not Harlan." Molly says. She extends her glass toward Porter and clicks it to his. A smile breaks across her face, the smile Grandpa called her "ear to ear." She feels a swelling in her chest, a burst of rediscovery, of personhood. She looks into Porter's eyes. He smiles.

"You look lovely tonight."

For the rest of the evening, Molly quizzes Keith about his job, his project filming cities for interactive laser disks. She tells him about Jed and the little she knows of his work in the travel field. They discover that Keith's office and Jed's are near each other.

After sharing desserts and drinking coffee, Pam offers an invitation to inspect their new house a few blocks away. Harlan calls a taxi and they all pile in, with Keith and Pam squeezed in the front giving directions to the driver. The car turns into a street lined with matching houses, brownstones, four stories, with wide stone steps They stop in the middle of the block, pile out of the car, and go in on the street level behind the stoop. Inside they scatter. Molly goes with Keith to the second floor, climbing up the stairs behind him and conscious of Grace's voice and Porter's echoing through the empty spaces.

Keith leads her to a room in back. Through the window she sees the backs of houses from the other street, their lights, and the shadow of a large tree secretly existing in the back-to-back backyards. She smells the dampness in the wood and notices the gas jets on the wall. This room is from another time.

"There's an elegance of eeriness," she says. "I feel I've stepped backward by a hundred years."

"You have. That's what I love."

"Will you furnish it in antiques?"

"Never."

Porter slips into the room.

"I love this house, don't you?" Molly asks.

"It looks in good shape."

"Not bad for a hundred plus," Keith says. "Did you notice the stair rails? The newel post on this floor is a beauty. Original, they say."

"It's very nice." Porter walks to Molly, puts his hand on her back, and talks to Keith. "It's unusual to have a house so preserved."

"We're the third owner."

Molly feels Porter's hand running along the small of her back. "Didn't Pam's grandparents live near here?" she asks.

"Her mother's parents owned a house on the next street. It's a great neighborhood."

"A great investment, you think?" Porter says.

"I'm not thinking investment. We plan to live here for a long time. It's a special place."

"I've enjoyed the tour," Porter says. "We must

not keep the driver any longer." He nudges Molly toward the door and leads her down the stairs, where the others wait in the entrance hall. They go through the double doors and descend the outside steps, Harlan shouting back good-lucks and thanks. Harlan gets in the front seat. Molly sits in back. Porter on one side, Grace on the other.

"Couldn't get me to live in Brooklyn," Harlan says.

"I agree with you," Grace says.

"I don't know," Molly says. "It felt good. I could feel the history."

Porter reaches for her hand. His touch drains the stiffness from her body.

"Give me the upper East Side," Harlan says.

"What do you think?" Molly turns to Porter.

"I'm afraid Brooklyn's not for me." He cups her hand between both of his. Molly closes her eyes.

She hears Grace talk, swordfish, salmon, slivered vegetables. She focuses on the tires riding across the bumpy pavement and imagines the cobbles and patchwork asphalt of the streets. She feels the car ascend onto the bridge and her focus shifts to her hand that lies warm inside Porter's.

She hears his voice. Harlan asking questions. The two deep voices of the men back and forth, back and forth. She digs her back into the scratchy surface of the seat.

Tomorrow is Sunday. The day to finish the proposal. Jed said he'd be there at eleven-thirty. She could be done by three.

"We dropping you two at Gramercy Park?" Harlan asks.

"Yes, please." Porter squeezes Molly's hand.

Molly opens her eyes and pulls her hand away. "I better not. I'm finishing a job tomorrow."

"I was hoping we could jog in the morning. It's Sunday."

"Tomorrow afternoon? We could meet at three-thirty."

"I jog only in the morning."

The car stops.

"Tomorrow night? A movie?" Molly asks.

"You're sure about tonight?"

"Go ahead," Grace says.

Molly hesitates. "We'll do it tomorrow."

Grace reaches her hands in front of Molly. Porter takes one and kisses it. "A great evening, Grace."

"I loved our conversation tonight," she says.

The car pulls away.

"You should have gone with him," Grace says.

"It's easier this way."

"Forget that. You should be there for him. I don't think you take Porter seriously."

"I do and I'll do it my way, thank you."

"Playing hard to get, is that what you're doing?"

"I'm not playing anything. I'm living my life."

Grace pouts. Harlan tells a joke about a dog in a bar. Molly looks out the window. Perhaps she should have stayed with Porter. She almost did. She'd like to know this morning's been forgotten. Best to sleep alone tonight, be up and wide-awake tomorrow. Tomorrow's just a job. She'll do it fast.

Siri Peterson is a woman who's vice president. Siri is a name from Norway. See Norway, Your Way. It's the poster above Jed's desk.

The car reaches Seventy-second Street. The doorman opens the door and Grace climbs across Molly. She kisses her cheek. "I don't get you," she says. "Sometimes you have no sense."

Harlan bends his head through the door. "Keep smiling, kid. Be careful downtown tomorrow."

The driver pulls from the curb and swings up Third Avenue. Aloneness feels like pleasure. Molly stretches her legs, unfolds the paper from her purse, and stares at it. She folds it back, making a triangle and another triangle. Spontaneous, she thinks. It's fun to be spontaneous. It's fun to be going home alone.

The flashing light on the answering machine winks in the dark as she enters her apartment. Without turning on a light, she moves the slider and pulls off her blouse.

"Checking on you. Jed Saunders here. All set for tomorrow. I'll be at the office about eleven. Come anytime."

Terror grabs her. It feels like going to a movie on Times Square with X's on the marquee. Pleasure cascades through her limbs—and guilt. She's sneaking into the barn with Rudy. She pushes rewind. "Checking on you. Jed Saunders . . ."

Eight

On Sunday, Molly wakes at six-thirty. She clicks on the television and finds a movie with Spencer Tracy and Katharine Hepburn. Propping her pillow behind her head, she watches as pink dawn creeps through the blinds.

Hepburn's great, definitely a spontaneous personality, filled with self-confidence. Molly peers close to the scene, scrutinizing Hepburn's movements, her hands, the tilt of her head, her walk. She listens to Tracy explaining baseball and laughs.

At the start of the credits, Molly pushes the power button, rolls onto her stomach, and pulls the covers over her shoulders. She sinks into the mattress and replays the conversation with Keith: divorced men make good husbands—it's fun to be me. Thursday was a "fun-to-be-me" day, especially at the Old Town Bar, drawing on the yellow papers, laughing, drinking beer, and being crazy—off the wall. Friday tried to be but failed.

She rolls out of bed and puts on her jogging clothes. Outside the air is damp and smells like fish; the streets are empty. She sprints to Second Avenue, heading south, letting her limbs set the pace and thinking of Hepburn and Keith and Grace. She passes Grace's apartment on Seventy-second and turns up Park. Yellow daffodils crowd the center island in the street.

Back on Second Avenue, she buys the Sunday *New York Times* and *Advertising Age* and ducks inside the luncheonette on the corner. She walks to the back and slides into a booth and orders coffee, scrambled eggs, and an English muffin. She opens *Advertising Age*. It's been eight years since she dared to read this paper. She flips the pages and scans each one. "Advertising's Spunky Upstarts." She stops and reads:

. . . then there is the wild man, Jed Saunders, who was on his way up at Dane Hollenbeck when he left with only one client (or was it two?) to make his way alone, Saunders and Associates. We can't report the names of the associates, (are there any?) or what happened to Peterson. We're all watching you, Jed—if you don't make it, nobody can.

She rereads, stopping at the word, "wild man," savoring it, saying it to herself. She puzzles over Peterson and the phrase, "If you don't make it, nobody can." She smiles at the phrase, feels pride. She gobbles her scrambled eggs, eats the bacon with her fingers, pays, and leaves, taking a toothpick from the counter. She lopes back to her apartment, chewing the toothpick, wishing she were fourteen and driving a tractor and rolling in the corn with Rudy.

She showers, blow-dries her hair, applies dark brown shadow in the creases of her eyelids, and pulls on her softest jeans and an old black T-shirt. She smiles in the mirror. Grandpa said her eyes would break a man's heart.

She wanders around the room, putting away the bed things, straightening magazines. It's too early to leave. She fills in the Sunday crossword puzzle and clips the article from *Advertising Age*. At 10:42 she puts on her black raincoat and heads out the door. The forecast says rain, heavy at times. In the taxi, the driver talks about the Mets.

She pushes the buzzer at 147 Fifth Avenue and waits, scanning the street and nodding to the Korean man arranging apples in front of the deli. The door opens, surprising her. She jumps. It's Jed. "Welcome, we've been expecting you." He grins.

She follows him through the door and up the stairs. "Who's here?" she asks.

"Just me."

"You said we."

"We is me. Do you object? Did you want a party, a crowd, a group of admirers, or will just me do?"

"You'll do." She laughs, feeling awkward, hearing the echo of their voices in the hollow space. The center room is gray and dark. There are no lights and outside the clouds are heavy with rain. She turns to Jed and notices a hole in his sweater right below his shoulder.

Jed turns the doorknob to her office and pushes it. Molly sees dark clouds between the buildings.

She drops her raincoat on the table. "Looks like rain," she says.

"Looks like rain," Jed says.

"You'll be in your office?" She clicks on the computer.

"Yes."

"I must finish today. I need to discuss some things with you."

Jed leans on the windowsill. "I'll be waiting."

She feels a blush along her arms and chest. She sits at the computer and moves the mouse along the tabletop. "I won't be long."

"Don't worry. I have lots to do."

She nods her head and keeps her gaze on the computer screen.

"Can I get you coffee from the deli?"

"No thanks." She studies his face. "Wild man," the paper said.

"I'll be in my office." He leaves.

She brings the file on the screen and stares at the darkness out the window. Everything feels empty: the street, the office, the office buildings all around. Jed is in his office, at his desk, waiting. There are lights across the street, the lamp lit in the window. She sees furniture and people and knows it's not an office but a place where people live.

She makes changes in the copy, runs the printer, and wanders to the center room—no Joe, no Angelo, nobody. Jed's door stands open, a light place in the somber wall.

She wanders over, leans against the doorjamb. "I'm waiting for the printer."

"I'm ready." He's at his desk. A single lamp hangs from the ceiling, making a halo where he sits. The rest is semidarkness. The space attracts her like forbidden food. "I read about you this morning in *Advertising Age.*"

"Jon Cohen's article? What did you think?" He leans back in his chair.

"Of the article, or what he said about you?"

"Either one."

"He's rude. Have you read it?"

"Jon's an old friend."

"He says you're part of a trend."

"Jon always finds something to say. He's a good guy."

Wild man, she thinks. *Why did he say that?* "Did you like it?"

"There were some digs in it. What can you expect?"

Molly hears rain splashing hard against the windows. She stares at the dark corners of the room, then turns and goes back to her office.

Torrents of water pelt the glass like a million beetles crashing on the panes. The building across the street is blocked from sight, only a faint glimmer of light gets through the downpour. Molly takes the papers from the printer, scans each one. She reviews her written notes, then gathers the papers and hurries through the center room to Jed. She pulls a chair up to his desk.

"It's raining hard," she says.

"It's good we're inside."

"Would you like questions or comments?"

"Comments first." He pushes back his chair.

"This is basically a PR proposal."

"You could say that."

"Who's doing the work?"

"That's a question, not a comment."

Molly bites her lip. "This office doesn't seem equipped to do the work."

"Not now. Good comment."

She scratches the side of her neck. "I guess it hung me up; I didn't know where to put some stuff."

"This is a very general game plan. We're not assigning jobs."

"What about a timetable?"

"The whole plan is a timetable," Jed says.

Molly pushes a copy across the desk. "We need Post-its."

Jed tosses her a pack. She listens to the rain and writes. "What do you think, is this a five-year plan?"

"Could be a lifetime."

The inflection of his phrase knifes through her belly. She feels a blush, a warmth somewhere. She feels confused and makes a doodle. She looks toward the windows and watches the splatter and the drips and the light across the street and writes on Post-its.

"What do we do now?" Jed asks.

"We play checkers."

"Okay." He wheels his chair around the desk and next to hers. They cut and paste and laugh and disagree. The splatter on the windows stops. The rain is fine and constant.

"Would you believe it's after three o'clock."

She thinks of Porter. She promised she would call, but calling him would break the spell. She leaps from the chair.

"I'll get this on the computer and we can have another look."

"Is something the matter?"

"No."

"Do you have to be somewhere?"

"Not really. This will take twenty or thirty minutes." She's by the door. "Don't worry, I'll be back."

She closes the door to her office and dials Porter. "I'm still at work. It will be another couple of hours. Do you mind?"

"Don't hurry. I sprained my ankle jogging. I've been sleeping."

"Are you all right?"

"It's not bad."

"I'll call when I finish."

Molly sighs, puts the papers by the computer, and begins to move and rearrange the copy on the screen. Porter sprained his ankle. What a stupid thing to do. She hears the door and jumps.

"I brought you some donuts and a Coke."

"You scared me."

"They had no potatoes." He sits in a chair. "Any problems?"

"Just you." She laughs.

"What does that mean?"

"Your presence is distracting."

"Thanks. I'm here to help."

His presence is distracting; it's hard to keep her

eyes focused on the screen. She sees his every move: feet on the table, feet off the table. He stands, he paces, he looks out the window.

"I see the neighbors are at home," he says.

"People really live there?"

"It looks that way to me. A man and a woman."

"Have you seen them before?"

"I never looked." Jed settles in beside the window. "You can see them now. That's a good-looking woman."

"Jed, I'm working. You're making me want to look."

"The man's tall and lean. Maybe a dancer."

Molly goes to the window, stands by Jed, two faces peering out the window like children gaping through a fence. "That's a crazy-looking chair," Jed says.

"I love the floor lamps. There's the man—he is tall and slim."

"She must be a dancer. Watch the way she moves," Jed says.

The man puts two dishes on a table. The woman sits on the couch. The man bends to her. They kiss.

Molly shifts her feet and rubs her neck. She leaves the window. "This is weird. I have work to do."

"Me too." Jed gets up. Walks to the door and turns around. "Enjoy your donut."

The job takes longer than she planned. She prints, makes changes, and prints again. Hard rain comes back and slams against the windows. She takes the final copy in to Jed.

"This is it. If you have changes, call. I'll come back."

"Sit, Molly. You can't leave in this rain. Didn't you have a question?"

Molly takes a chair and swivels it around to face the windows and the rain. "I wonder if anyone else lives in that building?"

"If they do, they're not at home."

"What do you think of morphing?"

"It's clever. We're not doing videos, not yet."

"Those drawings we did at the bar, they could be strung together like a comic but using the concept of morphing, changing digits, pieces, going from a potato to a bag. I've been working on it."

Molly leans across the desk and makes a row of pictures. "This is rough."

"Morphing is about reality," Jed says.

"Morphing is about nonreality—erase reality. Can a potato really be a bag and if it is, is it still a potato, especially when it biodegrades back to one? Is Michael Jackson the tiger?"

"If he thinks he is, he is."

"Or if the tiger thinks he is? Morphing scares me," Molly says.

"Is it powerful like the atom bomb?"

"Lethal by itself or only when it's in the wrong hands?"

"Whose hands are wrong?" Jed asks.

"Anybody's hands when they put them where they shouldn't."

Jed leans back in his chair. Molly scratches on the paper with the pencil. She senses Jed watching her: a feeling that she likes. She draws a hand with seven fingers and gives the paper to him and he makes an "X" across it and gives it back to her. She smiles at his semigrinning eyes. "Thanks," she whispers.

She folds the paper in four parts. "Do you think the plastic bags will be successful?"

"Absolutely. Bill is smart; he doesn't do foolish things. I like the product and I plan to give it a hundred percent." He puts his elbows on the desk and leans toward her. "I chose advertising to make a difference, not to push products at the consumer. These bags will make a difference."

Molly swallows and stares at the Norway scene above the desk, hoping the tears she feels will stay inside her eyes.

"I want you to meet Bill and Ellen. You'll like them. She's smart and perceptive like you. They're a special team."

"That would be nice."

"When can you come again?"

"I don't know. When's the next project?"

"You have a natural feel for this business."

Molly twirls her chair and looks back at the windows. "I had fun on this job."

"Me too. We need to talk some more."

She stands and crumples the neck of her T-shirt. "The rain has let up."

"It's six o'clock. If you can wait twenty minutes, I'll ride you uptown. My car's in the garage around the corner."

"I've got twenty minutes of cleaning up. I'll be across the hall."

Back in her office, Molly phones Porter. "How are you feeling?"

"The scotch has numbed my ankle. How about dinner Wednesday? I'm going to keep sleeping tonight."

"Are you sure?" Molly feels relief.

"I'm sure."

Molly puts papers in her briefcase, prints an extra copy of the proposal for herself, and checks the files on the computer. She stares out the window. Jed chose advertising to make a difference. So did she— once. This could be the special job to change her life. He's younger than she and driven. She stands and paces and looks across the center room, dark with white splashes from the street lights on the walls. Jed's door is closed.

She looks across the street; it's like a theater set spread out for her to view. Molly squints and laughs. She and Jed had stood like Peeping Toms. The man and woman kissed. The man is standing there right now, by the column in the middle of the space. He's not alone. The woman is against the column. Molly puts her face close to the glass. The woman's arms are wrapped around the man. He slithers like a dancer, like an eel, his hips making Elvis Presley motions.

Molly backs away.

She glances to Jed's door. She puts her raincoat on and ties the belt, turns off the light, and sits. She swivels in the chair. Without the light the scene is magnified. The couple stand enwrapped and kissing. A zing rips through her body.

The man unties the woman's hair. The woman lifts her leg and wraps it like a sash around the man.

Molly turns and looks away. The couple cannot know or care that she is watching. All she sees are hands and hair and swaying bodies. She thinks of Jacques.

She hears a noise. A voice: "Sleeping?"

She opens up her eyes and stares, confused. She pulls her raincoat belt and stands. It's Jed. She looks into the darkness for her briefcase.

"Sorry I took so long," he says.

"It's all right." She searches around the room, on the table, on the floor. It's hard to see. She hears the rain again.

"Are you all right?" He comes beside her and takes her arm.

She turns. His face is inches from her own. Desire overtakes her, stuns her, makes her dizzy. She feels hungry, a yearning in her gut, a desire to put her mouth on his, to taste. "I'm fine," she says.

Light from the street falls on his hair. She feels his breath. He smells of something she has smelled before and liked. She feels her body tremble. His eyes look into hers and search. She feels his hand around her arm. It's strong. She feels it through the raincoat. "I can't find my briefcase," she says.

"It's here beside the chair."

She bends and takes the briefcase and his hand no longer holds her arm. "I should have kept a light on."

"It's dark in here," he says.

She pushes back the chair, checks the room again, and turns toward the door.

"I'll treat you to the elevator."

He pushes the button and they wait, hearing the cables creak. The door opens. The space inside could hold a limousine. They stand close to the front, together, touching shoulders. The door closes with a scrape; the car descends. It's very slow. Molly feels her stomach stay upstairs. "It feels tired, this elevator," Molly says.

"It's old," Jed says.

The elevator jolts and stops. She hears the door and waits for Jed to move, to leave; he doesn't. She turns and meets his eyes. They hold her there as the door begins to close. They jump and laugh. They bump. He grabs her hand. They run.

"My car's around the corner. Wait here."

"I'll go with you. I don't mind rain." She feels tied to him, unwilling to break the link. They sink their necks into their collars and trot together down the street. His car sits by the wall, right inside the entrance to the garage. It's little and it's red. Jed waves to the attendant, opens the door for Molly, and goes around to the other side. Molly stoops and crawls inside. The seats are black leather, the dashboard wood and chrome. The smell is like the inside of the pocketbook her mother bought in Spain.

Jed starts the car and pulls around into the street. She hears the rain fall on the roof, watches it drip down the windows. She breathes in the leather smell, the oil. It's like a spaceship with the two of them together. The space is close, the road is close, the curbs, the water rushing to the drains.

The other cars are giants. She stretches out her legs beneath the dashboard and watches his hand on the gearshift between them, pushing and pulling. She notices the bits of hair along his wrist below the sweater cuff, the back part of his hand that changes shape each time his grip tightens and relaxes. She brushes back her hair.

"I'm on Eighty-sixth—right off Second," she says.

"Yep."

They enter lower Park.

"Do you feel safe driving this car in the city?" she says.

"Nope." He turns his head to her. "Do you?"

"I don't think I've ever been so close to the pavement. It's . . . It's . . ."

"Scary?"

"No, not exactly." She ponders. "I feel like a bug, or better a dwarf. Maybe this is the way it feels to be a dwarf."

"Or a child?"

"A child? That's it. That's exactly how I feel, small and vulnerable. How did you know?"

He doesn't answer. She sees his hand pull back and feels the car downshift. They climb the ramp at Thirty-eighth and sweep around the Pan Am building. She notices he drives with arrogance, weaving among the taxis and Lincoln Town Cars. The other drivers peer down at them. She likes it. At the stoplight, he guns the engine, then jumps the car ahead as through a starting gate. *Wild man,* she thinks, and feels a rush.

"Eighty-sixth, you said?"

"Yes, Eighty-sixth and Second. The corner's fine."

"Do you have a dinner date?"

"No, he sprained his ankle." She wants to bite her tongue, to take back what she said. It just came out. Jed is looking straight ahead. She sees the daffodils she saw this morning.

"When all at once I saw a crowd . . ." he says.

Molly's heart catches in her throat. "A host of golden daffodils," she says.

"Beside the lake . . ." he adds.

"Beneath the trees . . ." She stops and silence fills the car. The air could fuse a bomb. The car hugs the center island, the daffodils huge, like flowers in a children's book.

He turns at Eighty-fourth. Parked cars, like tall hedges, line both sides of the street. One pulls out; Jed brakes. The car skids. Molly falls against the door. Jed's hand reaches for her, reaches around her arm. "Are you okay?"

She pulls up, nodding her head. "I'm fine."

His hand stays while they wait for the car ahead to move down the street. He lifts his hand to shift. She rubs the place it's been. He turns up Third and onto Eighty-sixth. She sees the white brick building and loneliness flies in the door and drapes her like a sheet of ice.

"Is this it?" He stops the car.

"This is it. Thanks. I loved the ride. I love your car." She opens the door. "Call if you need me."

"I'll be calling you."

She slams the door and crosses the street in front of him. She waves and rushes to the other side. When she turns back she sees the car losing itself in traffic heading east. He's going somewhere that she doesn't know about.

Nine

Jed heads his car east, enters the Eastside Drive, and laces in and out around the taxis. He drives south to the Brooklyn Bridge. His fingers comb through his hair as he glances at the empty seat beside him and winces. Loneliness crawls up his back. He reaches for the radio and stops. The silence and the rain are better for his mood.

He taps his fingers on the dashboard. Damn, he thinks. This woman is dynamite, incredibly dynamite. First he sees her through the window and is dragged toward her like a positive charge in a negative field. She comes to the office, and is incredibly smart and clever and artistic and has a second sense about marketing and promotion. The man with the sprained ankle could be her lover, could be her fiancé. Women like her have fiancés or husbands.

That's his luck.

A taxi honks. He swerves and honks his horn. They always have another guy—like Siri, a serious other guy. He rubs his chest and bangs his palm against the wheel.

The office was thick today, rocking, steaming like the old days at Dane when George was there. "Cooking," George would say. "We're cooking, Saunders, keep it rolling, the pot's about to boil."

Molly is like George, but beautiful, with legs and brains. George followed Nancy to Chicago and married. Jed almost did that once—marriage—but Siri had another plan, another man, a fiancé. He'd never marry just to marry. She's got to be a woman who stands him on his head, gets to him in places he's afraid to go alone, or can't go alone. Places in his psyche he has dreams about, fantasies about that only one smart, crazy, sexy female can unleash. Siri could do it. Molly could do it, too. He knows it in his gut, the way he knows the fellow with the ankle is a serious guy.

His foot stomps on the brake, a near-crash with a taxi jumping into the space in front of him. He pulls the safety belt and lets it snap back on his chest.

It's good he likes to work. It helps. Tonight he has a bunch of things to do to keep him sane. He'll drown in words and push away the thoughts of Siri, the thoughts of Molly.

He speeds ahead and then into the right-hand lane. He found Siri in his desk today, a picture of her sitting on the grass in Central Park. It was the memory of the day—the memory of the week, the months they spent together. He had to close the door to keep his tears from Molly—and his thoughts. He saw the couple through the window and a reel of scenes went through his head, of Siri on the elevator, Siri in the park, Siri on the roof of her apartment and in the movies, with one hand eating popcorn and the other . . .

He brakes. The car in front stops, full stop, no warning. It is the exit for the bridge.

Siri was a nymph, the genie who broke the shield he'd built around himself. She tore it off and found him. "I'm saved," he cried, the time he saw the sun come up and he had never slept, she had never let him sleep but kept him making love and making love and squeezing every drop of passion from him, killing him with passion.

He guns the car up the bridge incline and looks for Molly in the seat beside him. He should have kept her there; driven on and never let her go. He could capture her, snatch her from her boyfriend. He laughs. It doesn't work. He tried it with his mother, tried it more than once; she always got away. There always was another man who came and took her out the door, to Paris, California. Perhaps that's why he picks the women that he does, women who have men already.

Siri had Mikail. She never told him till she left. How come he never knew? He walked around with glasses on that never let him see. Never put those glasses on again. Never get involved with someone with a fiancé.

He drives across the Brooklyn Bridge and rubs his palm in circles on the gearshift. There was something in that office that kept pulling him to Molly— in her office, his office, in the dark, on the elevator. For a moment on the elevator he thought that she was Siri—the same heat was there, the same tightening like a rubber band around their bodies. It had happened once with Siri, after rain, after dark, after she told him she was going back to Norway. It happened in the elevator pressed against the metal sides, the slow creaking elevator moving up and down . . .

Today he took Molly into the elevator. It was an instinct, a pull, like gravity he couldn't resist. He hadn't ridden it since the night with Siri. His eyes rivet on the red taillights in front of him.

She was an imp with blond curls and eyes that came from planets far away. She was an intern for a year sent to him by a client to learn the business, to help promote Norway. They worked together. She was smart and clever, and anxious to learn. To him she seemed naive; it was he who was naive. He showed her Barneys at her request and bought her dinner at the Union Square Cafe. She sang Norwegian songs and whispered in his ear and lured him to a taxi and climbed up on his lap and used her tongue. He melted and turned to liquid fire and drifted with her up the stairs to her apartment.

It was the games she played: the untying of the shoes, the rubbing of the feet, the hands along the legs, his legs, her legs, white and creamy legs she unveiled slowly, rolling down her stockings, each leg separately, each leg presented as a gift for him to touch.

It was the smallness of the room, the smell of cloves and roses, the tiny light bulb underneath the large pink shade. The deep ruby flowers on the black rug where they played like children with their legs spread apart, with her feet between his legs at his groin, massaging and his blood boiling, racing, hearing her giggles down a long tunnel and smelling her, and watching the moisture on her skin glisten and her body inch toward him, down the rug between his legs, rubbing him, touching him, teasing him with her saucer eyes. She smelled of woman, of shampoo and sweat that children have when jumping rope.

She sat on him. She lifted up and sat on him and it was velvet. Moving velvet, squeezing velvet, moaning velvet. He died, passed out into another world. Before he died he lived a moment, maybe two or three, screaming, yelling, throbbing with a life that had been hidden.

For six months she was his and then she left for Norway and Mikail, her fiancé.

He runs his hands around the steering wheel. He wishes Molly still were in the car. They would go and eat and laugh and talk of morphing and the aching in his heart, the need he has for her. There was passion there today, unspoken passion. It ran around the office after them, teasing them, setting snares.

At home he calls her number and hears her answer. "Thanks for coming in today. I'll see you next week. Maybe sooner."

Ten

The red car disappears. Molly stays at the curb, straining to get a glimpse between the other cars, to see him turn the corner. She runs for cover from the rain, rummages for keys, waves to the doorman, and rides the elevator. The phone machine is flashing. She passes it, dumps her briefcase on the floor, and beelines for the kitchen and the peanut butter jar.

She dips her finger in. The taste is better than a million steaks or chocolate ice-cream cones. She pulls away her raincoat and lays it on the couch. She wanders to the window and stares through the rain to the Eastside Drive. Her finger digs in goo; her mind sits in the car. Jed. She pictures him at the wheel, his hand, his knuckles curved around the gearshift. She feels the changing gears, the rain splashing on the window. She sucks her finger. She smells the leather, the dampness, the intimacy.

She sprawls on the couch. Her self-portrait stares at her. She squints and looks at it as if it were a stranger. The face is serious, the hair, long. The time, a million years ago. The painting shows a window, a table, an easel. She drifts into that space,

white and full of light. One wall a skylight always
filled with blue sky or falling snow or blasts of sun,
or stars. And Jacques. He was the presence in the
room, like Jed today. A power that she felt inside
her bones. Jacques goaded her to polish work, to
push, perfect. He made her unafraid to ask, to think,
to argue.

She felt like that today, unafraid, charged beyond
herself. She stretches her neck, gazes at the ceiling.
Jacques's presence made her sizzle.

It was her last semester, senior year. She posed
for Jacques. She was a model, nothing more. Then
one day he came behind her, touched her shoulder.
She was painting. It was a signal. She knew it was
about to happen. She knew it when his hand slid
down her back. He told her: senior thesis time, time
for sensuality, lessons in the art of feeling.

The senior thesis spoiled her. Jacques became the
only man she ever wanted, the man she still wants.
Grace says her dream of passion is unreal, an ado-
lescent fantasy. Grace is wrong.

Molly lays her head against the pillow and shuts
her eyes. Jacques taught her to let go, in painting
and in bed. To trust, to float, to feel. He thrust these
words at her. Pushed until she floated free from all
her inhibitions. Paint like that, he said, live like that.
Scream, dare, dive, push. Trust, strive, trust, strive.
It became her mantra. She lived by it until . . . She
stands. She lost it here in this apartment, that fatal
night, then sought it back with Jacques. It wasn't
there.

The phone rings. She jumps and turns her head

as if to scold the person who intrudes. It rings again. She rubs her eyes. It's dark, it must be Porter, maybe Grace. She stumbles for it, lifts it to her ear. She hears the voice; it's Jed.

"Thanks for the ride," she says. She hears the buzz and looks into the phone. The tears begin.

She picks up things and puts them down: a magazine, the peanut butter jar. She opens up the cabinets, the refrigerator door. She rearranges bottles, throws away a plastic box of ancient food.

She listens to the phone machine. It's Porter. She blows her nose, splashes water on her face, and dials. "How's the ankle?"

"Not bad. It was stupid of me."

"I hope you'll be all right."

"I will. I talked with my parents tonight. They're coming in two weeks."

"It's a weekend?" She lies down on the sofa.

"Yes, Friday until Sunday, maybe Monday."

"I'll mark the dates. Is there anything I can do?"

"I'd like them to meet Grace."

"Good. She'd like it. Harlan too?"

"Of course. How's your week?"

"I'll be working late most nights. Maybe Wednesday?"

"Call me if you're free."

Molly arranges the magazines in stacks on the coffee table. She gets a plastic bottle of blue glass cleaner and a roll of paper towels. Porter's parents are coming to New York, coming just to spend some time with her and get to know her. She sprays and rubs the rings left on the table by the glasses. She sprays again and wipes and on her hands and knees she checks to see that they are gone. She crawls across the floor and sprays the window. Porter likes his mom and dad. They look nice in the picture. She swirls her arm around, swiping at the spray that's dripping down the window. His father had a twinkle in his eye. She stretches up, sprays and grabs the dribbles with the paper towel.

She stops the cleaning, drops the crumpled dirty towels on the floor and phones Grace.

"Harlan Newberry."

"Molly Mitchell." She laughs.

"We've just finished supper or I'd invite you over."

"Thanks, I had peanut butter. I've been working all day."

"That's right. How'd it go?"

"I survived."

"Good." Harlan laughs. "I'll get Grace."

Molly waits. She hears Harlan's voice. "Pick up the phone." She knows he's at his desk. She hears him call again. She stretches out the phone cord to the kitchen and wipes the counter.

"Hello." Grace's voice sounds muffled.

"Are you asleep?"

"No."

"Are you all right?" Molly stops the cleaning and leans against the counter.

"Yes. I'm in bed." Molly hears her breathing. "I'm reading. I was going to call. What's new?"

"Porter's parents are coming to New York. I thought you'd like to know."

"When are they coming?"

"The weekend after next."

"For how long?"

"Are you all right? Go back to reading."

"No. I'm happy for you. Has he proposed?"

"No. You sound asleep. I'll talk to you tomorrow."

"Wait. Phyllis Robins called and invited us for Memorial Day. She's expecting Porter, too. You'll hear from her."

"Do you want to go? You don't sound sure."

"Of course. They live in splendor. It will be fun."

"Does Harlan want to go?"

"Harlan? You must be kidding. Golf at the Greenwich Country Club? Of course he wants to go."

"I've always liked Phyllis. Lunch next Saturday?"

"Fine."

Molly hangs up. Phyllis roomed with Grace in college. She was a girl who had her life all planned: Roland and a house in Greenwich and children. She has it all and more: dogs and fancy cars and country clubs. The weekend could be fun or terrible.

Molly opens the refrigerator and looks around, opens cabinets and bangs them closed, reopens the refrigerator, the freezer. She grabs her keys and wallet, takes the elevator, and goes across the street.

In the Korean market, everything looks good. She heaps a plastic tray with vegetables and salad. She waits in line. A daffodil-filled bucket sits beside the counter. A flash of Jed, Park Avenue, the poem. She rubs her arm and reaches for the daffodils. Back home she puts them everywhere.

* * *

Monday morning, Molly's back at the bank on Forty-second Street. Her legs and arms are jumpy. She glances out the window, replays the day when Jed came in. At noon, she puts on sneakers and zooms down Second Avenue. At Fourteenth Street she checks her watch and runs to First, then back uptown to try to beat her record.

The run has calmed her nerves. She works all afternoon. She hopes to finish Thursday and be free on Friday in case Jed calls with changes. At night she sits and draws: potatoes, plastic bags, potatoes fading into plastic bags. The hours at the bank seem endless. She checks her phone machine every time she has a stopping place. Porter's out of town. On Thursday night, while walking home, she stops and sees a film. Friday noon she runs the final copy. No messages from Jed.

She leaves the bank and walks to Fifth and then uptown. It's automatic. She knows where she is going, the place she always goes for solace. She passes Saks, St. Patrick's, Rockefeller Center. She turns on Fifty-third, goes halfway down the street, and pushes through the swinging doors into the lobby: the Museum of Modern Art, her home away from home, her first adventure in New York City.

The lobby teems with people, lines of people buying tickets, people sitting by the wall and watching, people standing looking at the people coming through the doors. She slows her pace and finds her card, then heads straight for the escalator. The members' dining room is full but, luckily, a table's free beside the black-framed windows. It's just the place she wants to be: Rodin's *Balzac*, Moore, David Smith, all out the window in the garden down below.

She breaks the whole wheat roll in pieces, spreads on butter, chews, and looks around. The tables buzz with chatter, waving arms and nodding heads. It's good to have a place that feels so good.

After broccoli soup and salad, she strolls through the galleries, takes the bench in front of Jackson Pollack, and plays her favorite game: searching for a line that stops, that doesn't move right to the canvas edge. She squints and moves her body on the bench to see around the people standing in her view.

Molly gazes at the man in jeans, the girl who wears a turban on her head. She gazes back at Pollack, pushes back her hair, and stands and turns and smiles at the painting. She strides to the escalator, strides through the lobby and through the swinging doors. She breathes the air and swings her arms and walks west to the subway. She rides to Twenty-third and Sixth and walks to Twentieth. She greets Angelo and Joe and asks for Jed. "He's in there, Molly, go on in."

Molly knocks, then pushes on the door. Jed is at his desk. He lifts his head and smiles. "Can I interrupt? Are you busy?" she says.

"Have a seat." He taps a pencil on the desk.

"I finished early at the bank. Thought you might have changes in the proposal."

"I've been thinking about you. I don't know where the time has gone."

"I know what you mean."

"I'm sorting through a project for Amtrak. Can you work next week?"

"Will Friday do?"

"Anything. Friday's fine. Have you ever slept on a train?"

"No, I haven't. Why?"

"I haven't either but I'd like to." He leans forward. "Lying in a bunk listening to the clickety-click."

"A porter making up the beds, or is that out?"

"Compartments, fold-down seats. Want to read something? Give me your ideas." He stands, goes to the desk, and gets a wad of papers. "Do you have time?"

"Sure." She takes the papers and swings her chair close to the window, into the stream of light. She glances at the windows across the street and smiles. The sun feels good; the room feels good. She reads. She sees Jed from the corner of her eye. The papers have scenarios of trips across America. She reads and feels adrenaline sweeping through her veins. She gets a pencil from his desk. "Can I write on these?"

He grins. She feels they are in a secret plot together. "Of course."

She writes and draws and taps the pencil. The ideas grow. The train is like a Disney World on wheels. She stares at the clouds floating between the buildings and lets the ideas run inside her head.

"Are you brewing?" Jed asks.

"This is great stuff. How did you get the client?"

"I've specialized in travel."

"This isn't travel; this is entertainment. I'm bursting with ideas."

"Bring your chair over here. I'll show you some projects we're proposing."

Molly moves to the desk. He pushes papers at her, then paces across the floor, his hands behind his back, his hands flying in the air. She spins her chair to follow him, talking, listening. She feels as if she's climbing up a mountain and Jed is climbing there beside her.

The door pushes open. Angelo's head comes in. "We're leaving, boss."

Molly checks her wrist. Jed does, too.

"It's after six," Angelo says.

"After six?" Molly jumps from the chair. "This is ridiculous."

"Late for a date?" Jed asks.

"No, not exactly. It's just . . . I don't know." She laughs. "It's just after six."

"How about a drink at Espace?"

The invitation rivets Molly, stops her from putting on her jacket. She looks at Jed.

"Well?" he says, looking at the ceiling.

Molly thinks of Porter; they haven't talked. "I'd love to." She pulls her jacket on and feels a twinge. She's sneaking into the barn with Rudy.

Jed grabs his jacket from a rack and opens up the door. "It's payment for this afternoon. This session was exactly what I needed."

They walk together down the stairs. "What about

Neo-Plastics?" she says. "I came to make corrections."

"That left two days ago. There were no changes." He pushes open the door to the street and waits for her to pass.

The bar at Espace is three-deep with men and women in business suits, with T-shirts sprinkled here and there and jeans. The room feels sparkly, Parisian and very trendy. Jed signals to the bartender, who hands Jed two beers through the crowd. Molly holds her glass in one hand, her briefcase in the other. She stands close to Jed; his jacket rubs her arm. She leans her face to his to hear his voice; she feels his breath and smells the scent she did before, a scent she can't identify that makes her heady. They talk of trains. People pass and knock them up against each other. They laugh and move away.

He puts his hand behind her back to keep her steady.

"It's like the subway," she says.

"It's Friday. The cages have been opened. How about some dinner? Shall I check with the maître d'?"

Molly checks her watch and hesitates. She sees his finger pull along his T-shirt neck. He grins. "Sure," she says. She's rolling in the cornfields and listening for her sister to sneak up.

She glances through the space noticing the sprays of tiger lilies in clay pots, the twenties' drawings on the wall. She watches Jed talking to the maître d'.

Waves run through her body; she hopes they can have dinner. The waves are interrupted by a pang of fear, of guilt, a picture of Porter calling on the phone and leaving messages.

She smiles as Jed walks back toward her. "It's an hour, but could be sooner. What do you think?" he says.

It's a signal to go home, or find a phone. A body bumps her from behind before she answers. She turns. It's Keith. "What are you doing here?" she says.

"Molly, what a surprise. I'm waiting for Pamela. What are you doing?" He looks at Jed.

"I'm Jed Saunders." Jed extends his hand.

"Keith McCarthy. Pam will be here soon. She'll love to see you."

"Jed and I are talking business," Molly says.

"Don't let me interrupt."

"No, I think you two have things in common."

Molly mentions laser disks and Jed and Keith take turns exchanging questions. Pamela arrives. The bar thins out and all four stand against it. The conversation moves among them. There's hunger for the information each one has to give. They laugh. Their tongues trip over what they have to say. Molly watches Jed, his laugh, the way he bites his lip.

The maître d' signals Jed; the table can seat four. The evening keeps on going, the pace the same, never letting up. Jed lives a block away from them in Brooklyn. They talk about the house and eat and linger over coffee. Jed suggests the Old Town Bar.

Molly walks with Pamela, Keith with Jed.

"He's nice," Pamela says.

"Jed?"

"He's different from what's-his-name."

"Porter?"

"You go together. You and Jed."

"What do you mean?"

"If I didn't know better, I'd think you two were married."

"We work well together."

"Are you sure that's all?"

"That's all, believe me. He is at least five years younger than I am."

They crowd into a booth. Molly feels nostalgia for the night that she and Jed were there alone. She feels connected to him, here, sitting as a couple in the booth. The bench is narrow; their arms touch. The glass globe lamps shine in the beveled mirrors. Keith tells about the trip he took when he was twelve, a train trip through Canada. They drink coffee with whipped cream.

"It was the greatest. I'd take my kids." He looks from Molly to Jed. "You know we have a secret. Pam's pregnant."

"Please don't tell Grace," Pam says.

The moment has a kinship. Special friends linked in the secret of the baby.

"Congratulations," Jed says. His hand rubs Molly's arm.

"I think we need to get home," Pamela says. "This has been a great evening." As they walk to Broadway, they wrap their arms around each other, the four together. The first taxi is for Molly. Keith and Pamela kiss her cheeks and pull her in and hug her. Jed leans down and puts his lips on hers. The kiss is brief.

The taxi ride feels short. She thinks about the afternoon, standing at the bar, the night with Pam and Keith, the kiss. The number on the message machine is three.

"Porter here. Where are you? Let's meet for dinner."

She sits on the couch and kicks off her shoes.

"It's nine o'clock. This is Porter. Grace is worried. Call when you get in."

A beep. "Eleven o'clock. Just thought I'd check. No message, but call if you get this. It's Porter."

Molly dials Grace.

Harlan answers, awoken from sleep. "Here's Grace."

"Sorry to wake you," Molly says. "Porter's message said you were worried."

"Where have you been? You're okay?"

"I'm great. I guess I should call Porter."

"He's been frantic. Where were you?"

"I'll tell you at lunch tomorrow. You'll be surprised who I was with."

"Who?"

"Pamela and Keith McCarthy."

"Pam? How come?"

"I'll tell you tomorrow."

Molly pulls the bed out and gets the blanket and the pillows. She drops her clothes and finds a cotton nightshirt. The phone rings.

"Did Pam invite you?"

"Invite me where?"

"Tonight for dinner?"

"No, I bumped into them. I have to call Porter."

"I want all the details tomorrow."

Molly gets in bed and pulls the covers to her neck. She stretches her legs. Her body washes with sensations. She wiggles her toes and reaches for the phone. The receiver feels hard and cold. She presses each button; the beeps are loud; the rings are endless.

"Drummond here."

"Sorry to wake you. I'm home."

"I was waiting for your call. Where were you?"

"I met some friends and had dinner. That's all."

"I was planning dinner."

"I'm sorry, I didn't know."

"Will I see you tomorrow?"

"Of course. We'll talk in the morning."

"I'll call. Sleep well."

Molly pulls the covers under her chin and tucks them in around her body. She clicks on the television. Garbo is Camille: the scene with Robert Taylor. She raises the volume and props up her pillow. She watches the picture, hears the voices, and drifts between Espace and the Old Town Bar.

Eleven

Saturday morning, at seven-forty, Molly's phone rings. On the third ring, she knows it's not a dream and lurches from her bed.

"Porter here."

"I'm asleep. What time is it?" Molly yawns and drags the cord and phone under the covers.

"I'm going jogging. Meet me in Central Park."

"When?"

"In thirty or forty minutes."

Molly looks at the clock. "I can't. I'd rather sleep. Is your ankle feeling better?"

"Seems to be. Maybe I'll stop by."

"I'm meeting Grace for lunch."

"What time?"

"Twelve."

"What are you doing then?"

"I don't know, it's too early to think."

"Come to my place after lunch."

"We may go shopping."

"Come when you can. I'll be home waiting. You had a good dinner last night?"

"Yes, I met Keith and Pamela. Remember them?" Molly gets out of bed and goes to the refrigerator.

"The people from Brooklyn? You should have called, I'd have joined you."

"I'm sorry. I didn't know you were waiting."

"Tonight? Is there something special you want to do?"

"I don't know. A movie?" She pours orange juice in a glass.

"We could just stay home. I'll make dinner."

"You? Make dinner?"

"Steak, potatoes. You make the salad."

"I am sorry about last night. I thought you'd be working." Molly sits on the bed.

"We'll talk about it later."

Molly hugs the pillow and tries to sleep. Pictures of her and Jed and Pam and Keith flash behind her closed eyelids. The four jammed in the booth, walking down the street, arms around each other, the kisses at the taxi. Jed's kiss. She thinks of Porter by the phone, calling, waiting for her call. It wasn't fair of her; she knew he would be waiting, wondering where she was. She doesn't like to hurt. Her body sinks into the bed. The pictures fade; she sleeps.

When she wakes up, her mouth feels dry, her head feels drugged. It's late; almost time for lunch. She puts on jogging clothes and jogs between the crowds on Third. She's heading for the sixties, a restaurant Grace has found. It's Mexican and down a flight of stairs beneath some stores. Grace is always looking for the newest place to eat.

Grace is at a table near the back. Molly scans the whitewashed room, the checkered tablecloths. There are no windows; lights shine through tin sconces on the wall splashing patterns on the dark brick floor. It's empty but for Grace and two couples at a table near the front. The room is hot and smells of stewed tomatoes.

Molly takes the bentwood chair across from Grace. "What's this?" she says, pointing to the pitcher on the table full of purple liquid and floating orange slices.

"Sangria."

"Fruit juice and wine? Too much. I need plain water." She signals the waiter.

Grace leans across the table. "So, you were with Pam and Keith. Tell me about it."

"Jed and I went to this trendy bar and I bumped into Keith, literally. I was really surprised."

"A bar with Jed? Where was Porter?"

"It was just one of those quick after-work drinks. Business talk. We got talking to Keith. Pam arrived and things went on. I had a great time." She gulps a glass of water.

"What's Keith like?"

"He's really smart and funny. What can I say?"

"Porter was frantic. He called looking for you."

"I know. Let's order."

"I'm having a burrito."

"A burrito instead of salad? What's the matter?" Grace's hair is tied behind her head. She wears a sweater Molly recognizes from college days. "You look beat or sick. What's wrong?"

"It's an off day."

"Are you pregnant?"

"No way."

"You could be and don't know it." Molly pours sangria in a glass.

"I couldn't be and I know it. We're not having children."

"What? We were having them together? What happened?"

"Kids are trouble. We don't need it. You have them."

"Wait a minute. Who's talking here?" Molly reaches out for Grace's hand. "Is Harlan feeling insecure? Don't you think he'll change his mind when he makes partner?"

"That's not it. I've changed my mind. No children." Grace pushes up her sleeves. "What are you doing tonight?"

"Grace, what's going on? You look upset."

"Nothing. Harlan's never home. It's that California deal."

"It's being an associate for too long in a Wall Street law firm. That will change." Molly pulls off her jacket.

"He's been acting strange. I can't explain."

"Strange? Like how?" They watch the waiter put down the food.

"I don't know. Forget it." Grace bites into the burrito. "And forget children for me. Harlan doesn't want them. I'll be the perfect aunt."

"I thought I was marrying Porter so we could have children together. That plan is over? Maybe I'll talk to Harlan." Molly picks at the lettuce.

"It won't do any good. It's done." Grace wipes her chin.

"Nothing's ever done."

"You don't know what you're saying. This is done." Her voice shakes. Burrito juice runs down her arm.

"Grace, what's wrong?"

"Harlan had a vasectomy."

"What?" Lettuce sticks in Molly's throat. "The bastard." She pounds her fist. "This is crazy. Who gave him the right?" She jumps from the chair and pushes it.

"Ssh. Sit down."

"I'd like to punch him. Didn't you talk about it?"

"I agreed."

"You what?" Molly pushes her chair near Grace's and straddles it. "Are you nuts?"

"It's better this way."

"Better?"

"It's birth control."

"It's mutilation."

"Stop it. You don't understand. Harlan did this for me."

"He did it for himself. I hate him." She turns the chair around. "You want children, I know it. Didn't you discuss it before you got married?"

"I just assumed we would. It will be all right."

"I don't get you. You should have talked to me."

"What for?"

"I don't know. I don't know what for." Molly pushes the salad plate across the table. "Maybe I won't have children either. I won't marry Porter."

Grace grabs Molly's arm. "You have to marry Porter. I'll die if you don't. You have to have the babies, one for me."

"Damn." She taps her fingers on the table.

"I shouldn't have told you."

"Damn. You were the one to have the children."

"You'll do it. You're not too old if you act fast. We'll still share. You have to make the family now. I'll become the big editor and the special doting aunt."

"I don't know."

"You have to, Molly. I want children."

"Let's get out of here and go to Bloomingdale's. I'm raging inside."

Molly finds the sunlight blinding as they climb the stairs. Anger sits like bad food. Grace links her arm. "Don't let Harlan know you know."

"When I punch him, I won't say a thing."

Bloomingdale's feels like a flea market. The aisles are crowded and people sit on stools, their faces lifted like baby birds while pink-smocked women apply eye shadow and face cream and rouge.

"Let's find the bathing suits." Grace sprays Charlie on her wrist.

"Don't put that on me. How about some Chanel No. 5?" Molly picks up the rectangular bottle.

"It might make me cry. It was the only perfume she wore."

"Dad's standard present to her." Molly sprays it on her fingers.

"Promise you will marry Porter and have at least one child." Grace grabs her hand.

"If he asks."

"Good. Let's find the bathing suits."

Racks and racks of bathing suits sit side by side. Molly stands by Grace and watches as her hand slides the hangers down the metal bar. She smells the perfume on her wrist. She's with her mother, buying clothes for school. It seems a million years ago.

"Let's try on string bikinis."

"You're kidding?"

"I've found a divine silver one for you and a pink one for me."

In the dressing room, they pull off clothes and pull on patches of color. Molly looks in the mirror. "This is definitely for someone under thirty."

"You look under thirty. It's fabulous. I'm buying it for you."

"You're throwing away your money."

"No I'm not. It's for your honeymoon. Wear it and you'll come home bursting with baby."

Terror seizes Molly like a jolt of poison. She turns from the mirrors and pulls on her jogging clothes. "I'll meet you out front."

Molly circles the bathing suits, walking back and forth and in between the rows and rows of racks as if they were a maze, a giant puzzle. Grace comes behind her and hands her a paper bag. "This seals our pact. You have the baby. I'll be the helpful aunt who spoils her."

Outside, Molly kisses Grace's cheek and watches her walk north. A vasectomy. What a crazy, selfish thing to do. What's wrong with Harlan? She waits for the light to change, then crosses Lexington and walks east. Too much noise, too much traffic. She crushes the package under her arm. What will Grace do? She walks on without looking, not caring where she goes and bumps her arm against a group of Asian tourists. She bows and smiles and stops and looks around. Too many people, too much smell of car exhaust. Every driver is leaning on his horn.

On the corner she pulls a dollar from her wallet and buys a pretzel. She bites and chews and bites and shoves the pretzel in her pocket and watches the people buying pretzels and the people crossing the street. She doesn't know which way to go. Harlan had an operation, got fixed like a dog. Grace will never have a child. No children. No babies. A taxi's at the curb; the passenger is leaving. She lunges for the door before it closes, dives inside, and flops onto the seat. She recites Porter's address to the driver.

Twelve

Porter opens the door. He wears a yellow T-shirt and navy running shorts. Molly hears Puccini playing in the distance on the stereo.

"I hoped you'd come. It's good to see you."

She goes inside. The large wood door closes behind her. The city's gone. The living room is warm and still and sturdy. She collapses on the leather couch and feels the comfort from the books and Oriental rugs. It's like a room in an English manor house.

"How was the jogging?" she asks.

"I went along the river. My ankle's still tender. How's Grace?"

"Grace? I'm not sure. I guess okay."

"Anything wrong?"

"She just looked tired." Molly feels stinging in her eyes.

"Would you like wine, a Coke, beer?"

"Water with lots of ice." Molly rests her head against the cool shiny couch. "Is this *Madame Butterfly?*"

"It's *Turandot*. What did you buy?"

"Grace bought it. It's sort of a joke." Molly pulls the bikini from the bag and holds it up.

"What is it?"

"A bathing suit. Can't you tell?"

"Prove it, put it on."

"Now?"

"I'd like to see it."

She drinks the water, sucks an ice cube. "You won't laugh."

"I might." He sits in the Windsor chair by his high-backed desk. His calm gray eyes smile. Molly smiles. She takes the package to the bedroom and removes her clothes. She works the silver triangle up her legs and hooks the patches between her breasts. She peeks into the living room and sees Porter's back against the spindles of the chair.

She tiptoes in. Her bare skin tingles. She yanks at the strings between her buttocks. The rug feels scratchy on her bare feet. "Porter?"

He turns his head. The love duet from *Turandot* soars. She feels cold and bare and funny standing in the room. "What do you think?" she asks.

He runs his hand along his forehead. "It's not a lot of bathing suit. Turn around."

She swivels on her foot like a child showing off.

"You're not planning to wear it in public?"

"You don't approve? Grace bought one in pink."

"I approve, but for private use only." He stands and moves toward her. "We need to talk."

Molly backs into the doorway of the bedroom.

"You worried me last night," he says. "I wanted to see you."

She folds her arms across her bare midriff.

"I thought of accidents. Thought you might be with another man."

"I should have called." She presses against the doorjamb.

He reaches for her, pulls apart her arms. His hands are warm. "I thought about the other morning. I'm not taking advantage of you, believe me."

"I know." She succumbs to his arms, comfortable arms. They wrap around her and hold her and she sighs and stays still, afraid to splinter the protection he provides.

"I think I love you, Molly."

She lifts her head. His lips press down on hers. They're warm and gentle. She feels his thumping heart. She wraps her arms around his neck; her legs mesh with the bareness of his legs. She closes her eyes and reaches for another kiss.

"I respect you, Molly. I don't want you to think I don't."

"I know."

He unwraps his arms. "Get dressed. You feel cold."

She splashes water on her face in the bathroom and looks in the mirror. *I think I love you, Molly.* She brushes her teeth and gets back in her leggings and sweatshirt. Her nerves cry to run, to swim, to get untensed. She slips back into the living room and sits on the couch, curling her legs up under her.

Porter hands her wine. "Are you warmer now?" He pats her head.

"Yes." She feels the start of tears.

"Will you make the salad? I bought the greens."

"Of course." She sorts through the magazines on the table, flipping pages. Porter puts cheese and Ritz crackers on the coffee table and sits on one of the matching love seats.

"What did you talk about at lunch?"

"Not much. Grace seemed depressed. Harlan's never home."

"I don't like his new California clients. He may be in over his head. I'm watching. I promise I won't let him get in trouble."

"Trouble?"

"He's ambitious and in some ways inexperienced. Grace should know a lawyer works long hours."

"She knows that. It's not the problem." Molly watches Porter light the lamps and pour more wine. He pulls the drapes. The room becomes a cocoon. Safe. He'll keep her safe, and Grace safe, too.

They cook, they eat, they rinse and do the dishes. They sit on separate love seats with their books and magazines. Piano music plays, Chopin preludes, Molly's favorite. She looks above the magazine she reads and sees his face, his glasses perched halfway down his nose. He wears a khaki long-sleeved shirt. She smiles. He thinks he loves her.

She thinks of Jacques, the way she'd watch his face when he was painting her, when she lay naked on the couch. Naked is the way she was this afternoon when Porter said the words. Her body had responded. She wanted him to pick her up and take her to his bed, like Jacques.

Jacques liked to tease when making love: to touch and pull away. He wanted her to beg. She did. She thinks about the places that he touched, about his fingers crawling up her body. She feels them now, feels the target waiting for his hands, craving for the touch. She stretches out her legs. Her heart is pounding as it did with him.

She looks across at Porter. His face is serious. She thinks about his body in the bed. Sensations run along her legs. She pushes out her legs and flexes back her toes. She stretches like a cat and arches her back. She needs a man, his strength, his warmth, his hands, the connection with his body. It's a reason to be married. She aches. She thinks of lying on the bed with Jacques, touching, taking turns, and meshing skin and palms and legs and tongues and begging for his body to come inside of hers.

"Tired?" She jumps at Porter's touch. He pushes in beside her on the couch. "I'm glad you're here."

His hand is on her thigh. She lifts her chin and looks at him.

"I'm making plans." He lowers his head to hers. She takes his lips like moisture for the thirsty and moves her leg to bring his hand up higher on her thigh. His fingers and his thumb grasp and release the flesh beneath her cotton pants. She moans and runs her tongue inside his lip.

"Let's go to bed," he says.

She waits and watches as he turns the switches of the lights. He pulls the bedspread back. She craves to feel the ironed sheets against her skin and pulls away her clothes. He follows her. Together they are naked. Her skin feels smooth; his body hard and ready. She wraps her arms around his back. She wants a man. His chest, his legs, his breathing all excite her. She likes the way he wants her, too. The moment doesn't last. It's quick, spontaneous, a miracle of matched responses. She keeps her arms around his neck. This may be love.

The morning light creeps underneath the drawn drapery. Molly blinks her eyes and reaches out across the bed. It's empty. She hears the bedroom door and turns her head.

"I've got coffee, croissants, and the *New York Times*."

She wraps herself in Porter's robe and goes into the living room. "You're up early."

"I'm always up early. I'd like you to see a co-op with me today. It's at Ten Gracie Square."

"How come?"

"I'd like your opinion. It's in the estate of a client."

"Sure. I'll need to stop and change my clothes."

At one o'clock the taxi drives under the sculptured entrance canopy of Ten Gracie Square. The doorman is at the car before the taxi stops. He opens the door. "Mr. Drummond, I presume. Mrs. Hirschfield is waiting."

A large woman in a large hat rises from a chair in the lobby. She extends her hand. "It's a pleasure meeting you, Mr. Drummond." She turns to Molly. "Mrs. Drummond?"

"Molly Mitchell."

They ride the elevator facing forward behind the man in uniform. Mrs. Hirschfield chatters about the spring weather. Molly watches Porter; he's in his business mood. It makes her feel important. She checks her posture, lifts her chin. She's glad she's wearing shoes with heels.

Off the elevator, they enter a tiny entrance hall. Mrs. Hirschfield works the key in the lock of the apartment door. "They don't come any better than this, Mr. Drummond, not anywhere in Manhattan." She opens the door. "You know you'll be sharing a building with Madame Chiang Kai-shek, Gloria Vanderbilt . . ."

Mrs. Hirschfield enters. Porter stands aside for Molly. Before them in the foyer is a winding staircase going to a second floor. "Your Christmas tree can go right inside the curve, all the way to the second floor."

There is no furniture or rugs and the bare walls show the marks of former paintings. They trail the woman to the far end of the living room where the windows look out on the East River.

"It's like being on a ship, don't you think?" she says.

"The view is very nice," Porter says.

"You've got four fireplaces, all working."

Molly stays by the window, a large bay window with a window seat, and watches a tug and barge going down the river. Porter follows Mrs. Hirschfield. Molly hears their voices in the next room.

"There are four bedrooms upstairs. Three full baths. Powder room off the downstairs entrance hall."

"We are going upstairs," Porter calls to Molly.

She follows, watching Porter open closet doors. She runs her fingers across the fluting on the mantel in the master bedroom.

Mrs. Hirschfield continues talking. "A fireplace, it's cozy . . . nice big shower . . . plenty of closet space . . . lovely view of the bridge." Molly follows in a trance, through the rooms and bath and down the back stairs to the kitchen. "Professional equipment . . . double sink . . . two ovens . . . freezer . . . perfect for entertaining . . . important for a man like you, Mr. Drummond."

They return to the foyer. Porter opens the front door. Molly starts to leave and Porter takes her arm. "Not yet, Molly. Thank you, Mrs. Hirschfield."

Porter closes the door. "What do you think?"

Molly feels moisture on her hands. She hesitates. "It's the biggest apartment . . . or co-op, I've ever seen."

"Do you like it?" He guides her into the living room.

She goes to the window and catches a last glimpse of the tug. "It has a lot of nice details: beautiful fireplaces, first-class wooden floors, wonderful moldings. What can I say? What do you think?"

"It's a very special place." He sits on the window seat and takes her hand and pulls her down beside him. "Maybe you and I could live here."

Molly pulls away. "This is a building of millionaires." She hears Grace: "He's looking at a big apartment."

He laughs. "If we lived here, I wouldn't lose you

on Friday nights." He slides across the window seat and puts his arm around her shoulder.

"What are you asking, Porter? You bring me to this unbelievable building, this unbelievable co-op, and now you're saying we should live here together. I don't get it." She leaves the window seat and escapes through the archway to the dining room. Her heart is beating in her throat. She's in a play and reading lines. The view out the window is all river and the bridge and the boats and barges. The dining room is huge with moldings on the wall the way she dreamed a room should be. She looks at Porter; he is smiling at her.

"Come back and I'll tell you."

She moves across the floor toward him, then stops in the archway and catches her breath. The living room is beautiful.

He unwinds his body from the seat and takes the three steps to her. His hands reach for hers and he raises them close to his chest. "I'd like to marry you and live here with you. We could think about a child . . . maybe two."

Her hands feel small and limp inside his. She looks down at the floor, then up at him.

"Will you marry me?" he asks.

She sees the furrows in his brow, the earnestness deep inside his eyes. She smiles. "I don't know what to say."

"Come, sit back down. We'll talk." He leads her to the window seat and faces her and takes her hands again in his.

She sees a sailboat on the river, a bare mast,

bucking the tide. One lone person stands holding the tiller. She watches the struggle. She feels the struggle in her stomach. "I need to think," she says.

"Of course. How much time do you need?"

"I don't know." The boat is banging into swirling waters.

"I'd like to know. I'd like to tell the office I can buy the co-op." He drops her hands.

"I see." She turns and follows the boat's transom. "I don't mean to hang you up, but it's something I need to think about."

"Of course. Let's take another tour." He hops from the seat.

She follows him. They wander in and out of rooms, up the stairs and down. Molly feels she's in a dream, another city with a stranger. She opens doors and looks out windows and watches Porter. *He could be my husband. I could have a child, a little girl with pigtails.* She thinks of Grace and Grace's plea.

The kitchen is brand-new, the woman said, good for entertaining. Molly notices the tiles laid into the wall above the counter. Each one different, each handmade. She runs her fingers over them, touching, examining the artwork. Porter comes beside her, his arm around her waist.

She feels his lips against her hair and shivers travel down her back. She turns and lifts her face and kisses him. He loves this place. It's like a fairy tale. She would have guests and parties and a maid and a nanny who would take the children to the park. The image of the boat leaps in her head, the person at the tiller. She runs her hand along his back. "This place is very nice."

"I'm glad you like it."

"I love these tiles." She bends across the counter to see better. "Look at the intricate work." He bends behind her. She moves to be a spoon inside his curve, to rub her buttocks on his groin. His arm encircles her, his hand cups her breast. She wiggles, she talks, she points, she teases him by wiggling. She hears her voice jump through the empty space. She feels her breast fill up his hand and feels the fullness in his pants. She wiggles. She pictures sitting on the counter . . .

He straightens. "We ought to leave."

She puts her arms around his neck, her tongue deep into his mouth. She rubs her hand across the bulge below his waist.

"Molly, not now—not here." He pulls her to the foyer.

She pushes him against the wall and leans her body flat on his.

"Someone could come in—the doorman. Please." He opens the door, jiggles his pants, and pushes the elevator button.

Walking back to her apartment, he holds her hand.

"Do you ever like to be spontaneous? Do crazy, wild things?" she asks.

"There's a time and place for everything."

Molly squeezes his hand. She feels like a child. Porter is the adult.

"Don't mention Gracie Square to Grace or anyone."

"I won't."

"We'll have dinner Tuesday night. You can say yes then."

Outside her building, he kisses her forehead and flags a taxi.

She struggles with the keys and gets inside her apartment. Nausea surges in her stomach. She holds the wall; the struggling boat, the whirling water, the tiles, bumpy and pink, tangerine, purple, fuchsia, aquamarine, water over the bow, water over the gunwales, swirling water. She sees the "1" on the answering machine and pushes the slider and goes to the couch.

"Jed Saunders. Enjoyed the other night. I'm counting on you next Friday. Give me a call if you can."

She pulls the phone to the couch and dials Jed.

"Molly, your input Friday was great. I need that kind of give-and-take and you and I do it well together."

"Yes."

"It would be great if you could work one day a week for me. More later. Not just the desktop stuff. I'd like to work you into the creative end of things. We think alike."

"Yes."

"Well, how's Friday?"

"Yes, I think so."

"Great. Pam and Keith showed me their house today. It's amazing. I made some suggestions. I think they liked them. Funny how they live around the corner from me."

"It's a great house." She leans against the back of the couch. The room whirls.

"Keith's got work for us. I want you to come with me to see his setup."

"I'd love to see it."

"Molly, are you okay? You sound strange."

"I'm fine. Maybe a little tired."

"See you Friday. I may call sooner."

Molly lies on the couch. She puts her arm across her eyes and sleeps and dreams. Grace is a little girl with a carriage full of baby dolls. She takes them one by one and throws them out a window. The window is the bay window in the living room of Ten Gracie Square.

Thirteen

Molly's radio plays at 7:40 Monday morning. She had been lying looking at the ceiling waiting to hear the click, the music, the talking, the weather. The blanket feels like an X-ray protection cover from the dentist's office. She showers and dresses by rote, carefully, step by step, like a well-trained, cognitively impaired person. All morning she feels like that: stuck in a body that moves automatically. At work, her computer is her enemy, eating copy, losing files; Pace Lewiston feels like a prison on a bad day.

At noon, she walks around the block, once, then again and again. The air is laden with water, either fine rain or heavy mist. It suits her mood. She buys lemon yogurt in the deli and eats it at her desk with a plastic spoon. She can quit all this. With her head resting in her hands, her elbows on her desk, she takes a mental tour through the rooms of Ten Gracie Square: she plans a party and dresses herself, she dines with Porter quietly in the dining room with candles, she lies in bed and gazes at the river. A lump is in her throat. She stretches, gets water from the water cooler, finds Tylenol, and swallows two. At three o'clock she leaves and goes home.

The doorman holds the door; she shakes her wet umbrella. "I have a box for you. It just came." He goes behind the desk and lifts a shiny box, long and white.

She takes it from his hands and rides the elevator. Balancing it, she finds her keys and opens the door to her apartment and puts the box on the kitchen counter. She sheds her corporate skirt and blouse and zaps the television. Donahue holds a book about women who choose wrong men. She watches, pulling the ribbon from the box and lacing it around her fingers. The box is full of roses, red ones. She lifts the box to her nose; it smells like satin bedspreads, pink wallpaper. She carries it to the couch and sets it on her lap, weaving the ribbon and listening to the women asking questions.

The phone rings.

"Molly, you creep, why didn't you tell me?"

"Tell you what, Grace?"

"Harlan just called. Porter told him. I knew it. I'm so excited I'm crying. Come over tonight. We'll celebrate."

"Porter told Harlan?"

"When did he ask you?"

"He shouldn't have told." Molly puts the roses on the table.

"How did he ask? What's the date?"

"That really annoys me."

"What?"

"It's not official."

"I called your office. Why are you home?"

"I quit early."

"Of course. You don't need to work anymore, ever again."

"Yes I do." Molly takes a small white envelope from the box.

"Come over at six. We'll have champagne. Shall I invite Porter?"

"No, just us."

Molly removes the daffodils from the vase on the coffee table. She replaces the water; then takes each rose separately from the green tissue paper and stands it in the vase. She watches Donahue, his microphone, the answers from the author. She sucks her bleeding finger, pricked by a thorn.

She runs a bath, slips inside, and falls asleep. She's on a train speeding down a mountainside, sliding from the seat, crashing down the aisle, slipping, reaching with her arms and feet, struggling with her arms and feet to find a place to hold. She hears a ring—another ring. She opens her eyes and looks around, then grabs a towel and dives from the bath to the phone.

"Did you get the roses?"

"Yes. They're lovely."

"Don't mention Ten Gracie Square. You haven't?"

"No. I haven't said anything to anybody."

"We're still on for dinner tomorrow? I'm counting on a positive answer."

"What did you tell Harlan?"

"That I asked you to marry me. I met him in the men's room."

"The men's room?" She bites her nail. "I wish you hadn't."

"I thought you would have told Grace."

"I wish you hadn't told Harlan."

"My parents are coming Friday. I'd like this settled by then."

"Wait, Porter I—"

"I know, darling, you want a couple of days."

"Yes, a couple of days." Darling sounds so strange. "I don't know why."

"Have you picked a restaurant for tomorrow?"

"Let's go to Greenwich Village."

"If that's what you want. I was thinking something more elegant."

"I'd like to go to Rosolio's on Barrow Street, just off West Fourth."

"I'll meet you at seven-thirty."

Molly hangs up the phone and takes the card from the white envelope: Awaiting your consent. My love always.

She puts the card under the vase with the roses and leans into them, smelling them, drinking in their elegance. It's five to six. She pulls on black leggings, a yellow sweatshirt and sneakers, and leaves. In the hallway, she hears her phone, digs inside her purse for the door keys and wrestles with the locks. As the door opens, she hears Jed's voice recording.

"This is Jed, I'd hoped—"

She lunges for the phone. "Jed?"

"Molly? Are you there? I just talked to Keith. He wants us at his office tomorrow. Can you get away? I'm going there at three. What do you think?"

"I think that's fine."

"Then you can make it?"

"Sure, I'll work something out. Where is it?"

She scribbles the address on the phone book. "Jed, if I'm not there at three, don't wait."

"I'd like you there; I like your ideas."

"I'll try my best."

Molly walks to the windows, to the kitchen, to the walk-in closet. She crushes the flower box and takes it down the hall to the compactor. She comes back and brushes her teeth, combs a nail through her dark eyebrows, and squints at herself in the mirror. She leaves. The sky has cleared and dampness hangs like tinsel on a tree. Water stands in puddles. She goes down Second Avenue looking in the windows, looking at the traffic. Now and then, she whistles.

Grace opens the door. "Here comes the bride," she sings.

"Stop. Not yet."

"This is the best thing that could ever happen. Harlan sends congratulations; he won't be home until late." She laughs. "He says you owe him."

"I'm furious with Porter for telling Harlan." She looks around Grace's apartment and makes a beeline for the couch, slouching into it, patting the flowered chintz fabric.

"Why? Were you planning to keep this a secret?" Grace is at the pine hutch twisting the wire from the cork of the Moët et Chandon.

"It was presumptuous of him." Molly unlaces her sneakers.

"I'm the one who should be mad—you promised you'd call." She hands a flute of champagne to Molly and raises her glass. "To my sister, the rich bitch."

"Thanks." Molly tucks her feet under her and picks up the *Bride's* magazine from the coffee table. "I'm not ready for this."

"Of course you are."

"I am not wearing white and I am not walking down an aisle. Porter did that once."

"You could be married here."

"Maybe City Hall."

"Have you made wedding plans?"

"I haven't even said yes."

"What? What's wrong with you?"

"I don't know. I was surprised, regardless of what you said. I have to think about it." She unbends one leg, stretches it, and wiggles her toes.

"You're scared. I know you." Grace refills the glasses.

"He's not exactly what I planned."

"He's better than you planned. You don't feel worthy."

"I feel confused." Molly glances at the picture of the bride on the magazine.

"Tell me the juicy part. Where were you when he asked? What exactly did he say?"

Molly looks around the room, at Harlan's desk, the drapes that match the couch, the pale yellow painted walls. "We were on this roller coaster at Coney Island."

"Really, where were you? I want to know. In bed?"

"Wrong."

"At dinner? Tell me."

"My secret. Porter's parents arrive this Friday."

"I know; I'm dying to meet them. Porter talked to Harlan."

"I want to meet them, too. It may help my decision."

"Why?"

"I don't know." Molly runs her fingers through her hair. "It will fill in some blanks. Give me a better picture. If I really like them, I may not feel this hesitation. You know what I mean?"

"No. I'd be saying yes all over the place. Porter is wonderful. Forget his parents. They could be hicks for all I care."

"You seem so sure. I wish I did." She rubs her foot.

"If I weren't married to Harlan, I'd grab him. No waiting, no parents. I'd get him to the church."

"You're funny, Grace. You think he's got everything."

"He does. Call him right now and say yes. Has he told you about the co-op?"

Molly fills her glass with champagne. "He didn't talk about it."

"He will and then you'll say yes. Molly, I want Porter for a brother. I really do. Remember you were always Molly-to-the-Rescue when I needed you. I need you now, I really do."

Molly clicks her sister's glass. "Molly-to-the-

Rescue here I am. I'll find your tricycle, Band-Aid your knee, take you to Boston when you're feeling sad."

"I'm feeling sad, Mollykins."

"I know, Gracie. Harlan's a bastard."

"He's not. But you can make it all right. You and Porter."

On Tuesday Molly arrives at Pace Lewiston by eight and works through lunch. At three, she takes a taxi to Laser, Inc. The building is an old factory just east of Broadway on Sixteenth. The sign says, Second Floor. The flight of stairs are steep and smell damp and sour. Inside is a surprise: the walls are stop-sign yellow with one wall glass brick. The furniture is black. The floors are black.

"Molly?" A voice comes from behind a waist-high partition.

"Yes, I'm Molly Mitchell."

"They're waiting. It's the second door." The man behind the partition points to the hallway next to a wall that is filled with black-and-white photographs. Tiny white lights make dots on the hallway floor. Molly finds the door and opens it.

Jed stands up from a black leather chair and reaches for her hand. "You're here. This is great. You're going to love what Keith is showing me."

Keith is at a bank of monitors. He waves to Molly. "We've just begun. You've hardly missed a thing. Coffee and Cokes are on the table over there."

Molly gets coffee and a donut from a box and

sits next to Jed. A jolt of pleasure hits her like a rod up her back. She leans forward, looking from Jed to Keith, listening to Keith, staring at Jed's foot on his knee, feeling like the female member of a secret trio.

"We're at the beginning of a powerful new industry. It's about digitizing pictures, sound, text, film. It's about delivering information. It's about interaction: people with information, people with people."

Molly watches the images on the triple monitors. The changes are hypnotizing. She opens her jacket and wipes the donut crumbs from her mouth.

"Here is Aspen, Colorado," Keith says. "We're going down a street. Notice the ambient sounds. Do you want to turn left or right?"

"Left," Jed and Molly say in tandem.

"Do you two ever disagree?" Keith asks.

Jed reaches for Molly's hand and slaps five. The show continues. They go up mountains and ski down, tour restaurants, boutiques, the music tent.

When the demonstration ends, Keith takes a seat and opens a Coke. "The possibilities are endless. The tech stuff is running wild: high-resolution monitors, fiber-optic cables, 3-D pictures, things we can't imagine."

Molly listens as Jed asks questions. She scans the midnight blue walls, the red metal chairs, and follows up Jed's questions with questions of her own. They pop into her head and out her mouth. It's as if her mind were programmed for this job at birth.

"We're talking information as adventure," Molly says.

"Film, photographs, text, audio at your fingertips," Keith says.

"To play with like a game," Molly says.

"And, this is baby stuff we're looking at. In five years . . ."

"Do you find that frustrating?" Jed asks.

"I look at it this way. If things aren't changing and improving, business would be dull. It's like life. I love being on the edge. Sure, Pam and I bought an old house, but we don't think of it as going backward, but updating. We're taking an old frame and putting in new technology. We're zapping that house into the twenty-first century. Have you guys ever been to Epcot?"

"I haven't," Jed says.

"In Florida?" Molly says, "I've thought about it."

"Let's go, the four of us. Soon. Before Pam gets too pregnant. What do you say?"

"I'd love it," Jed says, "Molly, you would too."

"I would, but—"

"No buts, Molly," Keith says. "It'll be great. We're in the industry so we get to play all the games without the waiting lines. I'll talk to Pam. Let me show you the rest of the shop."

Molly trails Keith and Jed follows. They go in and out of rooms and shake a lot of hands. Keith turns on switches, pulls things from shelves. The talk is continuous; Molly's mind buzzes. When they return to the front room, Jed says, "How about a brew at the Old Town?"

Molly looks at her watch, 6:20. She's meeting Porter at seven-thirty.

"I can't," says Keith. "But I'll be in touch and we'll plan a trip to Epcot."

"Come on, Molly," Jed says, reaching for her hand. "I guess it's you and me."

Molly follows Jed down the stairs. "I haven't much time, maybe one beer."

Molly bounces next to Jed down the crooked sidewalk. She feels like a time traveler coming from the twenty-first century back to Rome.

"Was that a turn-on?" Jed asks.

"Unreal," Molly says. "It's like you have to shift your glasses and throw away the old ways of doing things, or even thinking about things."

"That's exactly what excites me." He swings her around, grabs her arms and puts his face in front of hers. "You get it. That's what I love about you. You get it. It's like new glasses. Molly, how did I find you?"

He takes her hand and swings her arm. She's in a Woody Allen movie or with Gene Kelly: sailing down an old street in New York, beside the funky buildings and laughing and swinging hands and almost dancing. They turn the corner and halfway down the street they enter the Old Town Bar.

"There's no updating in this place," Molly says, threading her way with Jed through the standing drinkers, across the tiled floor, beneath the high tin ceiling.

They find an empty spot in back; he signals for two beers. He clicks his bottle to hers. "To a great future together." He drinks and wipes his mouth on the sleeve of his tweed jacket. "I think you're the creative brains I've been looking for."

"Thanks. I like working with you. If it works out with Keith, it will be amazing, meeting him through my sister Grace."

"There's lots of amazing things going on." He looks in her eyes and her face feels hot. "I think there are lots we can do with Keith. I've got good contacts. Things you and I haven't even discussed."

Molly watches the Budweiser clock above the bar. It's moving too fast and the beer on her empty stomach is making her dizzy. "Thanks for including me, today. I liked it. It's got my head whirling." She runs her hand across her hair.

"Me too. How did you ever get into desktop publishing?"

"What do you mean?"

"You're too smart. But women do that, don't they? They don't take themselves seriously. Don't go for the big job."

"Not true." She feels heat in her chest. "Women do go for the big jobs."

"Touched a sore spot, huh?" He smiles and licks his lip. "Trade beers?" He holds his bottle out to her.

She lifts it to her mouth. Her eyes close. She feels the moisture on the rim. She keeps it there and looks at the clock. The hand is on the three; she has to leave.

He takes her arm. "I like you, Molly. We share

beers. We share ideas. It's the perfect relationship, but you are looking nervous."

"It's the time," she says.

"The big date, again? Mr. Goodbar?"

"Mr. Goodbar." She laughs and hands him the bottle. "Friday? Are you expecting me Friday?"

"I hope so." He puts the bottles on an empty table and blocks her as she goes toward the door.

"Before you go, thanks for working for me." He kisses her cheek, then quickly on her lips. His lips are wet and cold and cover hers like whipped cream. The moment doesn't last. The kiss is not for passion, but passion is what Molly feels, like warm water on cold hands.

He guides her through the crowd to the street. "Cab?" he asks.

"Yes, too far to walk to Barrow."

"Rosolio's?" he asks, leaping into the street with his arm outstretched.

"How did you know?"

"I like it too." He opens the door of the yellow taxi. The cab waits at the light; she watches Jed walk down the street. He strides with confidence and purpose; his body has a lilt, a bounce. It makes her smile.

Fourteen

At 7:40, Molly is at Rosolio's. Porter isn't there. She goes to the ladies' room, wets a towel, and wipes her mouth. She puts on lipstick and brushes her hair. The dining room is small and square, the tables plain with starched white linen. The walls are white stucco with sculpted blue neon lights. A large plate glass window looks onto the street. She watches from her table. A taxi stops. She sees Porter, his long body emerging from the cab. His Wall Street suit looks out of place. She wishes she had picked La Grenouille.

He carries his briefcase, opens the door, and stops to talk with the maître d', who gestures toward her. Molly watches him approach. Her hands feel damp. She wipes them on her napkin and takes the hand he offers. His cool gray eyes smile.

"Sorry I'm late. We got lost; all those one-way streets." He sits and puts the white napkin in his lap.

"I was late myself. It's okay."

"How did you find this place?"

"I used to come here when I lived on Sullivan Street. I loved it then. I guess I'm being nostalgic."

"It's different. Italian, I presume?"

"Yes, good pastas, good soups."

"I'm not big on pasta—it's a yuppy rip-off. But," he says, "let's have a bottle of good red wine."

"Yuppy rip-off? The Italians have been eating spaghetti for centuries. It's real food. I love it."

Porter smiles. "You are being nostalgic. We could have gone to Le Cirque or Le Bernardin, a proper place to talk about marriage. Are you ready to accept?"

Molly blushes. "Porter, please don't push." She looks at her clasped hands hugging the edge of the table. "Grace was dying to know where you proposed. I wouldn't tell her."

"Good thing. The co-op looks like a sure thing. I talked to the firm today. It's wonderful, isn't it?"

"Yes, it is."

"It would be nice if we could announce our engagement to my parents."

"I'm anxious to meet them."

"They'll like you. They'll want you for a daughter." He reaches for her hand. "They're making the trip just to meet you."

The maître d' stands by the table. "Wine, sir?"

"What is your best red?"

"We have an excellent Chianti Classico." He points to the wine list.

"Chianti? Not for me. Something better."

"The Chianti is very special. Perhaps a Barolo?"

"That's fine. The Barolo."

Porter shakes his head and looks at Molly. "You look flushed. Busy day?"

"I had a great day. Remember Keith? I toured his office. He showed us some of the things going on with laser disks. It was amazing. It's got me very excited."

"Like those games at airports?"

"Yes, sort of but much more."

"I've seen things like that get hot, then fizzle. Keith didn't impress me."

A young man in black pants and white apron recites the specials. Molly orders pasta with artichoke hearts and prosciutto and Porter, veal chops.

Porter talks about the steel industry and the problems with import regulations. The maître d' pours the wine. Molly watches Porter swirl it, smell it, taste it. "It's fine," he says.

She lifts her glass and looks at him. She sees him glance around the room, stare at the two men in T-shirts at the table next to them. She fingers the button on her blouse. "Is the wine okay?" Molly asks.

"It will do."

Porter continues talking. She hears words: damn Japanese, yen versus the dollar, Washington, deregulation. She notices the dark outside, the neon glow bouncing off the glassware and the plate glass window. She remembers the nights she sat here by herself or with a friend. She was an artist in New York. This was the place she ate the yeasty bread and drank the wine and twirled the pasta on her fork. Today she felt like that at Keith's and in the Old Town Bar. Tonight with Porter she feels changed, a stranger.

"How's the veal?" she asks.

"Surprisingly good."

"Please taste my pasta." She scoops a spoonful on his plate.

"No thanks." Porter cuts his meat. His left hand holds the fork and lifts it to his mouth. She waits, expecting him to speak.

"No lunch?" she asks.

"I had a sandwich at my desk." He holds his fork in midair. "Molly, there is something I need to tell you. You know I was married before. We wanted children but Elizabeth waited, she wanted to get a start on her career—she was a lawyer . . ." Porter puts his fork on his dish and picks up the glass of wine. "It didn't work—she didn't get pregnant. Then she did this crazy thing—a woman in her office . . . I think she felt she was a failure as a wife."

Molly twirls linguine on her fork. She watches Porter. He sets the wineglass on the table without drinking.

He continues, "I would like to have a child. I know you would, too."

Molly rubs her cheek and pushes back her chair. The restaurant feels hot and crowded; uptown would have been serene.

"Where is Elizabeth now?" she asks.

"I'm not sure. She's in the city. She's a very confused woman."

Molly feels her heart beating. She drains her glass of wine and watches the busboy refill the water glasses. "I'm confused." She pushes the words at Porter, who works at the last morsels of meat on the bone. "I think you have asked me to marry you to produce a family, grandchildren for your parents and sons and daughters for you—people to fill up Ten Gracie Square."

"That's part of it." He looks up and smiles.

She runs her fingers through her hair. "I don't want to do that."

"Do what? I don't understand." His hand reaches across the table and covers hers. She pulls away.

"Be your . . ." She sighs. "Be a baby machine—a child maker."

"You do want a child, don't you?"

"Maybe. Maybe it's too late. You need a younger baby maker."

"That's not what I want. I have asked you to marry me. I am not that young either and yet I have a lot to offer a child, maybe two children."

"And if I'm like Elizabeth?"

"You are not like Elizabeth."

"If I don't get pregnant?"

"I'm not worried. I think you will. Women your age have children all the time today."

Molly rubs her hands across the linen in her lap. "Do you want dessert?"

"Do you?"

"I'd like to leave."

Porter motions to the waiter. Molly excuses herself and goes to the ladies' room. She frowns at herself in the mirror. Her face looks flushed; her stomach feels uneasy. She washes her hands and rubs them hard on the brown paper towel.

On the street Porter waves to a taxi. "Shall we go to my place?"

"Let's walk awhile. Do you mind?"

Porter sends the taxi on. "Where shall we go? This is your neighborhood."

"Doesn't matter. Let's just walk. I'll show you where I used to live."

The night is warm for early May. They turn down Waverly and walk along the edge of Washington Square Park. Dogs and people walk around them. The street lamps spot the park with globes of yellow light shining on the trees' new baby leaves.

She leads him past the bars and little shops to Sullivan and points her finger at the building where she lived. "What do you think?"

He puts his arm around her waist. "I bet you're glad you don't live there anymore."

"Not really. I loved it. I loved the village. I miss it."

"Now you're grown-up and live uptown."

"Only because my mother talked me into taking Grace's apartment."

"I'm glad she did. Where to now?"

"I'd like coffee with amaretto and whipped cream."

"Lead the way."

She takes him to a bar on Bleecker Street. They push through the swinging door and past the bar, the TV, and the baseball game. Molly sees a woman with a group of men, her eyes checking Porter, moving from his face down his body, to his face again.

She feels the glances from the men and slinks into a booth. Porter sits beside her.

"So?" Porter asks after giving the waiter their order.

"Would you still want to marry me if I didn't have children, if I couldn't—"

"I like marriage."

Molly moves the plastic ashtray to the corner of the table. "I'm not sure I've thought about marriage."

"Of course you have. Every girl does."

"Not every woman. Working women. It's not like it used to be."

"Marriage is man's natural state. Everybody thinks about it, even you. Marry me, Molly. It's you I want. Forget about children. If they come, they come."

The waiter puts the coffee in front of Molly and a small glass by Porter. Molly stirs the coffee and the cream with a straw. She sips. "I think you are dying to live at Ten Gracie Square and you want me there so you don't rattle around."

Porter laughs and jerks the glass to his mouth and back down. "Molly, I'm asking you to share my life." She feels his breath on her face. "I've thought of marrying you for a long time—before I knew about Ten Gracie Square. Finding it has pushed me into asking you. It was . . . I was . . ." His hand rubs across his face.

"What, Porter?"

"I was afraid. Things disappear if you want them. I want you for my wife and I want to give you everything to make you happy. I want Ten Gracie

Square for you. If you refuse me . . ." His thumb rubs the palm of his hand.

There's a roar of laughter from the bar, the smell of cigarettes, the ball game on the television. She feels Porter's arm around her shoulder, his fingers on her neck. "I missed you last Friday night. I was miserable. I love you. I love you and I want to marry you. I'm saying too much. I don't want you to feel pressured."

"I don't," Molly says. "I'm honored."

"There's time. Meet my parents." He moves his arm from her shoulder and adjusts his body in the seat. He pushes the tiny glass around the tabletop like a toy car. "I hoped you loved me."

Molly whirls the whipped cream with her straw. "I do." She holds the coffee in her mouth. "I don't know what is stopping me from saying yes. Grace says I'm afraid. Maybe I'm like you."

He turns and reaches for her chin, for her cheeks. He bends his head. The kiss is a surprise. She feels his teeth and tastes the orange liqueur. He pulls away and puts his arm around her shoulder. His hand rubs up and down along her upper arm. His other hand is on her chin, raising it. He kisses her again and now his hand is on her breast. She feels sixteen and at the movies. "You are wonderful," he says.

She slurps the coffee through the straw. He downs his glass of Grand Marnier. They leave the booth. Walking by the bar, she hears a whistle. "I'd like to be in her shoes," the woman says. "I'd like to be in her." A man's voice. A laugh. Molly feels Porter's tall body behind her. He's like a wall, a safeguard from the world.

"Come to my house," Porter says in the taxi, reaching for her breast, kissing her hair.

"I have to be to work by eight."

"That's no problem."

"I shouldn't." She feels the beating of his heart, the passion in his fingertips.

"If you refuse, I'll ride with you to Eighty-sixth. Stay with me. Move in with me. Don't be afraid."

He pulls her up the steps and kisses her before he turns on the light. She thinks of Jed, the stairs at Laser, Inc. Her mind whirls with thoughts of Jed, the bar, the street, the holding hands. Porter pulls her to his bed and pushes up her skirt. She feels his hands tugging at her underpants, her nakedness— his hands on her neck, her hair—his bare legs, heavy on top of hers.

"You're wonderful," he says, crashing into her. Her body lifts and comes alive. She tries to find his lips, tries to thrust her hips in sync with him. She's flying in the air, whirling through the park. She's in a bar and kissing Jed . . .

Porter's up and standing over her. "It's late. We must sleep. Do you want to shower?"

"I'll do it in the morning." She hugs the pillow and thinks of Jed.

Fifteen

Molly opens her eyes into the semidarkness of Porter's bedroom. The heavy drapes are closed, letting in only a sliver of the early morning sun. She sees Porter in the shadows, putting on a shirt, buttoning the buttons. She stretches. "Good morning," he says. "It looks like a beautiful day. Shall I open the curtains?"

She checks the clock. "I should be up. May I use the shower?"

"The bathroom is yours. There is coffee in the kitchen." Fastening his cuff, he comes to the bed. "Thanks for staying last night. My parents get in Friday afternoon. I'll leave the weekend schedule on your answering machine. We'll all have dinner Friday night, maybe drinks here first." He kisses her forehead. "We'll talk before then."

When she comes out from her shower, Porter is gone. The subway to Wall Street is crowded; she stays on the local train, sitting in a seat vacated at Fourteenth Street. A large woman shoves into a tiny space beside her. She smells sour, like a long-haired dog still wet from the rain. Molly sorts through the coming week. There is too much to do, too much to think about; it is impossible to complete the Pace project by Friday. Jed needs her then. She has to give Porter an answer. Last night she said she loved him. They were in the grubby bar, he was pressed beside her; she felt overwhelming tenderness. She will meet his parents Friday and she'll know. She hates the job at Pace, hates the bank job, hates desktop publishing. She'll call Sophia, give her all her work.

For two days she reschedules her life: Sophia will help with the job at Pace and with her other clients; the bank will hire someone to replace her if she can do the training. On Friday, she opens the blinds to the early morning sun. This is the beginning, she thinks. She stretches her legs, her arms. She thinks of Jed, of Porter. He thinks she'll marry him. She does too—she told him that she loved him, she must. It's a peaceful kind of love, not like the passion she felt for Jacques. That was youthful, lustful love. She brushes her teeth. Must get down to Saunders by eight. A thrill runs up her arm. Jed says that they work well together. They do. She pulls on jeans and takes a taxi down to Fifth and Twentieth. No time for subways. She arrives before eight and walks into the open space of white and green and polished wood. Angelo is at a drafting table.

"Did you have an all-nighter?" she yells.

"You're funny, Molly; I just start early."

Breezing through the room to the corner office, she feels whipped with energy. She tosses her coat, turns, and sees Jed standing in the doorway.

"Anxious worker, here so early?" he says.

She feels a blush across her face, relief that he is there. "You too, or did you spend the night?"

"Hardly. I have been working every night. Came back and worked till midnight when I left you on—"

"Tuesday. That was fun." Molly turns and picks up papers from the table. "Are these for me?"

"It's short. Should take an hour or so. I'd like you to work with me on the Amtrak job."

"When?"

"Ten o'clock okay?"

The deadline puts her in high gear. She marks the pages, sketches a layout, and boots the computer. She thinks of Jed's remark: you're too smart for desktop publishing. Good-bye to that. At ten, Molly finds Jed in the center room with Angelo. She stands and listens.

"The people aren't in the right spot," Jed says. "Too far from the train."

"If I move them, I block the train," Angelo argues.

Molly stays to the side listening to Jed, watching him wave his arms, watching Angelo defend his artwork. Impatience wears on her. She moves closer, studies the drawing. "May I suggest something?" she says.

Jed turns. "Sure. Solve the problem."

"First, the train is unfriendly. The windows are dark. You could use some light here and in the doorway. Anthropomorphize. Remember *The Little Engine That Could?*"

"The Little Engine that what?" Angelo says.

Molly takes a black pencil and sketches on a

piece of newsprint. "I would keep the people vague, use them to lead the eye to the train, to the door, like this."

"What do you think, Angelo?" Jed asks.

"Guess I should have read that Little Engine book."

"Pretend the train is a big friendly animal. That's all," Molly says. "And bunch this copy. It's in the way. The train's your focus. Copy is incidental." She grins slyly at Jed.

"I think she's got it, Angelo," Jed says.

"I'll work on it," Angelo says.

"We'll be in my office," Jed adds.

Molly takes a chair by Jed's desk. "Didn't mean to butt in. You said you weren't the visual one."

"I said I needed a creative director, an art person. You have the instinct. How come?"

"I guess Andy Warhol drove me to it."

"I like what you said out there. You're an enigma." He sits behind his desk and clasps his hands behind his head. "I hired you to do computer work and you're . . . I don't know. Let's get to the Amtrak business."

They lean over the large oak table, he on one side, she on the other. They hand things back and forth, printed papers, letters, pictures, drawings. They discuss, they argue. An hour goes by. "What have we done?" she asks.

"Done?" He laughs. "Moved things from here to over there."

"And what do we do now?"

Jed looks at his watch. "I'm meeting Candace for lunch."

"In that case I'm going to finish my computer job." She gets up, walks across the room and turns. "Is there something you want me to do with that mess? How about a plan? I think I know the solution."

"Can you do it today?"

"I need a half hour to finish what I'm doing. That means I can start at one if I don't eat lunch. I'm leaving at four. Will you be back by then?"

"Of course."

Molly clicks into her professional mode. She prints a draft, makes corrections, and prints the final copy. She checks her watch and leaves for her noontime walk.

Out on the street, she walks fast. Once around the block, then twice. She buys an apple. Back upstairs, she gets the papers from Jed's office. It feels strange to be in his room without him there. She looks at the couch where she sat the first day—where Candace sat. Jed is having lunch with her. Candace looks like Demi Moore—pert, young. Damn. Molly rushes past Angelo and back into her office.

At three-thirty, Jed walks in. "I've been thinking."

Molly swings her chair around and faces him. "About what?"

"About you—about your working here."

He hangs on the side of the table, swings his foot. She imagines him at lunch with Candace. She feels irritation. "You mean organizing your messes." She gets up and walks to the other side of the table. "I hate doing this and I hate desktop publishing."

"What would you like to do?" he asks.

"I don't know. I'm confused. I'm confused about me and my life and this and you and the whole mess." Her eyes sting. She turns her back to him and watches a taxi letting out a passenger.

"Decisions are hard." She senses him ambling toward her. Her eyes brim with tears. She digs in her pocket. His hand comes in front of her; it holds a large white cloth handkerchief. She dabs her face, her eyes.

"Thanks." She turns and hands the handkerchief back to him and moves away and takes the papers from the table. "I've given you an outline on the Amtrak material. I'll be back next Friday."

"Keith called. He has a project for us. I think you'd like it." He rubs the handkerchief on the back of his hand.

"I don't know." Molly sighs.

"It won't be cleaning up my mess. It's something that needs your creativity, your spark, your brains. If you can't do it, I'll turn him down."

She looks from his hand to his face to his eyes. Heat rises to her neck and face. "You're tempting me, Jed Saunders."

"I need you, Molly. I think you need this job as well." He stands. "Get someone else to do the desktop whatever. I can keep you busy with things that use your talents."

"I like it here."

"I know."

She takes her coat and puts it on and watches Jed pull the neck of his T-shirt. "I've got someone helping with the desktop publishing. Maybe I can—"

"Have you seen Angelo's new drawing?"

"No."

"It's amazing. You've got him going in a new direction. You and I need to make plans."

"We can talk Friday."

"Friday? Come with me to Connecticut."

"Connecticut?"

"I have a house there. Bill and Ellen are coming. We're going over the proposal. I'd like you in on it."

"For how long?"

"The weekend. I'm driving out late Friday afternoon." He taps on the table. "There should be fields of daffodils."

"I'm not sure." The pit of her stomach is tightening.

"This is work. You'll be paid."

"If I need to get back, is there a train?"

"A bus."

"I'll let you know." Molly stuffs papers in her briefcase.

"If you're going to work here full-time, you should come to Connecticut."

She turns and stares at him and listens to her heart. "I'll arrange to go."

His fist punches his palm. She gathers the papers, hands them to him, closes her briefcase, and heads for the door. He follows. As she goes down the stairs she hears him yell. "I'll phone you early in the week."

Molly dresses in red silk, a circular skirt below a tight bodice. Porter's message an the phone machine listed the schedule: drinks in his apartment with dinner at Laurent on Fifty-sixth Street; Saturday night, the ballet at the Metropolitan Opera House, *Romeo and Juliet,* preceded by dinner in the Grand Tier Restaurant; a "girl's lunch" with his mother on Saturday and Sunday brunch at Grace's.

Molly looks in the mirror and swirls the skirt. Her blood has been on fire since she left Jed. He needs a creative director and he wants her for the job. She pictures a vast meadow, stretching to far horizons, filled with new challenges. It's like coming out of a burrow, like a groundhog in spring.

She telephones Sophia and leaves a message: "I need you permanently. Give me a call."

She paces around her living room, waiting for the buzzer from the doorman announcing the car that Porter is sending. It's nice to have a driver. It's nice to have a great job. She stands by the window mesmerized by the orange and red colors smeared on the windows across the street—the reflection of the setting sun. Tonight she will meet Porter's parents. They could be her parents if she marries Porter. She could live the luxury life at Ten Gracie Square and have her dream job, too. She checks her face in the mirror, adds blusher, and dabs Paloma on her wrists. It's the New York smell of nightlife: taxis filled with dressed-up people, gold brocade and sparkling lights.

The buzzer rings and Molly grabs her coat. She sails through the entrance, nodding to the doorman holding the door, and into the car at the curb. She leans back in the seat, feeling the upholstery on the back of her legs and watches Friday night pass by outside the window: people scurrying on the sidewalks, standing in queues waiting for buses, straining at corners like horses at the starting gate. The pace is like her heartbeat, rapid, strong, waiting on the brink of a surprise.

The driver parks at the curb, leaps from his seat, and has the door open before Molly collects her purse. Porter is halfway down the stairs to greet her. He kisses her cheek and squeezes her hand. "My folks are here."

"I know." She notices the dampness on his palm.

"They're anxious to meet you. Did you get my message and the schedule?"

"Yes."

"Good." He stops halfway up the stairs and whispers, "I hope you'll spend the night with me."

Richard Drummond stands by the fireplace, a drink in his hand.

"This is Molly," Porter says.

Richard comes toward her and takes her hands. "We are so happy to meet you. Call me Richard. This is Porter's mother, Annette."

The woman on the couch stands and kisses Molly on the cheek. "We've come to New York especially to meet you. Please sit here beside me. I want to get to know you."

Molly notices her clean, pink manicured nails on the hand that rubs a gold watch hanging on a chain around her neck. "How was your trip?" she asks.

"I hate airplane travel, but it's the way the world is now and it's fast. Our hotel is wonderful and Porter filled our room with roses."

Annette asks Molly about her sister, her parents. They chat easily and Molly likes the conversation, likes telling Annette about her life, what she did in college. Porter stands by the fireplace and talks to Richard.

In the car to Laurent, Richard quizzes Molly and remarks, "We don't come often enough to New York; I enjoy the restaurants, the music. Annette loves the museums. I think we'll come more now."

The room at Laurent overwhelms Molly. It is small, gold-colored, and full of flowers. The chairs are high-backed and brocade. It's like a private club. The conversation flows between her and Richard and Annette. Porter hardly speaks, but Molly feels him watching her; he has the hungry look he had on Tuesday night in the bar on Bleecker Street.

"We look forward to meeting your sister Grace. Porter says you and she are very close," Annette says.

"She's the only family I have."

"Annette and I hope we can fill in and become the family that you are missing." Richard raises his glass of wine.

Molly touches her glass to his and looks above

it at his warm brown eyes. She turns to Annette and sees a kind and gentle woman. She clicks her glass to Porter's. He smiles. She sees self-assurance, smugness. She glances around the table. There is a safeness here, a security that's been missing in her life. The red wine is musky; she feels it on her tongue after she has swallowed it. "Thank you," she responds.

"We have a summer cottage on a lake with a canoe and sailfish. We have lots of fun." Annette laughs. "Christmas is a special time. We have a huge tree, a yule log. Porter doesn't always make it, but maybe he will now. We could all be together, including your sister and her husband. Would they like to come?"

"It sounds wonderful."

"Molly is an artist," Porter says.

"Painter?" Annette says, "I used to paint."

"Landscapes?" Richard asks.

"No, still lifes, lots of glass, reflective glass rather than transparent glass. I used to experiment with windows, mirrors, large glass vases. The objects on the canvas were depicting something that wasn't there. I've always been interested in the reflective, using it to examine reality."

"Yes, of course." Richard signals to the waiter to refill the wineglasses.

"Like Janet Fish?" Annette asks.

Molly turns to Annette. "You know Janet Fish's work?"

"It's like what you describe."

"Sort of. Her glass is not reflective. She lets you

see the object through the glass. She works with repetition, distortion, fragility."

Annette clasps her hands. "Do you have time to join me at the Met tomorrow after lunch? It would be such a treat for me."

"It would be a treat for me, too," Molly says. She likes this woman.

The car drops Porter's parents at Eighty-first and Fifth. Molly stops for clothes and goes with Porter to Gramercy Park. In the car, he holds her hand. "They like you," he says.

"I like them, too."

"Molly, you should start easing out of your job. Train someone else. There's no need for you to work. Return to your painting. I listened to you tonight."

"I am easing out of desktop publishing but I've become involved in something new. I'd like to continue that."

"Decorating Ten Gracie Square will be a full-time job."

"Has it gone through?"

"I'd like to get married this fall."

Molly looks out the window. "Maybe we should live together first."

"We've known each other long enough. Besides, I don't approve of that."

They ride in silence.

Later, in bed, his fingers touch her nipple through her nightgown. "I love you, Molly. My parents love you. Let's plan a wedding for September or October."

She looks at his soft gray eyes. They are like Annette's. Molly smiles and covers his fingers with her own and thinks of his father and the toast: We'd like to be your family. Warmth runs into her breast. She pulls away the cloth and watches his finger making circles. Her legs move next to his, her thigh against his thighs. The down pillow feels sturdy and smooth under her head. "Maybe," she says, "maybe in October."

Molly meets Annette for lunch on Saturday. They sit together on a banquette at the Stanhope Hotel, where Richard and Annette are staying. They eat asparagus soup. Annette tells Molly about her daughter Anne, Porter's sister. "When she was eighteen she died in a car crash."

"Porter never told me. Never even said he had a sister."

"I suspected that. He can't talk about it. He adored her."

"How old was he?"

"He had just finished his first year at Princeton. She was starting college in September."

Molly holds the spoon in midair. "How terrible. I can't imagine . . ."

"It's something you never get over." Annette pats Molly's hand. "We really lost one child and half of another."

Molly cocks her head.

"Porter didn't come home for years. He lost his joy. He always was a happy little boy. We hoped Elizabeth would help. She didn't."

"I don't know what to say."

"Porter needs a lot of love, an understanding woman. He is a precious person, kind as well as brilliant. He'll be a wonderful father."

"Yes, I think he will be."

"I fear another disappointment will set him back. Emotionally, that is. He can't have another woman leave his life."

Molly lifts the water glass. "I see."

"Have you made plans?"

"Plans?"

"He has asked you to marry him?"

"Yes."

"And?"

Molly puts the water glass on the table. Her thumb moves back and forth over the moisture condensed on the outside.

"Have you set a date?"

"October."

"Oh, thank God." Annette reaches for Molly, reaches for her hand, her arm. "You blessed girl. I love you. October? That's wonderful. We'll have a party this summer for our friends. Come to Minneapolis, to the cottage. Bring Grace."

Grace is fixing flowers when Molly arrives Sunday morning.

"So, how was it? I've been bursting all weekend to hear."

"It's been fun. Busy but fun."

Grace hands Molly a tray of flatware, plates, white

with wide circles of green and blue, green-and-blue-dotted napkins. "Put these on the table. Are they coming at eleven-thirty?"

"They want to meet you. They're adopting both of us." Molly tells Grace about Porter's sister.

"I knew something was going on with Porter. I could tell it. I thought it was just his wife but now . . . this makes sense."

Molly tells Grace about the museum and Annette's knowledge of art. "We argued about Matisse. I couldn't believe it. It was great, and at the ballet, at the end of *Romeo and Juliet,* we both cried."

Grace puts her hands on her hips. "You know, I think I'm jealous."

"Jealous? Don't be." She pulls Grace through the swinging door into the kitchen away from Harlan. "Your life is terrific."

"Except for one thing."

"Babies? I'll have one for you."

"I'm really happy for you."

Harlan bangs through the swinging door. "Time for Bloody Marys?"

"We're having champagne," Grace says. "This is a celebration."

"How are the in-laws, Molly?"

"I like them." Harlan's skin looks rough and red—so do his eyes. "Working hard?" she asks.

"Every night. Can't make big bucks any other way. My parents weren't rich."

Exactly at eleven-thirty the buzzer rings, announcing the Drummonds. Molly opens the door and waits. She watches Annette float down the hall, into the apartment, where she takes Grace's hands in hers. Molly kisses Richard and Porter and listens to bits and pieces of what Annette says to Grace: the darling younger sister, family, Christmas all together, Molly perfect for our Porter.

Harlan pours champagne and hands around the glasses. They stand in a circle and Richard makes a toast. "To our new daughters and happiness to our son."

Harlan lifts his glass. "To Porter, my friend and colleague, much happiness. Welcome to the family."

The men huddle on one side of the room. The women sit on the couch. Molly listens to Annette question Grace about her job, about New York. When Grace goes to the kitchen, Annette moves next to Molly and leans toward her. "I can't get over it," she whispers. "Grace is a replica of our Anne."

Sixteen

Molly stretches out her legs and pushes on the floor under the dashboard of the red Mercedes. Jed is beside her, hands clutched on the wooden steering wheel. Her body rides in tandem with the car: lurching when he shifts the gears, swaying when the car swerves to another lane, bracing when he speeds to pass a trailer truck.

She thinks about his house; they are going to Connecticut. She told Porter she had business; he is staying on in California. This is a business trip. She looks at her jeans and sandals, Jed's jeans. This is a business trip, she reminds herself. They have a meeting with a client: Bill and Ellen, Neo-Plastics. She rests her head against the seat. She's glad the week is over, the country will feel good. All week she felt pushed in all directions: training her replacement at the bank and Sophia on the other jobs and Porter on the phone about the wedding, the co-op, and the trip to Minneapolis.

She sighs. Her body feels it's floating; there's gentleness inside the car.

"I think the country air is what you need," Jed says.

"I don't feel I am on a business trip."

She sees him rub the steering wheel. "Let's call it an exploratory trip," he says.

She squeezes her arms across her body. Her face feels strained and red. Rudy used to say that, "Meet you in the barn at five for an exploratory trip." They would climb the hayloft and explore. At first it was their mouths, their tongues together—then it was her breasts. After a week or so she told him she had never seen a boy. He was different than she imagined, a surprise; she wondered how he fit inside his jeans. Her instinct was to put her fingers on it, then to squeeze. She liked to tickle him and hear him laugh. He intrigued her, the way he felt, the way touching made her feel. She was shy when she showed herself to him; it was something that she promised. She spread her legs and closed her eyes and gasped at his fingers playing with her folds; she kept quiet, lying still, following his fingers, listening to her heartbeats. Every day they played at five o'clock. They only touched or licked, like children having ice cream.

"Are you thinking business?" Jed asks.

"I'm thinking exploration."

"Good, I'm sure Bill and Ellen have some ideas we haven't thought about."

A huge trailer truck barrels by the car.

She looks out the window at the line of hissing trucks slowing for the turnoff to the George Washington Bridge. "This car is a joke," she says.

"Wait a minute, no insults allowed."

"Look at it. It's tiny. It doesn't belong on this highway."

"Feeling unsafe again?"

He knows. She hadn't named the tension in her body as unsafe but that is how she feels. "Tell me about your house," she says.

"The house is wonderful. You will love it. It was Lucy's."

"Lucy?"

"My aunt." His hand thumps on the gearshift. "She died two years ago." He downshifts and passes a Buick.

"She gave you the house?"

"She gave me everything." He settles back in his seat. "She saved my life."

"She sounds pretty special."

"She was—tough, warm, smart, and knew what to do with a twelve-year-old boy who was lost."

"You?"

"Yep."

The traffic's thinned; the trucks are gone. Molly stares at Jed's hands. "Did you live in the house? Did you live with Lucy?"

"My mother remarried again and was going to Paris. I didn't want to go."

"Your father?"

"Nonexistent."

Molly stares ahead. The trees are green with fresh new leaves. "Have you ever been married?"

"Came close once. At least I thought so. You?"

"I'm going to be."

"You're what?" His head swivels and looks at her. His hand grabs the gearshift and pulls it back.

"I'm getting married." She braces against the sudden change of gears. "October, I think."

"The guy with the sprained ankle?"

"That was nothing. He's okay. How did you know?"

"You mentioned him the other day."

"I did? I don't know why. You're the first person I've told, except my sister."

They have left the highway and are stopped at a light. Jed drums his fingers on the dashboard. He turns on the radio.

Molly watches out the window. The car angles left and enters a new highway. He speeds past the other cars, pulls ahead, and into the left lane. She chews her finger. Jed pounds the steering wheel in time to the music. The shadows are long and spread wide along the sides of the road. She glances at his profile, his concentration on the road.

"How far do we have?" She raises her voice above the music.

"Another hour."

"Will Bill and Ellen be there? When are they coming?"

"Not until tomorrow." She barely hears his voice above the music.

"Tomorrow. I thought——"

"Noon tomorrow. It should give us plenty of time."

She hears him sigh. He doesn't want to talk. She leans back and closes her eyes. The tension that she felt is gone, replaced by an anxiety she cannot name. She wonders about Jed: he seems nervous, focused on his driving and the music. She listens to the radio, the car engine, and watches the big hand of the clock move from the seven, past the twelve, and downhill to the three.

"Do you like Mexican food?" His voice startles her.

She sits up. "I love it."

"We'll stop for dinner. Any problem with that?"

"No, that's fine."

The car pulls into a parking lot beside a small low building. The sign shows a giant head of a man under a sombrero. Inside, the sounds of guitar music mix with the din of the crowd. It is stuffy and a group of people stand inside the door.

"It will be thirty minutes, do you mind?"

"Whatever you want."

"Let's get a margarita at the bar."

Molly reaches for the bowl of chips. She is driven by hunger and stuffs them in her mouth. Jed asks for guacamole and pays the bartender, who puts two large-bowled stemmed glasses full of frozen lime liquid in front of them. Jed gulps his without looking at her. She licks the salt around the rim and takes a sip. It is sweet and bitter and reminds Molly of a dive she frequented on winter Sunday nights in college. She looks around the room at the tables crammed beside each other with parents and children and couples and groups of teenagers.

"Have same guacamole," she says, pushing the bowl toward Jed.

"No thanks. I got it for you—you seemed starved." His eyes graze on hers and then look past her.

"I am." She laughs. "It must be the country air."

He takes another gulp of drink and excuses himself. She watches him walk toward the sign for rest rooms. She panics. He has changed into someone she doesn't know, like a person with a secret. Tonight she will stay in his house alone with him—Bill and Ellen may never come; it may be an excuse. She sips the icy drink and glues her eyes on the doorway he entered. Her nose hurts from the coldness and she feels dizzy. The article called him wild man. He emerges. His hair is combed; he doesn't smile; he climbs back on the stool.

"Why are Bill and Ellen coming here for a meeting? Why not New York?"

"Ellen has a cousin she is visiting in Danbury. Then they go on to Boston. This seemed easier. Besides, I need to check the house."

"You never use it?"

"Rarely."

"How come?"

He orders another margarita and one for her, stuffs the change in his pocket, and looks at her. His staring eyes make her nervous; she thinks of the window at the bank. He scratches his neck. "A lot of painful memories, I guess."

The hostess leads them to a table in the corner. Molly knows she wants chilies rellenos without looking at the menu. Jed orders the same.

"Why don't you sell it?"

"Can't. It would be wrong to have strangers living in it. It was Lucy's house."

"But if you don't use it . . ."

"Doesn't matter."

Her heart feels touched by the inflection in his voice. She slides the glass around on the oilskin tablecloth, the moisture from the bottom making it slippery. Platters of food arrive, and beans and rice. It smells like tomatoes and peppers and the plain aroma of boiled beans. She tastes the beans and cuts into the steamy cheesy poblano pepper.

She senses his gaze on her. "You can finish my margarita. It's gone to my head." She pushes the glass across the table. He lifts it and drinks. She looks up and smiles. His glance moves around her face; he bites his lips.

She wipes her mouth with the paper napkin, plays with the rice; she is stuffed.

"My mother died two years ago— Like Lucy." The words surprise her. They appeared without her thinking.

"How about some coffee?"

She nods her head and watches the waitress take the plates.

"Your mother must have been too young to die?" He leans across the table.

"She was young . . . she missed my father . . . he died two years before her . . . she had lung cancer . . . when it got bad we took her to a hospice . . . they were very nice—better than a hospital, I think . . . I miss her very much." She picks up the mug, puts it to her mouth, and smells the heat, the coffee smell. She looks at Jed. His eyes are intense, caring. She feels the tears well behind her eyes. They spill. "I'm sorry," she says.

He reaches across the table and takes her hand, then offers her his handkerchief. She holds the coffee mug. He moves his chair beside her and mops her face, one arm around her shoulder.

"I feel embarrassed," she says.

"It's late and you're tired and I've been moody. Let's go home."

He keeps his arm around her as they pick their way through the potholed parking area.

As they drive, Molly watches the arc of the new moon flit between the trees as the car changes direction.

"I find it hard to believe that I'll never see Lucy again. It takes time for death to sink in."

"It's more than that. I miss my mother, but I can't find my place in the world. Do you know what I mean?"

"Someone said when a parent dies, it puts you next in line."

"I don't feel that. It is something to do with not being anyone's child. With feeling . . . unsafe."

"Do you feel unsafe with me?"

"I don't think so. I sometimes feel unsafe in the whole world. I crave security. I never used to be like that."

"Were you a crazy, wild risk taker?" He laughs.

"Sort of . . . How about you?"

"Sort of . . ." Jed leaves the main road, turns into an unpaved one, then into a driveway. The white clapboard house is visible in the car headlights and then disappears back into the darkness. It is like a storybook: the house nestled among tall pines and oaks, no other house around.

"Stay here. I'll turn on an outside light." Jed gets out of the car.

Molly sits sideways on the seat, her legs outside the door. She watches the moon, smells the grass and the damp moss aroma from the black forests of trees. She stands stretching into the coolness of the night air, her body feeling like a butterfly emerging from a stuffy cocoon. She sees the yellow light flick on in the lantern by the flagstone steps. Jed stands at the door. She grabs her knapsack and bounds up the pathway. For one fleeting moment it feels like Rudy waiting in the hayloft.

"Welcome to my house." He takes the bag and walks into the living room.

The room is small and smells stuffy. Jed lights a lamp and Molly sees a couch covered in stripes, and oak chairs with slatted backs and leather seats. She sits in one and runs her hands across the flat wood arms. "These chairs were in my grandfather's house."

"They've been here as long as I can remember."

Molly laughs. "They feel good. Mission chairs."

Jed disappears around a corner. Molly follows. A round table is in the middle of the kitchen floor, a yellow light above it. She pulls the ladder-back chair away from the table and sits, taking in the room in one glance: the avocado refrigerator, matching stove, the glass front painted cupboard with stacks of plates, rows of glassware.

Jed opens a bottom cabinet and takes out a round dark bottle. "Would you like some port?"

"Maybe a sip." The house feels quiet, quiet like walls padded with thick mattresses. Molly listens. There is no sound. Perhaps her heart. She reaches for the glass that Jed hands her and laughs. "Where did you get this glass?"

"Would you prefer Donald Duck?"

"Goofy's fine, only"—she sips—"these glasses belong in my grandfather's house, too."

"They're good for drinking port around the kitchen table."

"We didn't do that at Grandpa's. I think it was milk."

"There is one bedroom downstairs. Bill and Ellen will have to sleep there tomorrow night. If you don't mind, you can sleep in my bed upstairs. I'll be next door on the daybed."

"That sounds good."

She follows Jed up the narrow stairs. They creak with each footfall. He turns left into a room with a sloping ceiling, a window in the eaves, and wallpaper with toy soldiers in red-and-blue uniforms. Jed goes to the sleigh bed and pulls back the covers. "No spiders, no centipedes."

"Do you always do that?"

"This is the country. The bathroom's next door. There's no hot water yet. Call if you need anything."

Jed goes back down the stairs. Molly feels abandoned. She listens to the opening and closing of doors. In the bathroom, she washes her face. A bronze streak runs down the middle of the white round sink. The water is like ice. The sheets on the bed are cold. She lies stiffly, looking out the small patch of window at the white crescent moon and the massive black triangles of pines.

She rolls on her stomach and pulls the hand-sewn quilt around her shoulders. It smells of must. It smells of Grandpa's house. She sees a figure in the doorway. He walks across the room. Heat flashes up her legs across her stomach. She stays still. She hears him lift the window. She hears him walk across the room again. The ache is there again. The door closes. She hears a click. A sigh comes from her chest and with it, tears.

Chirping sounds pop inside her dream. She opens her eyes. The sounds are at the window. She rubs her cheek and looks around the room. Wooden soldiers stare at her. She smiles and pulls her legs up to her chest reaching for her watch: 6:05. She wraps her arm around the pillow. The air is moist and smells of green.

She thinks of Jed asleep next door. She thinks of Jed at twelve, sleeping in this bed. She thinks of last night in the restaurant. She hears running water, then a step in the hall; she holds her breath. A click, the door opening. "Jed?" she whispers.

"Are you awake?"

"Yes." She sits up. "The birds did it."

Jed steps in the room. "Damn birds. Noisy creatures." He walks across the floor. His hair is tousled. He wears jogging pants, no top. His chest is thick with tawny-colored hair.

"Aren't you cold?" Molly asks, pulling the covers to her chin.

He runs his palm across his chest. "I guess. By the way, the water's hot."

"Good. I slept like a log. I needed it. How was your daybed?"

"Full of ideas." He sits at the foot of the bed with his back against the footboard. "I've been thinking about our meeting today. What do you think of . . ."

Molly tosses him a pillow. He props it at his back. She listens. Her mind tunes in. She throws back his idea, adds one of her own. She moves her legs under the sheets and watches his legs stretched out toward her. Her mind is glued to his, tuned in. The birds are the only other sound she hears. They talk and talk, like two old friends.

She picks up her watch. "I can't believe it's eight o'clock."

"I bet you'd like some coffee?"

"First a shower."

"Shower, and we'll hit the diner for coffee and breakfast and I'll show you the rural landscape."

The little car feels different on the narrow rolling roads. Molly looks across at meadows, planted fields, cows, and white clapboard houses. They have breakfast and on the way back they stop in the general store, another white clapboard building. Jed holds the door. A woman looks up from the counter, scurries around it, and kisses Jed's cheeks. "It's been too long. Who's this?" She looks at Molly.

Jed introduces Molly. The woman grabs her hand.

"This kid we've known for years. At twelve he moved in and took care of his Aunt Lucy. He's quite a guy." Jed buys beer and bread and other things. Molly stands and talks about the town.

At exactly eleven Bill and Ellen arrive. The day is nonstop conversation: sitting on the screened porch, around the kitchen table, hiking down the middle of the street patterned with cutouts of sunlight through the trees. They munch sandwiches and raw carrots and Molly talks to Bill, then to Ellen. It's Neo-Plastics and safe living. It's making ideas work.

At night, Molly and Ellen sit in the backseat of the rented car. They drive north to the next town and a tiny restaurant in a little house beside a lake. They sit knee to knee around a table meant for two and dip bread in olive oil and eat beans with garlic, penne, thin crusted pizza with caramelized onions and goat cheese. They drink wine. Molly wants to reach and touch the three of them. She feels a joy, an energy, a link with something bigger than the four of them.

Driving from the restaurant, Ellen says that they must leave tonight and drive to Boston for a meeting in the morning. They hug and kiss and talk about the next time they will meet and how exciting it is that the four of them will work together.

Molly flops on the stripe-covered couch in the living room. Jed sits at the other end. He hands her port in the Goofy glass. "Like to share?"

She takes the glass and rubs her fingers across the decal. Light comes through the doorway from the kitchen. The port smells sweet. She drinks and hands it back to Jed. She wants to sit like this all night.

"How come you know the advertising business?" Jed asks. His voice is like a priest's asking why she sinned.

"I worked for Hopper/Wang/McGrath."

"When?" Jed sits straight, and turns to face her.

"Four years ago. I was there for five years."

"Five years? Why didn't I know?"

Molly runs her hand along the back of the couch. "I don't know."

"Why did you leave?"

"I wanted to be on my own, I guess."

"I don't believe you."

She looks at him through the darkness, turns the glass in her hand. "There was a misunderstanding—with a client."

"You left over a misunderstanding?"

"Things got uncomfortable."

Jed moves down the couch close to her. He takes the glass and rolls it between his hands. "Was it sexual? Abuse of some sort?"

A knife tears at her wound. Her body springs from the couch like a jack from a box. "Yes. That's what it was. How did you know?"

"It's always that." He reaches for her hand.

She avoids him. Walks around the couch, paces, her body full of fury.

Jed gets up and turns to her. "Damn it. It's always that. It's always some guy who thinks women are . . . I don't know." He pounds the back of the couch.

Frozen, she watches him.

His fist pounds his open hand. His voice is harsh, scolding. "It was that bad? You had to leave?"

Molly starts to shake. Tears begin. They drop in splashes from her cheeks onto her shirt. "Yes. I was confident, successful. Then it was gone. Poof. I felt fooled. I felt foolish." She gasps. Her hand covers her mouth. "I'd been promoted. I was really proud. Then I realized it was a hoax. I had been misled to think it was my talent, my work. Instead it was his way to get me to . . ."

Jed's hands reach out and hold her upper arms. His eyes peer into hers. "And I bet you paid off because you didn't know how not to."

"I did and I didn't . . . I shouldn't have done what I did . . . No one knows. No one cares."

"Don't blame yourself. Men are bastards."

"Not all." Molly wipes the back of her hand across her cheek.

Jed drops his arms. "Not all, I hope." He sighs. "We all might be guilty." He moves backward and leans against the couch. "The bastard kept you from using your real talents. That's what's wrong. You left because you couldn't face yourself. You couldn't believe in Molly."

Her eyes brim again with tears. He reaches for the port and hands it to her. She dips her finger in the sticky liquid and licks it, dips it in again and puts it to his mouth. She feels his lips. She feels unburdened. "Thanks."

They stand in stillness. She feels the web around them. The invisible spider weaving. She dips her finger back inside the glass and licks it. He dips his and puts it in her mouth. He rubs her lips. She melts like a candle heated by a flame.

A crash rocks the house. Jed's hand grabs her arm. A whip of lightning slices through the room. "Oh my God," he says.

"Are the windows open?" Molly asks.

"Don't move. Forget the windows. Don't move." His voice shakes.

The storm is over the house—fighting giants, crashing clubs, blasts of weapons, thuds. Laser lights zap through the windows. Jed stands immobile, his hand cemented to Molly's arm. She wraps her other arm around him—pulls him in—holds him—holds his beating heart, his sweaty neck and arms. She enwraps him while they listen to the outer space invasion, to the cannonballs rippling through the sky, to the ray guns shooting through the darkness.

She folds her arms around him while the giants move their game away and take it to another town. When the sound is faint, he pulls away. "I'm sorry." He reaches for the glass of port. "I hate thunderstorms."

"What happened?"

"It was at summer camp. A storm. My friend and I were together, I was crouching, he was standing by the barn. He was hit—knocked down and dead. I can't get over the fear. It always brings it back. Especially out here. You were nice. Thanks."

"There's no light in the kitchen."

"Damn. The storm has knocked the power out." Jed flips switches. No lights. "Let's hit the sack. It's been a long day. You go upstairs. I'll find a flashlight."

Her room feels empty. The bed feels cold. She feels as if she's swum the English Channel.

It's nine o'clock when Molly wakes. She throws on clothes and goes downstairs. Jed sits at the kitchen table piled with papers. He looks up. "There's no electricity or water."

"I know."

"We'd better get back to the city. The phone is out; I can't call anyone. The lightning must have got the well pump." He runs his fingers through his hair. "If only I could stay."

"I'll take the bus back. You stay."

"I can't. I'm meeting Amtrak tomorrow. Get your bag. We'll stop for breakfast."

Upstairs, Molly stuffs her duffel bag. She's angry and disappointed. She wants more country, more being here with Jed.

She hears Jed on the stairs, going up, going down. She hears him in the basement. She waits in the kitchen.

"I'm really pissed." Jed says, coming up from the cellar. "I've got to get the pump man. Maybe I'll drive out . . ." He walks past her to the living room. She hears windows banging.

"Jed, I've an idea." She stands in the doorway to the living room. "I'll stay."

He turns and looks at her. "Why would you do that?"

"I don't know. It's like a vacation here. I'd really like to stay. To be alone for a couple days. I can get everything fixed."

He starts up the stairs, stops, and looks down at her. "You can't stay without water or electricity."

"Why not?"

He yells from the upstairs. "What would you do?"

"I'd hang out. Fix things. I really like the idea," she yells.

On the way back down, she hears him mumbling. "Crazy idea. Crazy woman." She watches him stuff papers in his briefcase at the kitchen table. "How would you get back to the city anyhow?"

"The red car. You take the bus."

He picks up his bag, his briefcase. "Come on."

They pile the luggage in the tiny space behind the seat. Molly stretches and looks around at the trees. "I really want to stay."

Jed flings the keys at her. "Then you drive. We're going to the bus station."

Seventeen

Molly drives up and over hills. The car is fun. She stretches her head to see the long vistas, the colonial houses, and white farm fences. She drives by a farm stand, catches the sight of red and pink geraniums, pushes the gearshift into reverse, backs up, and guns into the parking lot. She piles the front seat with geraniums and petunias and heads for the general store.

"Survive the storm?" It's the woman she met yesterday.

"We lost electricity. Maybe the water pump."

"Sloves is really busy. Are you on his list?"

"No. I need a phone."

"Use the one in the back."

Molly phones and starts to leave. The woman calls, "You take care of Jed."

"I will."

The woman comes from behind the counter. "Don't go treating him the way that foreign girl did."

"What did she do?"

"Up and left, that's what. Thought they was getting married and next thing you know she's back in

Sweden or someplace and married to someone else. Broke his heart."

Molly picks up the package of peanut butter, bread, and water. "Thanks for the phone."

"I mean it. Jed is special, like he's got wings or something. We don't want him hurt again."

In the garden, in the sunshine, Molly pulls weeds, digs in the dirt. Her thoughts are about Jed, what he said, what she said, how he looked and moved and the woman in the store—she said Jed was special, like a man with wings. She makes holes and sets geraniums and petunias in them and in the wooden tubs around the flagstone terrace, carrying water from the stream down the hill and dumping it on them. It's like Grandpa's house, ordinary, simple, loved. She sweeps the leaves off the flagstones and collapses in a weather-beaten canvas chair staring at the tubs of flowers, admiring them. Her back is stiff. A hot bath would be wonderful.

She gets a pail of water and works away the dirt and mud on her arms and down her legs. The phone rings.

"What's up?"

"How was the bus ride?"

"Terrible. How's the house?"

"Terrible. No, it's wonderful. I'm yearning for a hot bath."

"Did you get Sloves?"

"Left a message."

"Molly, you're great to do this. Have you eaten?"

"No problem, Jed. I'm a big girl."

"I know. By the way, I hired an office manager today."

"Today?"

"Met her on the bus."

"Stop kidding. Who is it?"

"She's the daughter of a senior guy at Dane Hollenbeck. She sat next to me. She is a beautiful girl."

"You offered her a job because she's beautiful?"

"She just got out of college. Worked summers at Dane. She's perfect."

"Perfect?"

"Smart. Organized. I'll check in later."

Molly smears peanut butter on the bread and gobbles it down. The sun is almost gone and the house is dusty gray, shadowy. She wanders in and out of the rooms, talking to the furniture, patting it, talking to the walls and pictures.

"Do not fear," she says, "Molly-to-the-Rescue is here."

Upstairs, she peels away her mud-caked clothes and lies on the bed. The house is like a little friendly nest into which she has crawled. She feels protected, unashamed to be naked like a child, spread on the bed with the wooden soldiers and a picture of Jed in a boat with a fishing pole—a teenager.

Her eyes stare at the photograph on the wall, obscured in darkness. She knows it's Jed; he's in her thoughts, almost in the room. He sat here on the bed in the morning with the birds. They were alone—they could have touched. She held him in the thunderstorm. Their bodies merged. Inside the darkness with the rain and lightning, and banging in the sky, they merged. It was a miracle—like love.

Silence. Heartbeats. Darkness. A ring. Another ring. The phone. She moves off the bed, the cover dragging on the floor. She flies through the hallway to the den. "Hello."

"Molly, this is Jed. Are you okay?"

"Yes, you startled me. I guess I was asleep."

"Is the electricity back?"

"I think so."

"Is everything all right."

"I was dreaming about you. I'm in your bed."

"In the dark?"

"In the dark with no clothes on."

"Don't tell me."

"Where are you?"

"In the light fully dressed."

"Of course."

"It's quiet here. I wish I were there."

"Me too. Is it hot in the city?" Molly pushes her feet to the bottom of the bed. She listens to his voice, hears about the city, the meeting with Amtrak. She turns on her side, props her head with her hand. He tells her what he ate for dinner. She asks about Brooklyn. She fingers the edge of the blanket, pulls up the sheet. He talks about Angelo, about Pratt, about the Brooklyn Academy of Music. She puts her nose inside the pillow and smells the way he smells.

"Time to go," Jed says.

"They asked about you at the store today."

"Were they prying into my life? They love to do that."

"They mentioned a girl." She hears him breathing.

"They love gossip."

"They said she hurt you."

"Well, it's a rumor."

"A true rumor?"

"Girls always hurt guys. We better hang up."

"Who was she? Peterson?"

"Where did you hear that?"

"I've heard it. She worked for you. Your partner?"

"Not exactly. She was a client from Norway."

"And?"

"Now who's being the gossip?"

"Sorry. When they said you were hurt, it made me sad. I thought about it all afternoon."

"It was a long time ago. Call it a disappointment. You've had those, right?"

"Right. I like it here. Thanks for letting me stay."

"It's midnight."

"Here it is just dark."

"I'll call tomorrow or call me when the pump's fixed."

Molly stays in Jed's bed. She sleeps there Monday night as well. On Tuesday she returns to New York.

Eighteen

On Tuesday morning, Bert Sloves finishes install-
ing the new pump for the well. Molly takes a proper
shower, washes the dishes in the kitchen, and
plumps the pillows on the couch in the living room.
Jed said Mrs. Somebody would come in to wash
the linens and clean but Molly wants the living room
looking tidy before she leaves. It's a room she has
fallen in love with. In a kitchen drawer she found
a picture of Aunt Lucy taken with an instant camera.
She assumes it's Aunt Lucy; it resembles the mental
pictures she has of her: a woman who would own
this practical, uncomplicated house, a no-nonsense
woman who would make a lost twelve-year-old feel
wanted without feeling babied.

Molly senses Lucy was one of those courageous
types, marching for women's rights, kowtowing to
no man. She probably fished for brook trout in the
river and played wicked tennis in the same outfit
she'd worn for twenty years. Whoever she was, she
gave Jed a sure sense of himself and probably a
sensitivity for loving and for women. Molly will
never know. She takes one last tour through the
house. It's a goodbye tour. A farewell to a friend.

As she climbs into the little red car she has an overwhelming sense that this house is more her style than the elegant apartment at Ten Gracie Square.

She avoids driving with the big trucks by staying on the west-side route to Manhattan, going down the West Side Highway. As she nears the George Washington Bridge she feels tension begin to build in her shoulders and her neck. The drive has been fun. The car and she are one: gliding like old friends on the smooth paved highways, downshifting on the Saw Mill River, and speeding in front of lumbering sedans. Her thoughts are fixed on Jed. She will walk into his office, drop into a chair, tell about the pump man, and the ride back to the city.

She pulls into the garage on Twentieth Street and unwinds from the seat. Jed will be at his desk. She'll walk into his room and see his smile.

The white and green and oak, the smell of paint and glue greet Molly. She swings past Angelo with a wave and a greeting and heads for Jed's office. It's empty.

"Where's Jed?" she yells back at Angelo.

"Out."

"Thanks. When will he be back?"

"Talk to Amy. She's in the corner office."

Molly goes across the floor to her office. The door is closed. She turns the knob and opens it. Fury rises in her stomach. "What's going on?" She doesn't recognize her voice. It's strident, accusing. She looks at the stranger sitting at the table covered with folders and papers. There is no computer, nothing that she left here on Friday.

"You must be Molly."

"Where are my things? Where's the computer? What are you doing here?"

"Didn't Jed tell you? I'm Amy Greenman." The girl pushes back her chair and plays with a strand of red hair.

"I didn't think you'd be in here. Where's Jed anyway?"

"He's out at a meeting. I don't know when he'll be back. Late, I think. Can I get you anything?"

"Did Jed say you could take over this office?"

"I'm sorting things. It's good space to do it in."

"What am I supposed to do? I need this office."

"I didn't know you would be in. You can have it, I guess." She starts to gather up the papers.

"Forget it. It's late, don't move. I won't be back till next week but I want it then. I'll use the phone in the other room. Do you expect Jed at all?"

"Oh, yes. I'll wait for him. It may be after five or later."

Molly circles around and returns to the center room. She stands with her hands on her hips looking at Jed's open door, out the window, to the corner room, across the empty space to Angelo, then wanders to his drafting table and looks over his shoulder. She makes comments, chats. She goes to the deli and gets coffee, then sits watching the door at the top of the stairs and dials Porter. "How's California?"

"Where have you been? I thought you were coming back Sunday."

"I took a vacation after the meeting. Didn't Grace tell you?"

"Yes, she called. She's lonely. Harlan's still in L.A."

"Do you want to meet for dinner?" Molly asks.

"Of course. Pete's at six-thirty. Grace will be there, too."

The computer sits on an empty desk. Molly looks at her watch. Time to kill; time to wait for Jed. She boots the computer and sorts through files. It's like a friend she can talk to when she feels unnerved. She wishes Jed were here. She wants to talk about the corner office. No sharing. No Amy Greenman in her space. He said that she was beautiful. She is. This office doesn't feel the same.

Amy walks across the room and goes into Jed's office. Molly watches. Her skirt could be a little longer, her breasts a little smaller. Her hair is like a rusty pipe. When Amy comes back, she stops and folds her arms in front of Molly.

"Jed says I should learn PageMaker. Can you teach me? We could do it after work."

"That's a good idea."

"I think it's great that Jed started his own agency, don't you?" Amy says.

"Yes, I guess I do."

"I remember him at Dane. All the girls had crushes on him. He's cute, don't you think?"

"I hadn't thought about it."

"Are you married?"

"Getting married in October. Read the Page-

Maker manual. Try it out. I'll make time for you next week."

Molly leaves at six; Jed has not come back. She leaves her duffel bag and briefcase. She'll walk to Pete's and come back later for her things.

Her city mood returns. As she turns on Irving Place, she sees Porter getting out of a cab and going into the restaurant. She finds him in the back room at a small round table with Grace. He stands and plants a kiss on her mouth. Molly bends down and kisses Grace's cheek. Her hair is different, more severe.

"This is a treat," Molly says. "Getting to see both of you at once."

"Why were you so long in Connecticut? It must have been quite a meeting," Grace says.

"Connecticut is gorgeous in the spring. I had a hard time leaving. How was California?" She turns to Porter.

"Not nice," Porter says, "not like Connecticut. Let's not talk about it."

"Harlan loves it, doesn't he?" Grace says.

"He's better at it than I am. That's for sure."

"He appreciates your helping out," Grace says.

"I'm not sure about that. I wouldn't be there except for the two of you. I feel I have a stake in Harlan's success."

"Thank you, Porter. That's nice." Grace reaches across the table and pats his arm.

Molly eats a hamburger slathered with onions and tomatoes and cheddar cheese. It's a respite from three days of peanut butter. She orders french fries and eats them with her fingers. They tell tales of California.

"Do you women want to come to my place for coffee or brandy?" Porter asks.

"I would," Grace says. "I can't stand that empty apartment."

"I'd like to but I think I won't. My bag is back at the office and—"

"Too bad, Molly. You and Porter haven't been together in a while. Do you want me to go home?"

"We have the rest of our lives," Porter says.

"Remember this is Memorial Day weekend," Grace says. "We're all going to the Robinses' in Connecticut. Do you know Roland, Porter?"

"I worked on a buyout with him once. A good man, smart investment banker. It will be nice for all of us to be together."

Molly walks back to the office. As she turns down Twentieth Street, her stomach begins to tense. She pictures Jed at his desk—alone—no one else there. He'll be surprised to see her. She sees the light from the street. As she climbs the stairs her heartbeats speed. His office door is closed. She wants to run across the floor, instead she walks and takes a breath and reaches for the knob. She hears a woman's voice. Through the crinkled glass, she sees Jed sitting on the couch; Amy's on a chair. She panics. She tastes the hamburger, the onions, the fries. She retreats across the floor. Her palms are wet. She grabs her duffel bag and briefcase and takes a taxi home.

* * *

On Friday night, Molly sits at the formal dining table in the house in Greenwich. Porter is next to her; Harlan and Grace across from her and Roland and Phyllis Robins at either end of the large table. Roland makes a toast.

"To Porter and Molly, our new good friends. Phyllis and I are honored to have you as our guests. We are providing you with two small children for the weekend to observe. May they be an inspiration."

Roland laughs. Everyone cheers and raises their glasses of wine.

"That's wonderful, Roland," Grace says. "When my sister and Porter have a child, I will be the number one aunt."

"Aunt and mother too, I presume," Roland says.

Molly looks at Harlan. He holds his napkin and red wineglass together in one hand. "I'll toast to Aunt Grace," Molly says.

"To Auntie Grace," says Harlan.

"Fill up Grace's glass," Roland says, pushing the bottle down the table. "Come on, Harlan, get started. Kids are fun."

"Tonight's the night." Harlan lifts his glass. "How about it, Grace?"

"To Porter, my new brother-in-law," Grace says. "The best one I could have."

Porter stands and clears his throat. "To Phyllis and Roland, our gracious host and hostess. We are delighted to be here and look forward to a wonderful weekend."

"Hear, hear," cries Harlan, standing, gripping the back of his chair. "To my beautiful wife."

Grace slides from her chair and kisses Harlan on the mouth. Molly notices Grace looking across the table and smiling at Porter.

Harlan's arm goes around Grace's shoulder. "Come on, baby, let's tango." He ushers her from the table through the archway to the hall. "Pardon us. We have things to do." Grace supports him like a ski crash victim.

"Let's have some port in the living room." Roland pushes back his chair and stands.

"Great idea," Porter says, pulling the chair back for Phyllis.

Molly takes a seat on the couch next to Roland. The smell from the port carries her back to Connecticut. She rubs the outside of the glass: no Goofy, no Mickey Mouse. She listens to Roland talk about buying wine; her mind is on last weekend. She looks across at Porter sitting in a wing chair.

The room becomes a blur, the voices too. She squints and sees a mixture of the rose and blue coming from the Oriental rug, muted colors from the oil painting of flowers on the wall. Porter stands. "Time for bed, don't you think?"

They climb the stairs. The room is on the third floor. It's square with windows in the eaves. The pine bed is covered with a multicolored quilt; the wallpaper has tiny yellow flowers that match the curtains. An oval braided rug is on the floor. Molly collapses in the rocking chair. She watches Porter bend and undo the laces of his shoes. "Thanks for tonight," she says.

"For what?"

"I don't know. I guess Harlan bothered me."

"He's all right. That flight from the coast can be a killer." He folds the quilt and puts it on a chair. "We have to set a wedding date."

"I know." She undoes the buttons on her blouse.

"The sooner the better. No reason to put it off." He removes his gray trousers and drapes them on a hanger. "My parents are planning a party in July; it could be a wedding party."

"That's impossible." Her mind races through her calendar. "I have too much to do."

"I'd like a quiet ceremony, do you agree?"

"Yes, absolutely."

"Good. Harlan and Grace will come to Minneapolis with us. I'll call Mother."

"Not a wedding then, Porter. Please. It's too soon."

"Sometimes you sound unsure." He goes to the chair where she sits and reaches for her hands.

"I'm not." She stands. "It's just this new job. I can't do two new things at once. October's better."

"Your job should not be more important than our marriage." He puts his lips against her hairline.

"It isn't. I just feel rushed."

He lifts her chin and kisses her. She tastes the port. He pulls her to the bed. His hand is in her blouse. His leg moves in against her leg.

"Wait." She pushes on his chest. "Let me undress, brush my teeth. You use the bathroom first."

He takes the towel from the rack and leaves. She removes her clothes. The moon shines through the window. It's bigger than it was last week. The window looks familiar, a tiny window in an eave.

Porter comes back. Molly tiptoes past the door to Grace and Harlan's room. The bathroom is small, under the eaves with a tiny round sink. There is a bronze mark where the water drips, like the sink at Jed's. In the hallway, coming back, she meets Grace, a tiny figure submerged in a long white gown.

"Are you all right?" Molly whispers. A slice of moonlight barrels by them, lighting up the dark-stained floor.

Grace jumps. "I didn't see you."

"Is everything okay?" Molly asks.

"Why?"

"I don't know. Harlan had a lot to drink." Molly follows Grace into the bathroom and watches Grace put water on her face.

"He was tired," Grace says.

"Did he fall asleep?"

"Not right away." Grace's voice shakes. She unties the ribbons on her nightgown.

"What did he do?"

"You know what he did." She faces Molly.

Molly sits against the ridges on the metal radiator.

Grace puts water on a washcloth and the washcloth on her breast.

"What are you doing?"

"I find this makes it better."

"What better?" She takes the cloth from Grace's

hand and opens up her gown. Blue marks are on her breasts. "What are these?"

"My skin is tender."

"What did Harlan do?"

"You know what men do."

"I don't. What?" She peers through the half-light. The small room is lit from just the moonlight and the tiny shell night-light on the wall.

"They like to bite. You know, suck hard."

Molly grabs Grace's arm. Her hand squeezes. "Normal men don't do that." She sees tears filling Grace's eyes.

"Molly, you're so lucky. I'd do anything to be in your shoes."

Molly sighs and rocks her sister in her arms. "Don't ever let Harlan do this to you again."

"I can't stop him, I've tried. He says sexy women like it."

"He's wrong." Molly pats Grace's breasts, closes her gown, and makes bows in the ties. She walks with her down the hallway, kisses her cheeks, and watches her open the door and disappear.

Porter sleeps. Molly crawls in beside him. The bed is narrow. She looks at the yellow flowers in the wallpaper. She moves close to Porter's body. She wants an arm, some comfort. She thinks of Harlan's mouth on Grace's tender breasts.

Chirpings wake her. She looks for the soldiers on the wall and finds flowers. The sun is beaming through the attic window. Porter is beside her. His arm reaches over her. She lifts it, places his hand on her breast. The warmth floods through her chest.

He moves beside her, his leg is over hers. His loose pajama bottoms feel twisted with the sheets. "Kiss my breasts," she whispers, "be gentle."

She feels his tongue. It's like a balm, an ointment. She runs her fingers on his neck. His large legs bump around beneath the covers. His hand pulls at the fastening at his waist, brushing up against her naked belly, making funny feelings in her groin. She runs her legs along his legs. His lips are on her neck, his chest is on her chest. Grace's words run through her head: you are so lucky. She pictures Harlan biting Grace's skin. Porter is making noises, soft noises. She runs her hands across his back and pushes up against his body. "Chirrup, chirrup" comes through the window.

Porter dresses, leaves. It's golf day. Molly stays in bed drifting in and out of sleep. She dreads getting up, seeing Grace, talking to Phyllis. The door opens. A tiny boy with coal black hair walks in and stands beside the bed.

"Hi," Molly says.

"What's your name?" He twists his finger in his hair.

"Molly. What's yours?"

"Ben. Are you spending the night?"

"I already did. Where's your room?"

"Downstairs." He rubs his hand across the sheet. "This floor is only for guests. This is the third floor. I sleep on the second floor with Mommy and Caroline. Do you want to see my bear?"

"Yes. Is it Pooh bear?"

"No. It's a teddy bear." He puts it next to her.

The cloth shows through the worn down fur. There's one glass eye.

"Where's Mommy?"

"Downstairs with Auntie Grace. They're drinking coffee."

"Auntie Grace is my little sister just like Caroline is yours."

"They told me to get you."

Molly finds Phyllis and Grace in the kitchen. They have planned a shopping spree on Greenwich Avenue. Molly says she'd rather stay and play with Ben and Caroline. Ben sits on a high stool and watches Molly eat bananas and Cheerios. He shows her his bedroom and all his toys. They sit on the floor and build a house with three garages out of smooth beige blocks. She teaches him to spread peanut butter on bread and they make sandwiches and eat them and explore the rocks down by the water.

They swim in the pool. Ben makes rat-a-tats and booms and noises with his tongue against his teeth. So does Molly. She lies in the chaise and Ben climbs in her lap and falls asleep. The sky is blue; the water of Long Island Sound stretches out in front of her. She follows a mass of sailboats and keeps her hand on his curly head and feels the warmth from his sleeping body penetrate her legs, her heart.

Mrs. Fitch, in a starched white uniform, comes down to the pool carrying Caroline swaddled in a light pink blanket. Ben raises his head and climbs down from Molly's lap. Molly reaches up and takes

Caroline. The baby's eyes open, her cheeks plump up and smile.

"She only just born," Ben says.

"She's four months old."

"I'm two." Molly sees Porter walk across the lawn. He sits and Ben climbs on his knee. Porter bounces him and says a poem. They laugh. The baby kicks her feet.

Molly takes a shower. She wraps one towel on her body, the other around her head, and goes down the hallway. Porter comes from their room dressed in a white dinner jacket, black pants. Molly stops. He is the picture of an elegant successful gentleman: his smooth face shines, his fair hair is combed neatly. Her mother would approve.

"You look great," she says.

"You do, too."

"You like my sarong?"

He follows her back into the bedroom. "I liked seeing you with Caroline. You're a natural."

"Thanks. If you don't leave you'll see all of me." She unwraps the towel, notices his blush, and laughs.

The Country Club has a special room for dances. It swirls with couples, men in black and women in assorted colors with dresses short and long, sleek and puffy. Molly wears white, very short, silk, straight, and cut to swing with her body. She feels good and notices the looks, feels the "who are they?" Phyllis introduces them around, taking them from one group to another.

Grace wears black, short and bouffant. "You look fabulous." Molly whispers. "Do you still hurt?"

"Harlan apologized. He said he was carried away."

"I see." Molly looks across the room at Harlan. He wears dark glasses. Porter is beside him shaking hands. Molly sits at the table and talks to Roland.

"You and Porter should buy out here. We'll get you in the club. Do you play golf?"

"No."

"Tennis?"

"Somewhat. I haven't for years."

"We have a super golf pro; you can learn. The women have a lot of fun."

The band plays. People dance, swing their hips, twirl under arms and smile at the people dancing next to them. Molly hears the clarinet, the saxophone, piano. They take turns soloing. She sips her vodka tonic and eats the shrimp that sits on lettuce.

Porter's hand is on her shoulder, asking her to dance. She's never danced with him before. He leads her to the floor. They glide; he turns each time the beat is strong. She follows him with ease; his arm is firm across her back. She is a debutante, in a movie, dancing with the leading man.

"I'm thinking of making reservations for Tanglewood for July Fourth," he says. "Just the two of us."

"Grace might have something planned."

"Molly, I'd rather not go with them. Not at this time. Trust me."

Molly sees Harlan come across the floor and tap Porter. "May I cut in?"

He whirls Molly to the edge of the dance floor, away from the tables. "So you have it made, Molly? Are you going to thank your big brother?"

"Thanks."

"Where's the enthusiasm?" He dips her back. "Porter's got lots of bucks."

"Jealous?"

"Who me? I'll make it." He spins her until she feels dizzy.

"Harlan, don't hurt my sister."

"Grace is talking, huh?"

"I found her in the hall last night."

"She's too tender. She needs to be tough."

"You need to be gentle."

"Sexy women like rough guys. Haven't you found that out?"

"No."

"You better give it a go before you marry Porter. If I weren't your brother-in-law . . ."

"Grace is fragile."

"Grace is my wife. She complains too much. It's frankly making me sick."

"Harlan, what are you saying?"

"I'm saying, don't interfere in things you know nothing about." He dips her back and swirls in a circle.

"I'd like to sit."

At the table, he holds her chair. "Remember what I said."

She makes designs with the string beans on her plate and looks across at Porter sitting next to Grace. Harlan is there, reaching for Grace's hand.

He leads her to the dance floor, turns his head back toward Molly, lowers his dark glasses, and winks.

Rineteen

Molly is in the backseat of the car with Porter. The weekend at the Robinses' is over and Harlan drives his newly leased Acura back to the city. Molly stares at the back of Harlan's head. He has erupted at Porter over the client in California and he drives the way he talks: jerking the car with the brake, tapping the horn.

Porter's voice is soft, even, and hard. He leans forward in his seat. "We are talking law here. California is still in the United States. It's a matter of what can and cannot be done. I'm telling you, you have no choice. There is no discussion."

Harlan flips the radio and sings country tunes. Porter crosses his legs and mashes one hand with the other. Molly feels sick. Grace looks straight ahead.

When the car pulls to the curb in front of her apartment, Molly untwists her legs, throws kisses to Grace and Harlan, presses Porter's hand, and dashes for the entrance. She unlocks the door, beelines for the water and the ice, and drops onto the couch. She leans against one flowered pillow, pulls the phone and phone cord to the couch, and dials. Jed's machine answers; she leaves a message.

She dumps her clothes from her bag on the floor, then goes to the closet and grabs armloads of clothes from the racks and drapes them on the furniture. She piles the long full skirts, the tie-dyes, the Indian prints in a pile on the floor. She sits on the closet floor, moving the shoes, matching pairs, and throwing the worn ones out toward the kitchen counter. She finds a black plastic garbage bag and stuffs it with shoes, old skirts, sweaters, a jacket from college. She finds a white man's shirt that has splotches of paint. She puts it on and cries.

She sweeps the closet floor. Jed must be in Connecticut. Perhaps he went with Amy and they sat on the terrace with the flowers and in the living room and he cooked for her and they swam in the pool and slept in the . . .

She calls Porter.

"I left the car without a proper goodbye. I'm sorry."

"I understand."

"I was feeling sick. What's going on with Harlan?"

"Harlan's got some things to learn. He will."

"He has been acting strange lately. Grace mentioned it."

"The glamour of Hollywood is affecting him. I've seen it before. We'll tap him down."

"I hope so. It worries me."

"Don't worry, I know what to do."

"I know. Without you I would feel lost—so would Grace."

"I talked tonight to the folks. We could easily be married in July. They would love it."

Molly jiggles the telephone cord. "Maybe. Let me think about it."

She turns on the TV and watches a group of lions and baby cubs. She carries the clothes back to the closet, arranging skirts with skirts, blouses with blouses. Chewing her nail, she returns to the TV and watches a lion with a group of hyenas, then continues in the closet, lifting hangers and putting them beside like colors with white and lights in front and blacks at the end. A brrring shocks her like a light switched on. She finds the phone on the couch.

"Just got in. Did I wake you?"

"No. I called to tell you I'll be in on Thursday. My other jobs will be done by then."

"Good."

"Amy Greenman has to vacate the corner office. I need that space."

"She knows that. She told me you were upset."

"Is there anything I need to know? What about the job with Keith?"

"Keith has the reservations for Florida the week after this."

"Who's going?"

"You and me—Keith and Pam. He'll be looking at the technical, we'll be examining the design."

"How long?"

"Three days. Two nights. Any problem?"

"It's part of the job."

"You don't want to go?"

"I do." She sits on the couch and bends over. Her stomach feels funny. "Did you go to Connecticut? How was the house?"

"It was great. The garden is terrific—bowled me over. Thank you."

"I liked doing it. I like your house." She listens to his breathing. "You'll have to weed now, you know."

"I'll have to learn. It felt like Lucy had come back."

"Did that make you sad?"

"No, not really. It was good. The people at the store asked about you. They think you're my girl-friend."

"I know. What did you tell them?"

"I said you were back at the house."

"That will confuse them."

"So what. It felt like you were there, sometimes."

"What do you mean?" Molly switches the phone to her other ear.

"I don't know. The house is alive again."

"The woman in the store told me not to hurt you."

"What did you say?"

"Nothing."

"You didn't promise?"

Molly laughs. "How is the car?"

"It missed you."

"I missed it, too. We got to be pretty good friends." She stretches out. "Is the pump working okay?"

"No problems. I saw Bud Greenman. Went to a party at his house. He has a lot of shop gossip. I'll tell you sometime."

"Good. I better go. I'll see you Thursday."

Molly ties the bag with the old clothes and takes it down the hall. She comes back and makes lists on a yellow pad for the rest of the week.

On Thursday, she gets to Saunders and Associates and finds her office transformed with a new table and a proper chair and a cabinet for files and drawings. Among her messages is one from Pam McCarthy: Reservations for Epcot confirmed. Room for two nights—nonsmoking—next to Jed's.

A week later, Molly sits at Kennedy in the boarding area for United Flight 365 to Orlando, Florida. The waiting area screams with children, adults, tourists, baggage, cameras. She holds the morning *Times* in her lap but looks instead at the crowd. She looks for Jed or Keith or Pamela and tries to ignore the bubbles in her stomach.

Her name flies through the air from the loudspeaker. It rebounds off the walls. "Ms. Mitchell, Ms. Molly Mitchell. Report to United's desk."

She reaches for her bag, drops the paper, and stuffs it under her arm. Her face feels hot. She pushes by a swarm of teenagers, looks up, and sees Jed. He grins. "Where have you been?"

Keith and Pam stand behind him. "We're boarding."

"I didn't hear the call."

"Change of plans. We're going first-class."

Jed takes the aisle seat. Molly sits beside him. He takes coffee from the attendant, the business section of the *Times* from Molly, and fastens his seat belt. "Nice seats, huh?"

"This is perfect." Molly refuses coffee: too many stomach bubbles. She looks past Jed at the people boarding. Jed's profile is in her line of vision, getting in her way, luring her to look at him and think about the trip. She shifts in the seat and reads the headlines on the paper. She has read them seven times before. She turns the page and turns her head to watch the stream of people going down the aisle. The flight attendants move like guppies in a fishbowl, the parents push the children, the engines ring. Jed looks up and smiles at her. She notices the swirls of brownish hair along his wrist, the hand that holds the paper.

The taxi pulls around the fountains and the large stone swans and underneath the canopy of the tall, white hotel. A uniformed man with epaulets on his shoulders piles the bags on a cart and disappears inside the opening doors. At the desk, they fill in forms, get door cards, and go up to their rooms.

"What do you think?" Jed stands in the middle of the pink carpet in her room.

"I think I've flown to Mars."

He walks through the connecting door. "My room looks like yours except the rug is green."

She pulls clothes from her bag and hangs them up. "A bed big enough for four?"

"A bed too big for one." He stands in the doorway.

She looks at him. His hand is in his pocket. He has changed his T-shirt. Her cheeks feel warm. They meet Keith and Pam in the lobby and take the bus to Epcot Center. They follow Keith going in and out and up and down and riding cars and trains and sitting on moving platforms. They eat Italian ice and Molly feels her vision charged by seas of purples, fuchsia, brilliant red, and scorching yellows. There are carpets of color and rivers of nodding flowers running through the walkways.

The day barrels by, the shadows grow long. The four of them walk and stretch and wave their arms and catch the warm and welcome breeze. They stroll around the lake and through the villages of Britain and India, Germany and Japan.

"Let's eat in Italy," Jed suggests. "I love olives and olive oil, spaghetti, tomatoes, and cheese. Even anchovies. Do you, Molly?" Jed asks.

"My favorite," Molly says. "Bread with hard crusts. Polenta."

They drink red wine.

"Is this fun?" asks Keith.

"I feel I'm on a high school science trip," Molly says.

"Nice, Molly," Keith says. "We have worlds to conquer. We're on the edge, guys. Can you feel it?"

Jed reaches for her hand. He holds it tight. His brown eyes glisten. Everyone's do.

"We're a great crew," Keith says. He kisses Pam who kisses Jed who kisses Molly. She tastes the wine. He lingers. She tastes Jed.

Outside the sky is dark and full of stars. Fireworks fly and spurt from boats and songs come out of nowhere, filling the air along the paths, teasing them to sing and dance and lock their arms and weave and laugh and skip and hop.

The crowds move in and break them up. They go in pairs. Molly's arms and Jed's are wrapped around each other. They weave and laugh and bump and sing.

"Like a New York subway," Molly says.

"Like a New York bar at five on Friday." Jed pulls her close and kisses her. It's quick. She stumbles and he holds her up. She wants to kiss again. She wants to stand and kiss all night. They reach the group of buses. She takes his hand. She holds it even when they board, even when she sits and he stands by the seat, looking out the window.

She pushes the card in the slot of her door; he turns the handle. The room looks dusty rose. He follows her and opens the door to his adjoining room. "We should get some sleep. Tomorrow's going to be a wild one. A meeting at nine. Keith's got us jumping."

"He's crazy." Molly sits on the edge of the bed.

"He's smart." Jed falls in a chair. "I like smart people. I like working with them. You're smart."

"So are you. It's good to be back with the smarts."

"How come you never let on about Hopper?"

"Because you would have wondered why I left."

"There was a story about a woman at Hopper, on the Better Bakers account. She made a real fuss about the word lite. Is that true? Who was she?"

Molly's hand moves to her throat. "How did you hear that?"

"Street gossip. We debated, was she right or not? What did you think?"

"I think she was right. How about you?"

"I loved the story. She was perfect in my book. Right on. Did you know her?"

"I did." She feels redness on her face.

"Wait a minute. Did you work on Better Bakers?"

"I did."

"Oh my God. Of course, it's you."

Molly nods.

"I love it. You're wonderful. I've had this secret admiration and I didn't even know it was you." He stands. He takes her face between his hands and kisses one cheek, then the other. He moves his lips to hers. The kiss is short; he backs away. "I knew when I saw you through the window you were special." He turns in circles and pounds the back of the wing-back chair. He goes to the door that leads to his room. "I'm going to bed. See you in the morning." He leaves and shuts the door between the rooms.

Friday repeats Thursday. They explore the science center, meet with engineers, designers, prowl behind the scenes. At noon rain falls. They duck beneath an awning and huddle close together. It smells like a zillion sour washcloths. The rain pours like water on a sluiceway. The drops are as big as quarters. When it stops, Keith says, "Who shut off the faucet?"

Children leap from nowhere and slosh into the puddles. Molly doffs her shoes and follows. The pavement is hot. So is the water.

"You want to take a train ride through a human body?" Keith asks.

"Not for me," says Pam.

"No pregnant women allowed. How about you, Molly?"

"I'll stay with Pamela."

Molly heads Pamela toward an empty bench. "How do you feel?"

"I'm fine. I can't believe next year I'll be pushing a baby carriage. This is a lot easier." She laughs.

"I could be, too," Molly says.

"You're going to marry that guy?" Pam shakes her head. "I can't see it."

"Why?"

"Cause you're in love with Jed."

"Don't be silly."

"And he's in love with you. You're great together."

"It's because we work together. We share so much. That's all. I'm too old for him."

"Come on. Plenty of women marry younger men. I see the way he looks at you."

"What do you mean?" Molly's gaze follows a pregnant woman and a little girl.

"He's crazy about you. It's obvious. Keith says so, too."

Molly stands and rubs her hands on her shorts. "I can't do anything about it."

"Don't be dumb, of course you can."

Molly pushes back her hair. "It's the work that's exciting."

"You're kidding yourself, Mollykins."

"Porter is different. He's serious but he's okay. Grace likes him."

"Grace is pushing you, right?"

"Of course not. She's my little sister."

"She has a way. I see it at work."

Molly spots Jed in the exiting crowd. She runs to him. "How was it?"

"We're feeling sick. I need a Coke."

Molly leads him under an umbrella. She buys a giant Coke, an ice-cream cone, a bag of popcorn.

Molly whistles in the shower. She's getting ready for the "night on the town" as Keith calls it. They are going to "Las Vegas." She puts on a jumpsuit, and a wide belt of colored rhinestones. New York and Grace and Porter, even the office, seem a million miles away.

At the restaurant they are Texas ranchers. They outdo each other with their drawls and talk about their cattle, their radio stations, their oil wells. They dance the Texas two-step and line dance with a crowd of other people. The fantasy becomes reality. Molly is a Texan, the owner of a ranch who flirts and dances and bumps and grinds and rubs her body against Jed's, and feels the part that makes him male and rubs it more. At two-thirty the music slows. Jed pulls her in and locks his body next to hers and rocks tight in sync with the wailing country song. She feels his breath, his chest, his thighs, the part that's hard below his waist. Lightning strikes her body. She feels his fingers on her neck.

The singer croons and moans and cries the sadness of the song about a lover lost, gone to another. Jed's fingers take her hair and hold it tight. His arm wraps around her body. She feels his beating heart, his mouth along her hair and now on hers. A million jolts surge up her arms and down her legs. She feels his tongue between her lips, the taste, the warmth, the taste that is her taste. She moans and crushes into him and puts her mouth in his and cries inside her heart and whirls inside in rhythm to their turning bodies locked together, moving with the moaning music, the strumming chords all minor, all sad, all pulling and raising the level of the yearnings in her heart.

The music stops. They pull away, blink, and wipe their hands across their faces and look around the room with eyes that come from darkness into light and hearts that come from dreams into reality.

At the hotel, he leaves her by her door, kisses her cheek, and turns away. "We'll see you in the morning, 9:25 in the lobby," Keith says.

She hunts for her card, inserts it in the door and waits for the green light. She turns back to Jed and sees him going in his room.

She flips the switch beside the door. It lights the lamp beside the bed. The room is big. It's empty. She sits in the chair Jed sat in last night and listens for sounds from his room. Nothing. She eats the chocolates on the pillows, unzips the jumpsuit, finds her nightshirt, and washes her face. She slips inside the turned-back covers and falls asleep.

Pelting rain and wind wake her. A green 3:47 shows on the clock beside the bed. The rain is like pebbles hitting the glass. She gets up and goes to the window. The rain is blowing like curtains in the street, swaying the palm trees, flapping the fronds. She creeps across the carpet to Jed's door, listens and hears the television. She turns the knob.

"Jed?" She sees him in the bed.

"Molly? What's the matter?"

"Are you all right?"

"Come in. I'm fine. I'm watching a colorized version of *Casablanca.*"

She walks to his bed, yanking at her nightshirt to cover her thighs. He wears a T-shirt and sits with his back against a pile of pillows.

"Have you seen this?" he asks.

"A hundred times."

"It's great. Come watch." He pats the empty spot beside him on the bed.

"I heard the rain."

"Me too. When it rains in Florida, it rains."

She climbs on the bed. Humphrey Bogart leads Ingrid Bergman and Claude Rains into a restaurant.

"Get under the covers. There's plenty of room." He tosses her a pillow.

She slips her legs under the covers. It's like getting in an envelope. She looks across the bed and sees the mounds that are his legs. The space in between could hold another couple. She stares at the screen. The words float above her head. She sees the streets of Paris. She's in the restaurant, slow dancing with Jed. She turns her head and looks at him. He's looking at the screen. She doesn't dare to move; her body is a stick. Her eyelids close. She drifts. She lifts her chin and pushes her head against the pillow. Bogart is a blur.

Nick and Ilsa stand on the runway, an airplane in the distance. It's raining. "We'll always have Paris." The credits reel down the screen. She turns her head toward Jed. He stretches out his arms. She looks around the room, at his suitcase, his pants draped on the chair. Her hand pulls the covers back. She stands. She stumbles around the bed, across the floor. "Good night," she says, going through the doorway, closing the door.

She dives through the dark for her bed and lies there like a board. Her heartbeats echo in her ears together with the rain on the window. She hugs the pillow and stares at the numbers on the clock. She must get back to New York and to Porter.

Twenty

Molly wakes to a banging at the door. "Come in." She pushes herself up against the cushioned headboard and rubs her eyes as Jed enters the room.

"I need to talk to you," Jed says. "Keith has a new plan. I hope it's okay with you."

She watches him brush his hair from his forehead. "Aren't we flying out at noon?"

"He wants to stay another two days . . . not here . . . on an island on the west coast."

"So?" Her fingernail scratches her hand. "We'll catch the plane without them."

"I was planning to go with them. I hoped—"

"That's fine. I can get back by myself." She diverts her eyes to her luggage, to the foot of the bed, and pulls on the sheet. She wants to leap from the bed and start packing.

He leans against the chair. "Maybe . . . I thought you would come, too."

"No. I can't. Why the sudden change in plans?"

"I'm not sure. A guy he knows in Fort Lauderdale, his father owns a house on this island. He's invited us for the weekend. It does sound like fun . . . might be interesting, too." He stretches his arms behind his head. "I'd like it if you came along."

"I need to get back. You go play. Let me get dressed. I'll meet you downstairs." She watches Jed shrug and close the door, then bounds out of bed and into the bathroom. The shower runs hard and hot. She stands under the pelting water biting her lip and resisting the tears that are on the edge of exploding. Two days on an island. She pictures herself on the plane, alone by the window. This trip is a disaster. She rubs the washcloth hard across her face and turns off the shower. Time to go. This is a business trip. She pulls her clothes from the hangers and folds them into her suitcase, rolling the jumpsuit from the night before into a ball. She puts on cotton leggings, takes them off, tries a skirt, changes to another. When she gets to the lobby, she sees Keith and Pam and Jed standing in a circle.

Keith dashes across the floor toward her. "We're going to change your mind."

"No, you're not."

"You're turning down two days in paradise? You'll enjoy Luke, too."

"Who's Luke?"

"A major player in our business. His dad has the biggest music business in Florida and Luke is putting together a project with Big Blast Video and Time Warner."

Pam comes from behind and puts her hand on Molly's shoulder. "You have to come."

"No, I don't. It wasn't in the plan."

"I've already changed the plane tickets. We'll fly back from Sarasota Monday night."

"I can't do that, Keith."

"Molly, listen! If you insist, I can get you back on the plane today. Think about it over breakfast."

Molly eats a bowl of fresh oranges and grapefruit covered with yogurt. She doesn't look at Jed or Keith. She feels like a bratty child. There is no reason not to stay. This is work. She can call Porter and Grace. The conversation bounces from Keith to Jed to Pam: Big Blast Video, Luke Fleming, the merger of Time Warner with a major television network. Her blood begins to stir. She notices the intensity in Jed's face, the excitement on Keith's. She tunes in.

Hot muffins in a basket go from hand to hand. Molly takes one. Talk is of the island, the Gulf of Mexico, the sailboat Luke owns. She smooths her hair and looks at Keith. "You're right, Keith. This is my kind of trip."

"I knew you would change your mind," Keith says.

"I'll make some phone calls." She downs her coffee and grabs her pocketbook.

Keith drives the rented car. Molly is in the back with Pam, who is asleep. The same message lies in wait for Grace and Porter: delayed on business, be back Monday night. She slumps into the seat and fixes her eyes on Jed's head, on the hair that grazes his collar. She can taste him, the kiss on the dance floor. It was another world. He was Jacques and she was a woman in a dream, in love. It was a movie, a DisneyWorld romance. She listens to Jed and Keith exchange sailing stories. This is a new side of Jed, the macho man on the spinnaker, racing sloops to Block Island, Bermuda. She smiles and drifts into a dream.

"Backseat wake up. Fasten your seat belts. We are about to land in Gasparilla."

"I can't believe I fell asleep." Molly shakes her head. Pamela groans and stretches out her arms. The water out the window is green. On all sides, going on forever. Sand and flimsy pines, and pelicans, and poles with osprey and sea green, like glass green, like emerald green, like the inside of a lime, like the outside of a Granny Smith. Molly smells the green, like salt spray and hot sand and lying around with no place to go.

"There is treasure on this island, in a cove, underneath the sand. There are secrets on this island if you listen."

"Only when the moon is full, I bet," Molly says. "Have you been here before?"

"Never. But I'm glad we came," Keith says.

"Me too. This place is beautiful. I have the feeling one of us might discover something special," Pamela says.

Jed looks at Molly. "Are you glad you didn't take that plane?"

"I don't know. I have mixed feelings."

Keith drives the car beneath a gigantic tree and stops. The tree trunks are long and gray like elephant legs.

Molly opens the car door and stretches out, crunching her feet on the crushed shells in the driveway. A hot wind teases her legs. The house beyond the driveway appears like a painted giant screen. It hides, tucked beneath arching trees. Its skin is pink coral stone with arches and a wooden balcony and openings filled with delicate iron gates. Bunches of purple jasmine, red bougainvillea, and yellow hibiscus crowd the driveway.

Molly's toes wiggle, anxious to be free of shoes. "Blue, the sky is so blue. I want to run barefoot on the sand."

"I want to run bare-bottomed into that green water," Keith says.

"And I want to float in the water like a balloon and be weightless and stare at the sky," Pamela says.

Molly sees a man, tall, wearing white shorts. She waves and he waves back.

"Yo Keith and Keith's wife and friends. Welcome to paradise. Dad's up in Tampa. He wishes he were here. Come inside. We've got cold drinks, a warm pool, lots of food in the fridge. Tonight we'll do the local scene and eat at The Temptation."

"Let's do it, Luke," Keith says.

Luke leads the way through the jungle of blooming bushes to the house. Molly picks her way from tile to tile inset in the broken shells. Huge gray branches span out above her like the limbs of a gentle giant. She glances up through the tangle, expecting a face, a smile, a welcome but finds only clear hot blue sky. Inside, the house feels intimate, warm and rosy and pink like the inside of a giant coral shell, round and curved with rooms flowing into rooms, and tile floors like an indoor roofed pavilion with painted ivy climbing up the walls and white-eyed flowers and wooden beams that look like old ship's planking marching across the ceiling.

Molly and Pamela glide from room to room. Hiding in a niche is a stairway, going partway up, then disappearing around a corner. Molly imagines the rooms above and blushes. She's in a barn; the stairs lead to the loft.

The men are in the kitchen, sprawled around a large table with an open bag of pretzels and dripping bottles of beer in cardboard six-packs. Molly sits by Jed. "I'm underneath the sea, in a magic castle," she says.

"You like it?" Luke hands her a short brown bottle of beer. "This is a place where no one does anything they don't want to do. You'll find a long white beach out front, beds upstairs, a pool in the courtyard. Tomorrow we'll take the boat out."

Molly follows Pamela up the winding stairs to a long passageway with a series of weathered wood doors.

"Choose a door," Pamela says. She squeezes Molly's arm. "Pick a room and sleep with Jed."

"Are you the tempting fairy godmother?"

"I tempt only where I see desire."

"I've been repressing that . . . or trying to at least."

"Go native. Forget being stuffy."

Molly opens the first door, a king-size bed, a chaise, a large master bedroom. They move down the hallway: a utility room, a room with a queen-size bed, a room with twin beds, one unmade. "Looks like tonight's the night." Pamela laughs.

"Spare me, gentle godmother." Molly leans against a doorway, caved in by the tremor in her chest. "I shouldn't have come here."

"Consider it fate."

They rejoin the men in the kitchen. The talk is all of Big Blast and Time Warner. Molly nibbles pretzels. Later, all five walk the beach and wade into the water and splash and kick and use their hands like buckets until everyone is soaked and dripping and Keith and Luke and Jed drop their shorts and shirts and swim like dolphins and Molly makes a mermaid out of sand. Pamela floats on her back in the pool.

When dusk comes they sit under the large thatched roof on the terrace looking at the still water turning into ink and the pasted globe dropping to the sea screaming softly with purple, red, orange, and hot pink slashes across the sky and they sip dark rum mixed with pulpy orange juice and sift hot sand between their tired fingers and become hushed by the big sky and big sea and the cove of the house nestled into the giant trees.

Later, in the restaurant, Molly sits squashed between Jed and Luke. Her face and arms are hot from the sun and the rum and the touch of Jed's bare thigh on hers. Luke tells stories about the frumpy murals on the wall, the fisherman, the old buildings and phosphate dock and oceangoing ship. Jed makes up a tale about the woman in the Scout uniform standing on the railroad platform. They share fried oysters and fried grouper and Jed feeds Molly long fried potatoes and the bottle of beer becomes theirs, not hers or his.

After dinner, they move to the bar, and press against the fishermen and the fishing guides and the local residents and drink port and Molly feels Jed's arm around her waist and she moves so that his arm goes all the way around and his breath is on her cheek. She melts. She becomes a piece of sand scooped by a crab. Walking home at 1:00 A.M. they sing, lock arms, weave around the spreading banyan trees, and zigzag through the carless streets.

They turn into the courtyard of the house and split apart. Molly seeks the breaking waves, the moonlit water. She continues on, passing by the pool, the covered terrace, stumbles on the stretching roots of trees, and finds the sand. Her toes dig in. The sand is hot. Blue light falls inside the shadows, like theater for the fish. Her mermaid lies unguarded, untouched. She lies beside her, lines her legs up with her tail, and stretches out. The sky is full of tiny lit windows.

A body lies beside her, legs in line and fingers by her own. She lies between the two, mermaid on one side, Jed on the other. She listens to his breathing and the lapping water. Her head feels heavy. She moves her hand to fall inside his. A ripple like the waves flies up her arm. A ripple like the waves moves up her legs. Be still. She breathes. She watches the moon swallowed by a cloud. She feels the darkness cover them, the theater lighting dim. Sleep falls like a safety net.

At dawn, with pink reflections in the sky, she wakes. She's lying on her side. Jed is on his back. She feels the heat coming from his body. She lifts her back and sits cross-legged, looks out to sea. The terns scurry in the early morning surf. Jed sleeps. She tiptoes to the water's edge and follows yellow-beaked birds down the beach. Farther down she drops her clothes and swims and floats. The water's like a sauna. The gentle waves like playmates. She loses time and thoughts and watches pink sky turn to blue and pink sun turn to yellow. She covers her wet body with her skirt and shirt and wanders back. Jed is gone. The mermaid is alone. The night had been a dream.

Luke makes eggs and Pam stirs the pancake batter. Molly enters like a creature from the sea. Heads turn, smile, and return to breakfast making, paper reading. She drifts upstairs and to a shower and lies down on a bed. At noon, Pam shakes her and asks if she would like to go out sailing.

Luke starts the engine, takes the wheel, Jed handles lines, Keith fends off. Pam has stayed at home floating in the pool. Molly watches people on the dock and sees a man running toward the boat with waving arms. He shouts, "Luke, phone call. The caller says it's urgent." Luke swings the boat around and lays it back against the dock. Jed secures the lines. Luke comes back to say he cannot sail. "You guys go out."

Keith turns to Jed. "You guys go out. I'll go with Luke."

Luke tosses Jed the lines. "Motor through the pass. Then unfurl a sail or two and have a blast.

You'll find life jackets underneath the starboard seats."

Molly stands stunned. She watches Jed take the wheel. He glows with confidence, daring, a pirate man with bronzed skin and wind-tossed hair. She is his mate. They are alone, leaving harbor on a sailboat.

The pass is filled with boats. "Stand in the companionway," Jed commands. "You can steady yourself against the current." Molly obeys; the captain has spoken. Warmth and safety flood her. She glances at the sea, the boats, at Jed. She stands sideways. A glimpse across her shoulder and she sees him at the wheel. She thinks about this morning, sitting by him, wanting just to touch. Lying in the water she had wanted more. The power of it scared her. She dared not go on land, back to him. She fantasized his body, his mouth. She fantasized his body locked with hers, shoved inside and rolling on the sand. The water was her balm although it didn't prevent the tears. She wondered if she cried for him or something she has lost or something she can never have. A new sadness catches in her throat, sadness for a wasted life. She should be glad that Porter wants to marry her. She isn't. She knows the emptiness she feels will not be filled by him. She knows she yearns for something that she cannot have. Time has been her enemy.

Jed turns the boat and heads out to the empty sea. Molly finds the sunscreen tube and takes a seat near Jed. She lathers lotion on her arms and legs and face.

"Can you do that to me?" Jed asks. "I've got the wheel."

Molly reaches for his knees. They seem the safest place to start. The cream is white and smooth; it comes out of the tube and sits like worms along his skin. She rubs. She runs her fingers down his leg, first one, then reaches for the other. She puts a blob of cream inside her palm. His thighs are pink; they must not burn. His skin is hard and taut. Be careful not to touch the tender skin between his legs. Be fast, be clinical, be like a nurse or doctor. She does his arms, the forearms first. His triceps bulge, contract. She rubs them once, then twice. The rubbing makes her legs feel weak. She stretches out her toes.

"Put some on the back of my neck."

Molly slips behind him. The warm smell from his body mingles with the smell of coconut. Her fingers massage and put cream behind his ears, along the bone that goes into his scalp, along the tendons going to his jawbone. Her fingers dig in skin and slip and slide. Her body eases close, merging as it did last night, lost in touching. The boat is all alone at sea. They are all alone. She's in a barn, touching, feeling, smelling, tasting, sensing heat flowing through her blood, watching changes in the one she touches. Her fingers glow with passion. They cannot stop their rubbing. Fire in her belly has a hold on her, a welcome friend returned.

She squeezes cream across her palms. The horizon sits before them, the sea wide all around them, the boat slides far away from land. Both hands take his neck, run across his shoulders, flow down his back. She rubs her skin on his and feels him swallow, feels him pull his neck up from his shoulders. The sun is warm and so is she.

He turns his head around. His face is close to hers. He starts to speak and stops. She sees him blush. She holds her hands, palms up for him to see. The boat flounders, rocks. He steps out from the wheel. "You steer," he says. "I'll put up the sail."

Her hands feel naked, lost. She wipes them on her shorts and takes the wheel. He's at the mast uncleating lines, wrapping them around a winch and pulling. Slowly, coming from the bow, a large white banner moves along the leeward deck and back beyond the mast. "Head up," Jed shouts, and points in a direction where black clouds lie.

Molly turns the wheel. The sail flutters. Jed yanks the halyard. "Go off. Head back where you were . . . slowly."

The rail moves down into the sea. Water flicks along the inside edge. Molly's foot braces against the seat; she grips hard on the wheel. "What's happening?"

Jed laughs and flashes her a smile. "You're sailing, that's what." He cuts the engine.

She feels the quiet and the power of the sail. The tension in her body now is in her arms. "This is amazing. I've never done this before."

"You are great. Head up until the edge of sail close by the mast starts to fold, then fall off slightly."

"You are talking Greek to me."

"We've got a nice breeze. You're a natural sailor."

"I'm going native." The wheel is alive, a force she must control like the one that grinds inside her belly, between her legs, and shoots up through her breasts. She watches Jed, then the sail, then Jed. He is like a little boy, at the mast, at the bow, scurrying down one side, then the other, hanging off a shroud, uncleating a line, recleating it, moving the boom, tightening the boom cover. He has become a boatswain, a sailor. He has left her kneading fingers.

She holds tightly to the wheel, controlling it from rounding up into the wind. She must be master of the sail which fights to have its way. She must be master of herself. Control, she thinks. Keep control.

Jed is back beside her. "I'll ease the sail. Head off. You can relax. I'll get some beer."

The boat straightens. The sail billows. Jed swings down the companionway and disappears. He returns with two beers and flops on the seat, resting against the cabin top and watching Molly. She concentrates on the horizon, the sail, the feeling in her gut and Jed.

"What do you think?" he asks.

"I think there is a storm coming for us. I think we will drown."

"Together?"

"Together."

"Good. We will live under the sea."

"What will we do there?"

"Swim"—he gulps the beer—"and make mermaids."

"How do we make mermaids?"

His tongue licks across his lower lip. He scratches his neck. "Do you like being the skipper?"

"I won't if the storm comes." Molly nods toward the one dark spot in the banks of huge white clouds.

"Sail into it. Let it crash around us."

The grin on Jed's face makes tingles in her breasts. He is having fun. She sees her nipples pushing through the thin cloth lying flat against her chest. She lifts the bottle to her mouth and lets the cold fill her throat. The dark clouds scare her.

"You don't like lightning," she says.

"Maybe this time I will."

"Why?"

"You don't know why?" He sits up. She sees his hands fall between his knees. "When did you leave?"

"I haven't left."

"Last night . . . this morning, on the sand."

"It was dawn. You were sleeping."

"Why did you leave?"

"I . . . I don't know."

"I think you do."

"Why . . . did you leave?" she says.

"Leave where?"

"Leave the wheel, leave . . . I don't know."

"To put up the sail?"

"I don't believe you."

"Why did you stay?"

"To meet Luke."

"I don't think so."

Jed swirls around and crashes back inside the boat. Molly's heart thumps. The sail thwacks the mast.

Jed is up again. Molly grasps the wheel and heads toward the storm. Jed is at the mast. He's leaping back and down inside again. He starts the motor, uncleats the halyard, and furls the sail. "The storm is getting close." He slides along the seat and takes the wheel.

Molly retreats to the companionway. She braces against the cabin top and watches the bow bounce up and down. Jed is back behind her. Tension covers the boat. She swallows. A lump is in her throat. She turns and faces Jed. "I thought we were going to sail into the storm."

"I don't think you are ready for that."

"What do you mean?"

"Only people who know the right answers can go into a storm."

Molly pulls her arms around her chest. She squeezes her eyes. Jacques is there. "You must leave and find your storm and make it happen."

She turns around, her back to him. She watches the pass approach. Her sight is blurry, her thoughts scrambled like a staticky radio. She follows one boat, then another, she hunts for leaping tarpon, she finds people on the beach, and umbrellas coming down, and children trudging with their pails. The sky is getting darker. The white lighthouse sits on legs above the sea, looking like a wise old woman. How long does wisdom take? This island has a secret, Keith said. Molly shivers. She turns back to Jed. He is the captain, stern and focused. "What did Luke call this island?" she asks.

"He calls it paradise."

"Yes. He calls it paradise."

The word resonates in her head. Paradise. This has been a paradise. She will think of it that way: Jed in the bar, Jed on the boat, Jed on the beach. She will call it paradise. She ambles from her safety spot and back to Jed. She sits beside him. "I think I know why, why Luke calls it paradise."

His eyes graze her face, then look away.

Twenty-one

Molly flips the page on the desk appointment calendar. July 1. What happened to June? Gasparilla seems eons away. She looks at the oak table piled with material: all current, all going projects, all steaming with ideas. She looks beyond to the nineteenth century buildings, her friends, each cornice, each decorated lintel etched in her memory. It's her three-dimensional wallpaper, her inspiration. This room has held meetings, think sessions, late-nighters. Ellen sat at that table for three days. Keith brought in a new client. Jed and she batted around morphing ideas. She grins. It's a great life.

She pushes up from her chair, goes through the center room, and leans against the door to Jed's office. "Got some time?"

"Fifteen minutes." He checks his watch.

She takes a seat beside his desk. "I want you to okay some stuff for Neo-Plastics before you leave for the weekend."

"I'm leaving tonight."

"Tonight? It's only Thursday."

"Little red cars hate weekend traffic."

"Connecticut?"

He raises his hand like a Boy Scout. "I promise I'll weed. I promise I'll water."

Molly laughs. "So what about this?" She flings the pages across the desk.

"I'll take it with me."

"Check Angelo's drawing before you go and look over those photographs I've chosen for the Amtrak article. I'll be here tomorrow morning. I'm leaving at one."

"Long Island? Connecticut?"

"Massachusetts. I'm going to Tanglewood."

"With your fiancé?"

"Actually, I'm meeting him there. I'm driving up alone."

"Stop by on your way. You can help me weed."

"Thanks." She stands and backs to the door. "I'll be back Tuesday. How about you?"

"Same."

Friday morning, Molly gets coffee from the deli and carries it and her suitcase into the office. She's planning to rent a car on Twentieth Street. The office feels empty, like the holiday has begun. She waves to Angelo. He leaves his drafting table and follows her to her office. "Where's Jed?" he asks.

"Didn't he tell you he's not coming in?"

"He never checked the drawings. I'm working tomorrow, maybe Sunday. What do you think?"

"I think you need his opinion."

"So?"

"Fed Ex them. Then call and give him hell. Where's Amy?"

"She's gone, too."

"Amy's not here?"

"She left last night. She and Jed . . ."

"Did they go together? Drive up together?"

"They walked down those stairs together. I'm no detective."

Molly rummages through the papers on her desk. She boots the computer, makes changes on a summary report. She goes downstairs to the deli and gets more coffee and a chocolate-covered donut. The street feels empty. Holding her brown bag, she wanders across the street and looks in the shop windows. Back in her office, she watches the clouds, munches the donut, sips the coffee.

She drifts out to the center room to Angelo and watches over his shoulder. "Have you sent the Fed Ex?"

"It's over there. They haven't come."

She chews her finger and picks up the parcel, turns it over in her hand. "Cancel Fed Ex. I'll take it. I'm going in that direction."

Molly drives along the Major Deegan Expressway. The giant trucks are backed up in the right lane, edging up the ramp to the bridge. She should get to Jed's by one. Porter expects her at six, at the inn in Lenox. He said he'd rent a car and drive from the airport in Springfield. He sounded exhausted when he called last night. He hates Los Angeles.

Molly reaches for the radio, dials until the music sounds right. Porter's an angel. Being there with Harlan. It's Grace who worries her. She canceled their last lunch date. She must be working hard. Funny how she met Porter on that plane back from California. It was good that he could talk to her. Grace is getting thin. She must call more often, insist on lunch. Hurray for Minneapolis, five days on the lake and she and Grace together.

She hums and taps her hand against the steering wheel. The music's like the night at Epcot. What a crazy night. She thought she was in Texas. The night was fantasy, a couple thing. Keith and Pam. She and Jed. Now she and Jed are business partners. That's all. Since Florida, he treats her the way he treats Keith or Ellen. She'll check the flowers in Connecticut. So what if Amy's there.

She checks the map, reading it while looking through the windshield. Two weeks and Minneapolis. The party. Annette says there will be a hundred friends. A party makes it all official. Then the wedding—a Saturday in October; they haven't set the date. Porter's getting nervous. He's doing all these things for her: California, Harlan. She'll tell him how important all that is. She appreciates him.

She slows the car. The unpaved road is up ahead. She turns and turns again into the driveway. The red car's parked beside the old garage. She parks behind it and looks around. Jed would not be standing in the driveway. She laughs and gets her purse and reaches in the back and gets the package, opens the car door, closes it without a sound, and walks around the back to the kitchen door.

Colors stop her in her tracks. Reds and pinks and yellows burst from the wooden tubs. The flagstone terrace could be the cover of a magazine. She drops her purse and package on a chair and runs and stands among the flowers. She reaches for the dead ones and plucks and goes from one tub to the other plucking, tossing wilted flowers back beneath the bushes.

"Whoa, look who's here."

She turns. His grin looks splashed across his face. She smiles and motions to the tubs. "Aren't these something?"

"What's up?"

"Checking on your watering."

"I'm waiting for the gods. Look over there." He points to the sky in the west.

She plucks a dead geranium. "Got to get rid of these."

"Seriously, why the visit? Anything wrong?"

"Nothing wrong. The office was lonely and you forgot to check Angelo's drawings. He's working this weekend. Is Amy here?"

"No. Should she be?"

"I'd like to discuss the drawings."

"Come in. I'll make us lunch. Tomato sandwich with fresh farm tomatoes?"

She pulls out a chair and leans against the ladder-back. The muted green refrigerator feels like home. She peeks into the living room. Sun streams across the floor. She watches Jed slicing the tomatoes, putting mayonnaise on the bread. She opens the package. "I've got Angelo working on morphing ideas."

"Like we talked about."

"Potatoes turning into bags. He really went with it. Like the *Nude Descending a Staircase*. Little minor changes, a cartoon in action across the page. I love it. Look."

Jed holds a knife and looks at the pictures spread across the table.

"You've got this guy hopping. These are great." He puts down the knife and wipes his hand.

"He's working all weekend, he is so turned on. You must call him."

Jed lifts one of the drawings. "This is miracle stuff. We've got to fax it right away to Bill."

"I'm glad you like it. I knew you would."

"I love it." He hands her a dish and a sandwich.

"This morphing thing is weird," Molly says. "Makes a person think about what's real and what isn't."

"You mean the potato becomes a bag and then in the garbage heap it degrades into a potato again?"

"Something like that. Everything sharing the same chemical basis. Just glued together in a different way."

"How about this tomato. What's it?"

"Lunch."

He puts a sandwich on her plate. "Now it's a gift"—he smiles—"from me to you."

She watches him across the table. He bites into the sandwich, picks up a drawing, then another one. The tomato tastes like sunshine and summer, like

Grandpa's house. She reaches in the refrigerator and pours a glass of orange juice. She drinks half and puts the other half in front of Jed. "I've got to weed before I leave."

"Don't let me stop you. I'll study these drawings."

Back in the yard, Molly pulls at the petunias and geraniums. The dark clouds close in. She goes along the path at the back of the house. The daylilies are in bud. The coreopsis is in bloom. She stoops and pulls the chickweed. A big drop hits her head. She looks up. The plops start to fall. She stands. Jed calls. She turns and waves. His arms whirl like a windmill. Lightning flashes. He calls again. She starts up the path. The rain is heavy, like Florida. Thunder rolls. She starts to run. A stone is in the way. Her toe. She is falling over. Both her knees hit hard. The pebbles dig in. Damn. Lightning streaks across the sky. The rain pours on her neck and down her front. She tries to stand. A hand pulls underneath her arms, lifting, dragging her along.

In the kitchen, they stand together, making puddles on the floor. Her shirt sticks to her skin. It hurts. Blood with rain runs down her legs.

"Upstairs," he says.

"We're wet."

"I'll get some towels. Go up the stairs."

She follows him. He turns into the bedroom with the wooden soldiers. "Sit on the bed." He pulls the shades. It feels like dusk, the room is almost dark. Her legs dangle from the bed. She shivers. She hears him in the hallway in the closet. He's back again with towels, cotton, cloths. He tosses her a T-shirt and turns his back.

"I'm wet all over."

"Wrap yourself in a towel."

She pulls the towel around her waist and sheds her shorts and underwear. She sits back on the bed. He kneels in front of her and picks the pebbles from her knees and wipes away the blood. She listens to the rain, the thunder getting more intense. Her eyes stay focused on his head, his hand that quivers, the mopping motions that he does. She jumps. "It stings," she says.

He holds her calf and dabs. "It's good for you. I'm almost—"

A crash. The house shakes.

"Good God," he says. His hand tightens on her calf. She reaches for his head and hair and swirls her fingers in the rumpled brown. The sky above the house is full of rolling rumbles.

They do not move. She feels his tenseness, his fear. The blast shakes the windows. A crack in the sky. She feels it in her chest; she grabs his hair. Another crack. The storm is on the roof. It tears the air. Bolts of lightning knock against the window. Her arms reach down, dragging at his arms, lifting him, pulling him with her to the bed. She lies with him. She holds him close and stops his shaking.

His clothes are wet. She works his T-shirt up his chest, above his head. He wraps the blanket from the bed around his waist and pulls away the dripping clothes. They lie, his head against her arm. They listen. The storm is moving east. She shivers. He pulls the blanket up around his shoulders, opens it and pulls her in against his naked body. She feels his mouth brushing on her temple. Her hand sits on his chest, feels the crinkles of his hair. The storm moves on. The rain plays softly on the window-panes.

Beneath her hand she feels the thumping in his chest. It calls to her like a time bomb she can't escape. The thumping is inside her chest as well. She moves her hand and puts it on his thigh. His skin feels good, his bareness, the hardness of his thigh, his matted hair. She wants to keep exploring. His lips are on her hair, her ear, behind her ear and on her neck.

She's a puppy reunited with its mother. She licks his arm and tastes the salt. She licks his chest. The towel around her waist is in the way; she pulls it off and tosses it. She's naked just like him. She wraps her legs around his legs and lifts her chin. She wants her food. She licks his lips, his teeth and tongue. This mouth is hers. It tastes like hers and feels like hers. She wants to climb inside. His fingers tremble on her cheek. She puts them in her mouth and rubs them on her body. She feels insane, her nervous system screaming, crying, jumping in her body like a starving baby at her mother's breast. She feels his kisses on her ears, her nose, her eye-lids, eyebrows, lashes. She seeks his eyes. They're inches from her own. They are part of her. She is melting, morphing. "I'm you," she says. "I know," he says. "I'm you." She probes his mouth. Their tongues get mixed up with each other. She doesn't know whose mouth it is, whose tongue it is, whose hand. Her hands are everywhere. She cannot stop their touching. The chains have broken. Her hands are free to touch, let loose from months of yearning. She gasps and stops.

"Wait," she says.

"For what?" he asks.

"I don't know."

"For reality?"

"Yes, reality."

"I think it's in the bed with us."

She wants to see his body, every pore, every part. She wants to have him look at her. She sits and lifts her arms above her head, watches his glance move from her face to her breasts, to her navel. She is making him a gift—this is yours. She watches his body stretch across the mattress, an animal letting down his guard, giving her permission to use him as a toy. She gazes at his chest, the tightness of his belly, his stiffness, pinkness, his throbbing plaything.

She touches it. He watches as she touches. Her palm slides across the stiffness. She wants to taste. She wants to know and savor all the parts of him she hasn't known. His hand is on her back, her buttocks. Rub your hands on me, the hands that drive the car, that rub along your sock. She sits and faces him. Looking in his eyes makes tears in hers.

His hand reaches for her thigh and holds it like it's something that belongs to him. "It's you. My thigh is you," she says. His hand moves along her silky inner flesh. She watches. His fingers lace among her private hair, and slip deep into her hidden parts. She looks up for his eyes. A grin is on his face. Her eyes close, her mind turns inward to the folds that feel his fingers, the moistness. This is reality. She reaches for him. "Jed," she cries.

"You are Jed," he whispers.

"You are love," she says.

She takes his hand and licks the back and lays her body all along the top of his. Her skin has found its home. She doesn't want to move. She waits. The moment holds a tremor, a gasp, a wonder. She breathes it in. Her face is at his face. Her eyes close and open and gaze on his and merge with his. Her heart merges into his.

Their bodies slip together. The blanket covers them. Covers their moans, their cries, their tears, their rocking ritual of love.

Twenty-two

Molly drives north on Route 7; Cornwall, Salisbury slip by like painted scenery in a movie. She feels fastened to the car, propelled on its own, disjoining her from Jed.

Her nerves are at the edges of her skin, all of them: her arms and legs and chest, especially her chest. They hurt. They tug and stretch like rubber bands attached from her to Jed. Each mile is torture. The car keeps going. She keeps her focus through the windshield, on the bumper of the car in front of her. Jed. She feels his mouth, his hands. She sees his body, all of it. His body still is there, inside hers. They merged like fuel and oxygen and blasted off to Jupiter. She was a goddess, enveloped in light, raised upon a platform with her mate. They soared. She existed in a way she never had before.

Ahead she spies a sign, two rows of pumps, a tiny store. She drives behind a pickup truck, finds the gas tank on the rented car, and pumps the gas. Inside, she pays and wanders among the pretzels and potato chips. It's five-thirty. Porter said be there by six. Impossible. She sees a public phone. She reads the words on cookie boxes, digs in her pocket for some change and for the piece of paper with the number. She dials. She must hear Jed's voice. Tell him all the things she wishes she'd said. Perhaps, go back. Just turn the car around. Go back. That's what she'll do. Call Porter and say she cannot come, she can't explain but she will later.

The phone feels sticky in her hand. She dials; her heart is hammering. She waits; she hears the rings. Jed. Her pulse is bursting in her veins. There is a click, an answer. She wishes she could sit or lean against a wall.

"Hello."

A woman's voice. Who is this woman's voice? She checks the number on the paper in her hand.

"Hello, hello."

It's Amy. She holds the phone and stares at all the tiny holes; a flat tone answers back. Her arm is rigid. She holds the phone. Her fingers all go slack, the phone bangs on the wall. She reaches for it. Grabs it. Slams it back in place. She limps across the room. The cookie boxes look like grinning spiders. She springs across the pavement for the car. The key is causing trouble; she cannot find the lock. She smells the gas. She hooks the belt and snaps it on her chest. Damn. Damn. She knew it all along.

The traffic's heavy going north. Her fingers grasp the wheel, hold tight, a life ring in her hands. Her stomach is entangled, full of tiny squirming snakes. She licks the salty water that lands drip, drip around her mouth. Her eyes keep looking at the car ahead. She sees the road, the red round mass of Amy's hair. Jed. His body wet beside her in the shower licking off the water on her cheeks. Laughing as the soap skids from his hands and lands across the room. She laughs and cries. She drives. The road is like a tunnel sucking her away from where she wants to be.

She passes Stockbridge, next is Lenox. The inn sign sits discreetly on the left. She parks and takes her bag. She's numb. The inn is large and sprawling with porches on all sides and beds of flowers, yellows, pinks, and purples, snapdragons, cosmos, mounds of ageratum. She climbs the stairs and goes inside the door.

"Are you Ms. Mitchell?" The woman is behind a counter.

"Yes."

"We've been worried. Mr. Drummond is waiting in the bar."

Molly follows the pointing finger. Porter springs to his feet, hurries up to her. "Where have you been?" He looks down at his wrist. "It's after seven."

"Yes, traffic. I don't know. Have you waited long?"

"Of course, I said six. Why didn't you call?" He takes her arm and leads her to the table. "Luckily I could postpone dinner."

"I'm sorry, Porter, I truly am." Tears hover.

"Wine?" He asks.

She sees a frown between his eyes. "Please." She smooths her skirt and looks around the small dark room. "I'm glad I'm here." The words sound strange but oddly true. "How was California, your trip back?"

"California was tedious. We must talk about it.

Harlan is causing a lot of problems. If he weren't married to Grace, I would have him fired."

"But you just made him partner."

"Doesn't matter. He could easily be disbarred for what he's done. I think I've taken care of it. I can't believe I've done that. Look, Molly, it's for your sake I'm doing this. I hope you understand."

"Yes," she says. A lump presses between her ribs. "What has he done?"

"I'd rather not say and it's best if you don't know. It's why I went to L.A. I had to stop him before the firm found out. I think I have."

"Does Grace know?"

"Of course not and she shouldn't—even you shouldn't know." He lifts the short squat glass and puts it to his lips. "Molly, you look different, maybe tired. Was the drive all right?"

"I need to change. What time is dinner?"

"Can you be ready in twenty minutes?"

"I'll try."

She takes the key. The woman leads her to the room. It's large. Molly sees the bed, the white lace canopy. The woman pulls the drapes across the floor-to-ceiling windows. Molly watches, notices the greens and burgundies, the same print on the cover on the bed.

"We'll be back later to do the bed. Is that all right?"

"Thank you. That's fine." The woman leaves and Molly feels a rage inside her body. She's not sure what it is. She wants to scream, to pound the bed. She hates herself. Why did she go to Jed's? Jed.

Her throat erupts and sobbing sounds emerge. She goes into the bathroom and turns the water on. She soaks a cloth and holds it to her face. A fool. Always the fool. Amy. She knew that Amy would be there. Damn. She sits against the tub and rubs her hands along the cold white porcelain. Tonight is special. Don't spoil it for Porter. Forget this afternoon. Put it in a secret place. It was a secret time. A one-time-only time. It was okay. Now it's Porter time.

She dries her face and gets the kit with creams and eye shadows. It's automatic. She does her eyes and runs the brush hard through her hair. Jed had dried it with the towel after they showered. She'd done the same for him. He'd kissed her neck. She dried his back. She kissed his back. Don't think. Don't remember. Think of Porter. He's waiting in the other room. He's special, very special. Tonight is special—don't spoil it.

She pulls on white silk pants, a skinny top with tiny straps. She puts on pearls. She glides back down the hallway, back to Porter waiting in the front room of the inn. He stands and smiles and puts his lips on hers. "You're beautiful."

The dining room is small. The floors are polished wood. The tables all have candles, stiff white linen and pink roses. Pewter service plates sit on the table set for two; on hers, a small black velvet box. "What's this?"

"Open it."

She knows it is a ring. She sits and takes the box and hesitates. This is the final ritual—the ring. She feels him watching and she feels her palms react.

The box is soft and fuzzy. She pushes with her thumb and gasps. The pear-shaped diamond glows, and emeralds, green and vibrant, sit on either side.

He reaches for the box and frees the ring. Between his fingers she sees it poised and fragile. He reaches for her hand, which she extends across the table. "The other hand," he says. She feels the ring slip on her finger, bump into its place. She feels his hand on hers and hears the champagne cork. The maître d' is smiling. The couple at a nearby table smile and lift their wine. "Congratulations."

"Thank you," Porter says and lifts his glass. "To love and happiness." She smiles, nods, and looks down at her hand. Her stomach churns; the snakes are back again.

"Do you like it?" Porter asks.

"It's beautiful," she swallows. A lump is in her throat. She glances up. The candlelight makes mystery of the room. His face is all she sees, the clean line of his nose, his eyes worried, waiting her approval. His glass, a flute of golden sparkles, hovers in his hand. She raises hers and smiles. "To love and happiness."

Their glasses touch and then she drinks. The sparkles make her sneeze. She laughs. "I feel like a child."

"A happy child, I hope?"

She smiles but does not answer. She touches the ring, traces the outline of the stones. "It is beautiful, very beautiful."

"The emeralds were my grandmother's. My

mother wanted you to have them. She likes you very much."

Molly eats but doesn't taste and pushes food across the surface of the plate. She shakes her head against dessert. "I'm tired." He pulls her chair back from the table. She feels his hand against her back and rubs her thumb against the gems, the stones that make her different from the person that she was before she came into the dining room.

The bed and canopy is all she sees, a mattress, pillows, silken covers. Deep in her soul she aches and yearns. She hides inside the bathroom and with the shower running water at full force, she masks the sobs she can't control. She tries to scrub away the smell of Jed, the feel. She cannot look above the sink, into the mirror. She pulls on the robe the inn provides, the terry cloth, deep-piled and white. Tomorrow will be better. The secret she will bury like a dream, a detour in her life.

The room and Porter suit each other. The wing chair holds his body tall and straight. *Country Life* sits on his knee. The lamp beside the chair gives off a glow. It's like his co-op, like an English manor house: the tall wood chest on chest, the shiny pulls, the small round candle table. Molly smiles. Her body now is scrubbed; she wants to sleep. The bed, stripped of its cover, is piled high with boxes. "What are these?" she says.

"Things I bought in California." He stands and comes around the room to where she is. He lifts her face and kisses it. "I need to kiss my fiancée. I wish we'd marry soon."

His lips are chaste and gentle, almost ticklish in their touch. She pulls away. "Let me see the presents. Which one shall I open?"

"Whichever one you want." She takes a box, lifts the cover, and smooths away the tissue paper. Her fingers touch the gown, the lace. She pulls it up. It's white and delicate and long and sheer. "A nightdress. Did you pick it out yourself?"

"With help."

"It's lovely. Shall I put it on?"

"I'd like that."

Molly goes into the dressing room. The cotton gown feels clean and pure. Small, pearl buttons start at the round deep neckline. She walks back in the room, her naked body barely covered by a scrim. She wants a robe. She doesn't want her body bare. Keep walking. Stand tall. This is a present. Smile. Let Porter see the gown, the present he has bought his bride-to-be. She goes across the room, stands before the chair. He pulls her to his lap. She feels warm on her breast. His lips. His tongue. She squirms. She doesn't want to kiss. Her eyes close. Her nipple hurts.

She pulls away and stands.

"What's the matter?"

"It's the food, the drive—something. My stomach is a mess. I'm sorry."

"Should you take something?"

"I just need sleep. Do you mind?"

"We have all weekend. I'm sorry you're not feeling well."

She climbs into the turned-down bed. Two boxes

sit unopened. They rock and one falls on the floor. She watches Porter pick it up and set it on the chair. He sits beside her, puts his palm against her forehead. "You do feel hot."

"I'll be all right tomorrow." She rolls onto her side and rubs the ring against her thumb. Pictures jump into her head. Jed. Amy. Her heart pounds. Porter's body is in the bed. He touches her. She doesn't move. He rolls away. She looks out at the moon. Her fists clench. She touches the buttons on her gown. The sex was a surprise. A jillion jolts of pleasure. A merging, a mighty merging. She morphed with Jed. He morphed with her. It is a secret. She has a secret. They have a secret.

Molly opens her eyes. The room is dark. The drapes let in no light. Porter is not there. An ache runs up her body. Jed. It never happened. Erase the memory. She pushes back the covers and gets the boxes on the chair, dumping what's inside onto the bed. Another gown. Antique lace with rosebuds, tiny, pink and mossy green, with a matching peignoir with satin streamers. She holds it up before the mirror and puts her arms inside the sleeves. She'll pretend that she's living in another time. Porter is a lord. This is their house, her bedroom. She'll dress for him. He'll visit. She must be nice; she cannot tell him no again.

She notices a green garment on the bed and picks it up. It's skimpy and lacy, one piece. Porter bought this too. Impossible. She pulls it up her legs underneath her gown. It is a sexy thing. She drops the gown and puts the tiny straps up on her shoulders. The satin part sits flatly on her stomach. She's like a courtesan. She's waiting for her lord—he comes three times a week. This is the day. She prances by the mirror. Brushes her teeth. Brushes her hair. A courtesan is always willing; she knows how to pretend.

She hears a click. The door opens. A waiter walks into the room. She dives beneath the covers. Porter follows. She sees the tray, the coffeepot, the juice, the buns. She watches Porter. He is the lord. It's nice to start with food.

"How do you feel? Awake?"

"I like the presents that you sent."

"You mean I brought. You opened them?"

"I did." She slinks from the bed and pours the coffee. She feels his eyes on her. Her legs feel long and white and bare. Be nice.

"The saleswoman suggested it."

"I thought you'd picked it out yourself." She turns and faces him.

"I picked the color."

"Why green?" She plays the part. Her eyelids close and open slowly. He's taking off his coat.

"I like green."

He approaches. He trembles. His arms are large and strong and all around her. He is the lord, the baron, the knight. She is the lady. He kisses. He paws. She unbuttons his shirt. She unbuttons and unzips his khaki trousers. He lifts her onto the bed. The green garment is off and thrown across the sheets. There's no surprise. He is the lord; she is the courtesan.

The inn is perfect for her play. They walk through avenues of tall and stately trees, rose gardens, red and white and pink. They sit on wooden benches. Play croquet. He talks of houses, trips, a son he hopes to have. She's walked into a novel and it's good. A happy story. Her secret will be safe. She'll work. She loves her work. She'll have a baby and a nanny and Porter will adore her.

They walk among the crowds strewn on the lawn at Tanglewood, the music tent, the Boston Symphony. They sit close to the stage on wooden chairs inside a box inside the patron section. The Wagner music makes her cry. She is Isolde. Porter is King Marke and Tristan . . . where is he? What does he think? Does he ache too? The thunderstorm was like a magic potion. That's all it was.

They drink tea in a glassed-in room. They talk of Grace and Harlan. Porter is the one to keep her sister safe. He is the lord. Her heart stirs. It's nice to be with him. His head sits proudly on his body. His mother said he used to laugh a lot. He will again. She reaches for his hand. "Let's set the date," he says. "We'll call and tell my parents."

Monday is a hot and sticky day. The chorus fills the space behind the orchestra. The concert is all-American: Charles Ives, folk singers from the sixties, the records Grandpa liked to play. She feels twenty-one, long-haired, and ready to reform the world. She stretches up her neck to see the people on the stage. The music starts. Shivers rise inside her veins. Never compromise, Grandpa told her. Smile your wide smile and be yourself. She twists the ring, looks at Porter. "It's hot," she says.

"Let's leave." Porter takes her hand and guides her down the aisle. The people clap and stand and sing along. They all are doing it: the ones inside the tent, those standing on the grass. It's Arlo Guthrie and "This Land Is Your Land." Men hold children on their shoulders. Their bodies bounce. It's Woodstock. The men have beards. They clap. The tune climbs up a half step on the scale. The heads rise up, the voices and the volume. They clap, they stamp, they sing. Porter keeps moving through the crowds, from the tent, from the music.

Twenty-three

Porter's hands hold the top of the wheel. His head is an inch from the roof of the car. Molly smiles to herself: he looks like an oversize teddy bear stuffed in a doll carriage. Four hours to New York City.

"Anytime you want, I'll drive," Molly says.

"No problem. You should have rented a bigger car."

"It's what they had." Molly can still hear the stomping, clapping crowds at Tanglewood; the song pulses in her head, the words running like a tape recorder. "I loved that concert," she says.

"It belonged in Central Park, not Tanglewood."

Molly's finger taps her arm. Grandpa sang those songs. He had cassettes and played them in the kitchen. He'd sing. They sang together. He loved Pete Seeger, Woody. She has those tapes. Porter's right: today was like a concert in the park, not serious, not Wagner, not like the inn in which they stayed. All weekend, she played the lady for Lord Drummond. Tomorrow she'll be back at work. Friday is a secret. It's tucked away. Jed will never mention it.

"Two weeks and we go to Minneapolis," Porter

says, flooring the accelerator and passing a rickety truck. "Four days at the lake and then the party. Mom sounded happy about October. She can now tell her friends, make plans. She likes the idea of a church. What do you think?"

"A church would be pretty. As long as we keep it simple. I don't want to walk down an aisle with you waiting at the end. You know what I mean?"

"Not really, but it's up to you. There's St. Paul's on lower Broadway. It's a beautiful simple colonial church."

"I'd like that." Molly rubs the ring. She lays her head back against the seat. She hopes Jed talked to Angelo about the pictures. She'd like them done. She wants him on the Amtrak job.

"Tired?" Porter asks.

"Thinking about work."

"You work too hard. It's not necessary. Cut back."

"That's not always possible. Besides, I like it. I'm finally doing what I love. We're getting into new technology. It's exciting stuff."

"You've only been there a month. How do you know?"

"We've got new clients. We're dreaming up new advertising schemes. Amtrak's an example, and morphing—"

"You can forget Amtrak. They have no money."

"That's not true, Amtrak's doing great. You sound like you hate my working."

"No. Only if a child comes, I'd like you home. Children do better with a mother, don't you think? Money's not the issue."

"I guess. I never pictured myself as a mother. A good nanny might be better. Anyway, raising a child involves everyone, the whole family: mother, father, aunts, uncles, teachers, grandparents, doormen, everybody."

"Someone has to make sure the jobs are done. That's the mother."

"Like a cop?"

"Like a manager. Kids need consistency." Porter reaches for Molly's knee and pats it. "It's a very creative job. You'll be great at it."

Molly looks into the windows of the cars on the highway. They move in a stream, like robots, the people, robot people facing frontward. Porter is so logical. She wishes she could think that way. It makes her stomach hurt. She can't argue. She lifts her hand and glances at the ring. Emeralds are her favorite.

She reaches for the radio and turns to the news. The Mets are winning; tomorrow will be hot; twenty minutes and the news repeats. Porter reaches for the knob and turns it off. "Look, Molly, you'll be able to hire anyone to help with a child and the house. I really need you to entertain, to organize."

"I'm not good at organizing."

"It's running the ship. I can probably get you on the board of a museum. I have connections at the Whitney. You can go back to painting and decorating our home . . ."

"I like the job I'm doing now. It excites me, I wake up energized." She pulls at the seat belt. "I wish I could wait for marriage and children."

"You know you can't." He laughs. "It's time to grow up."

"Grow up?"

"Stop letting whims rule your life."

Molly swallows. Whims? Friday? Was that a whim? She pushes hair behind her ear. "Maybe you're right."

"Growing up is hard."

"I really hate giving up this job. It's like a dream come true."

"Maybe it's a choice."

"What do you mean?"

"Marriage or the job?"

"That's not fair. Would you make that choice?"

"I don't have to."

"That's what's unfair."

"Molly, is this job that important to you?"

"I think it is. It makes me feel alive. It's challenging. I feel in the middle of a giant revolution."

"Is it something you want to do for the next twenty years?"

"That's a hard question but right now, yes."

"Then make a commitment. Ask for half the business. Get this Jed, is that his name? to make you a full partner."

"How can I do that?"

"Simple. Tell him that with the time and effort and talent you're providing, you'd like to be a partner. Don't be an employee. My wife shouldn't be an employee. I'll put money into it, if that's what's needed. I'll even do the papers."

Molly looks at Porter. He's right. She and Jed

should be partners. It makes sense. It even feels good in her gut. Will Jed agree? "It can be Saunders and Mitchell."

"I like Drummond and Saunders."

"Mitchell and Saunders."

Porter laughs. "Is your name so important? If we have a child, we all need to have the same name. Besides, it's my money going into the business. Grace uses Harlan's name."

"And they're not even having children."

"Give them time. They will."

"No, they won't. Harlan took care of it."

"What do you mean?"

"A vasectomy."

"I find that hard to believe. Grace would be a perfect mother."

"I know."

Porter stretches. He reminds Molly of a large snake trying to move inside a small box. He reaches for a knob on the dashboard and turns to public radio, the evening news.

Butterflies descend in Molly's stomach. Partnership with Jed? They can build the agency together. It will be wonderful. Friday will stay a secret, like a dream. In ten years she'll buy him lunch, champagne on the anniversary. Will he remember then? They'll laugh. They'll joke about the thunderstorm, the pebbles in her knees. She holds her breath. The butterflies are dancing. It was his hand, the way he touched her. His skin against her own. The merging, the soaring. It was like becoming someone else for an instant.

Porter pulls into the spot in front of the apartment reserved for taxis and carries Molly's suitcase to the lobby. He kisses her lips lightly and leaves. She follows him back out. "Porter," she calls. He stops and turns around. She runs and takes his hand. "Thanks for a wonderful time. I love you."

Molly calls Grace. "How was your weekend?"

"Long Island's crazy. Lots of parties. Lots of booze."

"How's Harlan?"

"He had a great time. You know, everybody dancing with everybody else. It's the scene."

Molly sits on the floor by the phone. "Can we have dinner next week? Is Harlan working?"

"I'll let you know. When is Minneapolis?"

"Two weeks. We'll finally get to spend some time together."

"Harlan may not come—only for the party. He'll be in California. He wants to move out there."

"California? You can't. I need you here. I can't have babies without you."

"I know."

"Is he serious?"

"I'm afraid so. He's had an offer. It's lots of money. He says he can't refuse."

"How about you?"

"He says I'll find a job."

"No." Molly stands. "No, no, no. He can't do this to us. We have to stay together."

Molly hangs up and paces around the room. She

dumps the clothes from her bag. Damn. What's Harlan doing? What's the job? She'll talk to Porter. He'll know, or does he? She better keep it to herself. In her closet she sees a skirt she did not throw away—the one she always wore with Jacques. She pulls it on. The cloth against her finger is a memory. She whirls before the mirror. Her hair's too short. She feels the passion that she had back then, feels a rumbling through her veins. She felt it Friday. With Jed, the sex was passioned by their dreams, the world they have created in their heads. It was acknowledgment that she is more than just herself with him and he with her. Can they work together now and keep that passion hidden? She cannot let it go. Yet, Jed was there with Amy. She must keep her feelings to herself and put her passion in her work.

On Tuesday morning, Molly gets up early and goes to work at seven-thirty. She wants her day in full swing when Jed comes in.

At eight-thirty she hears a knock. Amy walks into the room and leans against the windowsill. "I thought I heard some noise in here. You're early?"

"Getting ready for a short, busy week."

"Anything you need? How was Tanglewood? You and your boyfriend have a blast?"

"It was nice." Molly writes on a yellow pad.

"I went sailing with my dad."

"Overnight?"

"No. I wanted Jed to go but he didn't."

"Oh?"

"I was there Friday night."

"Friday night? At Jed's?" Molly's face feels hot.

"We saw this great Italian movie. It was a laugh. I stayed the night. Jed's amazing."

"I have work to do. Get me a second coffee if you go to the deli."

"Okay. It's just I've never known a man like Jed. It was all night. Honestly."

"What are you talking about?"

"You know." Amy twists her fingers in her hair.

"I don't want to know. Let me work."

Amy leaves. Molly reaches for a pencil. Her fingers do not move. They feel disconnected from her body. The pencil slips away. She stares at the buses. She stands, she sits, she stands again. She throws the pencil. Her mouth is dry.

She flies through the door, slams it, and tears down the stairs. On the street she bumps into a man. He curses. She stops and looks around. She walks south. Midway in the block, she turns and walks back toward the deli, hesitates before the door, and walks around the corner. Her pace is brisk. Her arms swing. It's hot. She feels moisture on her face.

She turns at Broadway and walks south. The sycamores at Union Square look comforting. She buys coffee, takes two napkins, and sits beside a woman on a bench. She wipes her face. There's work to do. Amy couldn't have known. Jed's a playboy. A bright, creative playboy. Why be upset? It was a lark—nothing more. She walks along the park. She stops and looks at Gandhi, small and peaceful in a grove, a statue in a small oasis. The noise, the traffic, Fourteenth Street and Gandhi.

Hollow out a place, like this. Keep the memory. It was four hours in a life, a special time. Keep it special—an oasis—a carved-out moment.

She walks to Fifth, back to the office. She smiles at Amy, who hands her pink slips. The day has begun—the phone rings. Her mind gets back to work: Ellen, Robert Greenberg, Miffy, Keith, Amtrak. The work takes over: energy, ideas, connections.

At five, she hears a knock. Jed. Her body jumps. He grins and pulls his fingers through his hair. "May I come in?"

"Of course."

She makes her body tall and sucks in her breath. She notices the looseness of his frame, the casual way he sits against the table, and she blinks and sees him spread across the bed, naked. "I have a long list," she says, speaking slowly. "I've made a bunch of appointments. I'm leaving in two weeks and want to make sure some things are under way before I go. I may work part of the weekend . . ."

"Wait a minute. One thing at a time. How late can you stay tonight?"

"What do you need?"

"I have a list myself. Can you stay?"

"Of course."

"Amtrak. Let's talk about Amtrak."

She pulls her chair to the table. He gets his files and the layouts. They discuss the project, switch to Neo-Plastics, switch to Keith. The world outside is dark. Lights, like cutouts, sit on the buildings down

Fifth Avenue—patches of light, here and there. The reds and whites of taxis leave paths along the street.

"It's nine-thirty. Shall we quit?" Jed says.

"I guess we better."

He gathers papers on the table. She opens the file drawer.

"Something new on your finger?"

"Yes."

"Congratulations. What's the date?"

"October, I guess." She goes to the door and waits to switch the light.

He brushes past her. Their arms touch. She feels electricity.

He stops, turns, his brow knits. "This was good work tonight. Thanks for staying. It helps to have your feedback. It's a good time of day, don't you think?"

"No phones? No interruptions?"

"Exactly. Need a ride?"

"A taxi will do. Thanks anyway." They go down the stairs. He opens the door to the taxi. She watches him amble down the street.

By Friday Molly has a stack of projects. She needs to talk to Jed. He's free and she is busy. She's free and he is out. At five she finds him at his desk.

"Amy says you're leaving at six-fifteen. Can I have the time until then?"

"Be my guest. Are you happy with Amy? Is she doing things okay?"

"Amy? Sure." A knot plops in her stomach. "She's fine, well organized but giggles too much."

"I know." He laughs. "What's up?"

"I met with Greenberg and discussed morphing again. I still find it creepy."

"How so?"

"The way it blurs reality."

"Sometimes that's nice," Jed says.

"Not in everyday events." She sees his smile. She's on the bed. She swallows and takes a breath. "We used it with Neo-Plastics. I'm wondering about Amtrak."

"Do you feel you're turning into someone else?"

She bites her pencil. "Sometimes."

"Is it good?"

"I'm not sure. Growing up is turning into someone else. Don't you think?"

"No. I don't. Growing up is getting to be more you. It's not abandoning the child."

"Back to Greenberg."

Molly keeps her eyes on her watch. She wants to finish before Jed leaves. At 6:10, she gathers the papers. "I'm working tomorrow. Will you be here?"

"Can't."

"Thanks for this time. It helps. I'll work with Angelo tomorrow." She gets up and starts toward the door. Amy is there waiting.

"Good night, Molly," Amy says.

"Good night." Molly walks through the center room. She turns and sees Jed turn off his light, take Amy's arm. It's like a hammer in her chest. She sits at her desk, her feet on the top. She watches the man in the apartment across the street. She calls Porter. He has work to do. She calls Grace. They're leaving for Long Island. She walks, she rides a taxi, she cries. Amy with Jed. Connecticut? Did they go to Connecticut?

Twenty-four

Today is Sunday. Molly lies on the blue leather couch in Porter's living room. The air conditioner hums. The newspaper falls on the floor and her mind drifts. She is back at her desk, on the phone to Ellen planning the launching of Neo-Plastics' bags. Her legs are tight from this morning's jog and she stretches her toes to touch the armrest at the end of the couch. She worked yesterday with Angelo. She likes the way he listens, bounces his head, runs his pencil around on the paper and then comes up with a dynamite drawing all his own.

"I'm signing the papers on Ten Gracie Square next week." Porter looks up from his paper.

Molly props her head on her hand. "Next week?" Hints of cheese omelet come into her throat. "I thought—"

"I found a way to close before the final settlement of the estate. This way we can start painting, decorating, buying furniture. We can be moved in by spring."

Molly bends her knee to her chest, then to the ceiling. "It's a big job."

"It is. You're going to have to make some time.

I wish you would quit your job or take a leave of absence."

"I can't. There's too many new projects that depend on me."

Porter folds the paper. "People always feel that way but it isn't true. No one is indispensable."

"Then someone else can decorate. You can do some of it."

"You know that's not possible. The law is a constant. Not much spare time. I thought you'd love decorating, with your artistic ability."

Molly sits up, putting her feet on the floor. "The timing's wrong, that's all."

"Quit your job. Married to me, you don't need to work."

"You keep telling me that but I do need to work. Besides, a professional decorator can do a better job."

Porter leaves his chair and sits on the couch beside Molly. "What if you were pregnant? Would you quit your job?"

"I don't know."

"We need to start. Time goes fast." His hand is on her shoulder, his finger twirling a strand of hair.

Molly scratches her forearm. "I understand that."

Porter's fingers wander from her lock of hair to the curve of her breast. The chimes of the wooden clock on the mantel color the silence. She nestles against the side of his body.

"How about now?" he says.

"Now for what?" She looks up into his face.

His hand reaches under her T-shirt. "Let's make

love with no protection. I want to make you pregnant."

Her nipple delights to the finger that worms its way under her jogging bra. She stays quiet. Her eyes stare at the dainty coffee cup on the table; her focus is on the glowing in her breasts and the sensations on her neck from his lips behind her ear, along the edge of her hair. She shivers. The coffee cup becomes the window at Ten Gracie Square with the bridge, and the river, and the struggling sailboat. She stays still when he pulls off her shirt and unfastens her bra and her breasts feel the cool, then warm from his tongue.

Her eyelids close, she lies limp, letting his hands pull off her shorts and bikini underwear. The slick leather of the couch is cold on her buttocks and the back of her legs. She is cold underneath and warm on the top with his body over hers, his waffled T-shirt on her chest and the zipper of his shorts at her knees. Her mental window holds Jed's face, his begging brown eyes, the crinkled intense look he has when he's thinking.

"No, Porter, no," the words rush from her.

"What's wrong?"

"Let's not. Not yet." She grabs her clothes from the floor and goes to the bedroom. She finds what she wants in the drawer beside the bed and breaks the package seal.

When she turns, she sees Porter, in his shorts, taking up the bedroom doorway. "You've ruined it," he says.

"No I haven't." She pulls back the covers and sits on the edge of the bed.

"You broke the mood. Get dressed."

Molly reaches for her clothes, tosses the bra across the bed, and pulls the shirt over her head. She untwists the lavender underpants from her jogging shorts and puts them on. Porter emerges from the bathroom.

"You are being unfair," she says. "Would you like me to go home?"

"Why would you do that? We can go back to reading the paper. I'll make more coffee. There is no point talking about it."

"Maybe I would like to continue. I just don't want to get pregnant right now."

"You seem to have a problem."

"My problem is that we are not married."

"If you get pregnant, I'll marry you. Right away."

"Are you trying out the cow before the marriage."

"That's crude, Molly."

Porter turns his back, walks through the living room and to the kitchen. He runs water in the celery-colored sink.

Molly stomps after him. The light cloth of her T-shirt annoys her sensitive nipples. Damn, she thinks. Her body doesn't know enough to quit. She watches Porter scoop and measure coffee with a plastic spoon; her mind stays magnetized on the places that ache beneath her shirt and pants. She bites the edges of her nail. "Damn it, Porter."

"Did I hear you right?" He turns and looks at her.

"You can't do that to a person."

"You were the one who pulled away."

He takes two cups from the cabinet. "Would you like coffee?"

"I suppose. Why did *I* ruin everything?"

"You should figure that out." He pours the coffee and passes her a cup.

She holds it in her hands and lets the aroma drift into her nostrils. The yearnings and aches have ebbed. Disappointment floods throughout her chest. She curls her hair behind her ear. "I've got some work to finish. Guess I'll go home."

"Think about the co-op. I'd like to make a budget for each room."

"You want me to inquire about a decorator? Grace knows all about those things."

"Yes. Ask Grace."

"She and Harlan went to Long Island for the weekend. I think Harlan has found a party scene."

"They'll be back tomorrow, won't they?"

"Of course. They were there last weekend, too. I worry about Grace. Do you see much of Harlan?"

"I've been keeping tabs on him. Harlan is very ambitious. That can sometimes trip a man up."

"What do you mean?"

"Ambition can get in the way of clear thinking."

"And you're watching that it doesn't in Harlan's case?" Molly lays the warm cup against her cheek.

"I'm watching. Let's leave it at that."

"You're nice, Porter. You are nice to my sister. Thanks."

"It's my pleasure. You know Grace and I had a long talk on the plane from California. Life isn't easy with Harlan."

"She told you that?"

"People tend to tell lawyers things they don't tell anyone else. We're like ministers sometimes."

"Grace likes you. She feels comfortable with you."

"I like her, too."

All week Molly tries to track down Jed. He seems to have perfected the art of disappearing. She must talk about partnership. Porter planted the seed and she is starting to choke on it. By late Friday afternoon, she is desperate and barricades the door to his office with her body. "You may not leave this office until I talk to you."

"Come in Molly. Client trouble?"

"No client. It's me. I need to talk to you."

"What's up?"

Molly drags a chair from the couch to the desk. "Are you leaving at six-fifteen today?"

"Don't worry about me."

"Have you been to Connecticut?"

"No. I'm going to Long Island tomorrow morning. What's the problem?"

Molly feels jealousy creep up her arms. She pictures Jed with Candace. Her fingers grip the wooden back of the chair. "I don't have a problem," Molly says. "I want to talk about a partnership."

"Partnership?"

"Between you and me."

He lifts his leg and puts it on the desk, stretches out his arms and cracks his knuckles.

"I want to talk about a business partnership. I don't want to be just another employee. I want part of this. I bring in business. I make decisions. I'm the visual part of the agency. I can put in money." She sits down. "What do you think?"

"How much money?"

"Equal to what you put in."

"Do you know how much that is?"

"No, but I can match it."

"The new husband, a generous fellow, huh?"

"It's only fair."

Jed stands and thumps his fist against the desk. "Fair? My favorite word."

"You agree?"

"I agree that you are a major part of this business. I agree that your ideas are original, creative, wonderful sometimes and . . ." He points his finger in her direction and swallows, "You put in a lot of time. I agree that we make a great team and with more good people coming aboard, we can become a major agency. I agree with all of that, but partnership between you and me . . ." He swings around and puts his hand behind his head. "Not now. This isn't the time. No. Not now. Do you understand? The answer is no."

"Why?" She uncrosses and crosses her legs.

"Why?" She feels her face flush and tears well in her eyes. "What's your reason?"

"Those are the reasons."

"What if I quit?"

"Quit, if you want. You always do what you want. I like that about you. Do what you want."

Molly stands and walks to the windows. Her heart is pumping fast. She closes her eyes and breathes deeply. "Could we talk about it again in six months?"

"We could."

"Do you have a problem with me?"

"No. Your work, as I said, is excellent."

She leans against the windowsill. She feels the string, the one that runs from her to him. She wants to reel it in. "The money could make a difference. There are things—"

"No, Molly. I don't want your husband's money."

"My money?"

"Any money. Look, it doesn't feel comfortable to me right now. That's all I can say."

"Comfortable? My God, Jed. What do I have to do?"

"Wait." He picks up a pencil.

"Until you feel more comfortable?"

"Perhaps."

She walks back to his desk, leans on it with both her hands. "I want a commitment."

"Make or get?"

"What do you mean?"

"Do you want to make a commitment or get one from me?"

Molly turns in a circle and then stands, feet apart. "I want to be committed."

"To what?"

"To . . . to this. To this office." The loudness of her voice surprises her.

"You know what I want?" His whisper has gravel in it.

"What?"

"I want you to make a commitment to yourself . . . to Molly Mitchell."

"That's what I'm saying." She scratches the side of her head. "What's the difference?"

"When you find out, we'll talk. I have to leave."

Jed stands and walks by her. He stops and runs the back of his hand along her cheek. At the door, he swings around. "Molly, it's like morphing. You can move the digits yourself or let others do it for you."

She watches him go out the door and follows his back through the middle room. She waits for him to turn and wave. He doesn't. She pushes the chair across the wooden floor, goes to the window, and stares into the apartment across the way. Morphing? Turning into someone else or something else through technical digitizing. Does Porter digitize her? Grace? Do they rub away her face? Jed doesn't. The room across the way becomes Connecticut, the living room of Lucy's house. The stairs are up against the wall, long stairs, dark stairs, leading to a place she doesn't want to think about.

She goes back to her office, a room awash in golden light. She drinks in the warm rays shooting through the windows. Next week is Minneapolis. Her hands go to her face. She feels the morphing taking place. Feels the way her face will be, her body, even her mind when she is Mrs. Porter Drummond. Where will Molly go? She hears the door and turns.

Amy stands, her hand grasping the knob. "Are you leaving Sunday?"

"Sunday morning. I'll be in tomorrow and leave you notes. How's life with you?"

"Great." She giggles. "Set your wedding date yet?"

"October. Sometime in the middle."

"You inviting lots of people?"

"Only family."

"Too bad. I wanted to come."

"Too bad."

"I want to tell you something. Do you have time? Can I come in?"

Molly drops in a chair next to the table and motions to the other one. "Sure. Sit down."

"It's about what I said about Jed. About that night I was there. You'll forget I told you, won't you?"

"I already have."

"It was an accident. I mean it was just that one time."

"You don't have to explain."

"Have you ever had sex with someone because you felt sorry for them?"

"I don't think so." Molly feels her face burn.

"It has to do with vulnerability, something like that. Some women get into it. It may have been why

I seduced . . . I initiated . . . I don't know. Jed was definitely upset."

"Upset?"

"I dropped by his house. He wasn't home. Then he came back looking awful. Like he lost his best friend. I suggested the movies. Afterward I tried to talk to him, make him laugh."

Molly straightens the edge of a pile of papers. "He wasn't in the mood for laughing, but he was for—"

"Nothing. I thought he needed a woman's body. My roommate says women often do it." She giggles.

"Do what?" Molly stares at the orange light sweeping the windows across the street.

"Give themselves to men they feel sorry for."

"Did you do that?"

"Yes. I've always had a crush on him but this was something different. He plainly needed loving. I mean he was bad. He just grabbed ahold of me."

Molly reaches for a pencil and bounces the eraser part on the table. "You're nice, Amy. It's hard being a woman."

"I know. My roommate put a sign on the refrigerator, 'Rock the Boat.' "

"What does that mean?"

"You know, women tend to go along, do what others want, never rock the boat. My roommate says, rock it." Amy giggles. "She says, 'Rock that boat, Amy, those who really matter will hang on.' Like you, Molly."

"Like me?"

"Like when you told Jed to get me out of your

office. I liked that. You didn't care if I liked you for it. You knew what you needed and asked for it."

"Yes, I did."

"I'm practicing to be like you."

"Thanks." Molly pulls a paper from the stack and starts to doodle. Amy stands, exclaims about the sunset and leaves.

After a few minutes, Molly leaves, too. The street feels warm, empty, like the world has left. She walks south down Fifth Avenue, smelling the bus exhaust, hearing the groaning of the yellow monsters stopping and starting. She stops and rifles through the books on the tables in front of Barnes and Noble. *Don't let anybody move the digits. Don't let yourself be morphed.*

She turns off Fifth and goes east to Broadway and picks her way along the square slate sidewalk. She turns at Eighteenth Street. The Old Town Bar is filled with people and colored light, red and pale yellow and the smell of beer and cooking burgers. She squeezes up to the bar, between the crowd, and orders Anchor Steam and french fries. She sees herself in the mirror on the wall between the rows of bottles. She is thirteen and climbing in the tractor. She's twenty and walking proudly and naked to Jacques's arms. She's twenty-one and in New York at Hopper. Her chin goes up, the bottle to her lips. Cold, harsh beer pours down her throat. She looks right and left at groups of drinkers in twos and threes and fours, laughing, talking, making a mosaic of collective din. This is her town, her place. She is woman. She is Molly.

Twenty-five

The highway in Minneapolis looks like every other highway in the country. Molly glances at Porter, then at Grace in the backseat. This morning they were in New York. It is still morning and they are in Minnesota. Porter looks serious, his eyes straight ahead on the road, his hands gripping the wheel of the rented Subaru. Molly thinks about the plane ride, the talk she had with Grace, unlike any other talk they ever had. She feels good, scared but good. Porter sat behind them with his briefcase open and a yellow pad and pencil. How puzzled he looked when he came by their seat before they landed and saw their faces smudged with tears.

"We're almost there," Porter says. "I spent every summer at this lake when I was a kid."

Molly sees the lake between the houses, the houses flanked with pots of pink and red geraniums. Porter toots the horn as they turn into the driveway, and, before they stop, Richard and Annette are on the lawn, waving, smiling, hugging each other. They all hug and kiss and go inside and Molly smells the pine and woodsmoke and closes her eyes: she is back with Grandpa.

"Just in time for lunch," Annette says. She holds Grace's hand and leads her to the screened-in porch. Molly sits by Grace and faces the lake. The sun is bright, and yellow and white sparkles dance on the water and the mast of a small boat bobs by the dock. She can see a green canoe and a float on the water, with young bare-skinned boys diving from a diving board. "It's good to be here," she says.

"We want you to relax," Annette responds. "It's a good place for that. A good place to get to know each other."

Molly takes the plate of sliced tomatoes Richard hands her. They are thick and red and smell like summer. She notices the zinnias stuffed in a tiny pot sitting in the middle of the table: exact and geometric, the purples, oranges and pink. She bites a piece of bread; it's thick and doughy. She fills her plate with ham and chicken salad, cheese and grapes, and sighs. She is a million miles from New York.

Grace tells about Grandpa's house. Molly drinks the herbed ice tea and wonders how their world will change when she begins to rock the boat. The idea makes her stomach churn, but not from fear. It's like the feeling just before she turned the key in Grandpa's tractor, anticipating the power that let her move the big machine across the field.

"Anyone for a swim?" Richard asks. "A canoe ride. What do you say?"

"The water looks wonderful. I'd love to have a swim," Grace says.

"Me, too." Porter rises from the bench and stacks the dishes on a tray.

"Would anybody mind if I take a little lie-down, as Grandpa called it?" Molly asks.

"Everybody does what they want. That's the rule at the lake." Annette folds her napkin and smiles at Porter.

In the bedroom, Molly props her head against the wicker headboard. The pillow and geometric-patterned cover smell of burning wood—a summer smell, a vacation smell. She yawns. it's nice to be alone and think and plan and get unwound from all the talking on the plane.

She can see the lake outside the window. Grace is on the float with Porter. Molly cranes her neck and notices that Grace is sitting just the way she always sat when she was small, her arms around her bent-up knees. Porter's lying on his back, his hands behind his head. His body's large compared to Grace, who looks so tiny. He looks relaxed and happy, like a boy. She's never seen him look like that before.

Molly takes the pillows on the bed and plumps them up behind her head. She sighs. She looks out the window, and wonders if her stomach will ever stop the churning. On the plane she told Grace how she felt.

"I have hated your apartment. I have lived there hating it for too many years."

"It's not my apartment."

"It looks like you, feels like you."

"Why? It sounds like you hate me."

"I don't want to live like you—in an apartment with your imprint."

"Do you hate the way I live?"

"It's not my style. It's fine for you—perfect for you."

"Why are you telling me this?"

"I think you want me to live like you—to be like you."

"Well . . . what's wrong with that?"

"What's wrong with that is that I'm not you. I'm me."

"So? Is that so different?"

"Somewhat different."

"Is Ten Gracie Square your style?"

"I'm not sure."

"It's the best co-op in all of New York."

"I know, but I don't want to live in the best co-op."

"You are being rebellious again and I hate it when you act like this."

"Exactly. Because I am not being you."

"What are you talking about?"

"You and I get along fine when I'm your twin. Otherwise, you put up this wall and I feel left out."

"You feel left out? Think of all the times I have felt left out. When you get into your art mood—when you go off and don't include me and have secrets—I'm left out. You can be very mean."

"Do I always have to do what you want to get your approval—your affection?"

"Of course not."

"I don't believe you. I want to be Molly and still have a sister who is my best friend."

"But I am your best friend."

"My best friend would let me be me and still be my friend. For the last three or four years I have been . . . I don't know . . . tailoring my life to you. I want so much for us to be close that I do what I think you want me to do."

"You do?"

"I go where you want, live where you want, wear what you want, sleep with who you want . . ."

Molly straightens the pillows. She remembers the look on Grace's face: embarrassment, thoughtfulness, a little-girl shame. She remembers hugging her, protecting her from her own words. She remembers her response:

"You do do what I say."

"I do . . . and you like it. If I don't, will you still like me?"

"I can try, Molly. I can try. I'd like to try."

"Will you like me if I don't marry Porter?"

"What? You can't do that. You can't do that. The party is this week."

"What did you just say?"

"But you can't. This is different. For God's sakes, he is sitting behind us. He will be devastated. I will be devastated. I—"

"I will be devastated if I do."

"You will?"

"Believe me. I will."

"Let me understand. You don't want to marry Porter and you want me to cheer you on."

"I know you are disappointed. I am too. He's not

my man. It would be unfair to him. In a way, I'm trying to be you again."

"Yes. Yes. I think I see."

Molly looks out on the lake. Grace's eyes had filled with tears. She had squeezed Molly's hand and laid her head on her shoulder. They had sat quietly for a long time and then Grace kissed her cheek and whispered, "I love you, Mollykins. You will be happy and we will always be best friends."

Molly sees Grace dive into the water. She acts like a little girl, her sister from her childhood. Porter swims after her. They play like dolphins, flipping and splashing and showing off.

Grace had kept her hand in hers, even as the plane was landing. "I'm confused," Molly said. "I've been afraid to tell you . . . ashamed to tell you. I need your help."

Porter has the towel and he's rubbing Grace's back and hair and she is laughing and chasing him and running with the towel and they are fighting for it, pulling at each end, and she falls down and he is lifting her and carrying her across the lawn. Molly closes her eyes.

Grace comes in the bedroom and peels off the wet and dripping suit. She takes a towel and puts it on the bed and then lies naked on it, on the double bed beside where Molly lies. "The water was heaven. I love this place. You should have come swimming."

"I watched you. It was almost more fun."

"I can't believe you're breaking your engagement. I'd marry Porter in a second."

"Why don't you?"

"When are you going to do it?"

"Do what?"

"Tell him. Time is getting short. Are you going to sleep with him tonight?"

Someone knocks. Molly throws a towel over Grace.

Porter stands in the doorway. "Molly, I thought you were alone. I came to see if you're all right?"

"I'm fine," Molly says. "Grace and I thought we'd sleep here tonight. Is that okay?"

"It's good. I'll stay in the loft." Porter leaves.

"Does that answer your question? Can we manage in this bed together?"

"It will be like Grandpa's." She touches Molly's arm and tears brim in her eyes. "I'm so emotional. I haven't felt this way in years."

"I love you, Grace. You're part of me." Molly smells the water from the lake on Grace's skin. It smells of leaves and flowers. She rubs her fingers along her skin, on her arm. "It's like being children again, before the boys and all those things."

"Before the competition."

"Are you jealous of me now?" Grace props her head on her hand, her elbow on the bed.

"For what?"

"I don't know. I'm afraid you might be."

"Should I be?"

"There's something you could hate me for."

"Try me"

"Today."

"Porter?" Molly puts her hand on Grace's back.

"Maybe."

"Tell me, Grace."

Grace lifts her head. "I'm in love."

"I know."

"I've never felt this way before. I'm scared. I don't know what to do."

"If I don't marry Porter—"

"When he dried my hair, I had sensations I've never had with anyone. I had this feeling with him the first time I met him when he came to my apartment. That's why I thought of you. Never for me. I never thought that way. On the raft today, he was lying there and I had this terrible desire to touch him and . . . I had to dive in the water. Have you ever felt that way?"

"Yes, but not with Porter."

"I didn't want you sleeping with him tonight. What am I going to do?"

"You may have to start rocking the boat."

"Rocking the boat?"

"There's this very wise woman in my office and she said . . ."

In the morning, Molly pulls on shorts and climbs the ladder to the loft. Time to tell Porter. Time to rock the boat. She sits cross-legged on the floor beside the cot. "We need to talk."

"What's wrong?" He props his head on his hand.

"Maybe we should walk or . . ."

"Is it Grace?"

"No, it's me. I've been thinking about us."

"Let's take the canoe." He pulls back the covers and grabs the khaki pants from the chair. She watches the sun hitting the wall from the skylight in the peaked roof. He takes a baseball cap and puts it on his uncombed hair. It doesn't look like Porter.

The morning brume rises from the water. Molly breathes the moist air, the newness of freshly bathed plants and grass. Porter paddles. With each stroke, the houses, the green lawns, the docks fade farther in the distance. They move into a scrim of mist. She feels unbound from Grace, Annette, and even Porter, who pulls the paddle through the water with a steady, even motion. Porter. This is a hard thing to do. She gazes at him, a strong, quiet man. "He could fall apart," Annette said. She cannot marry him to save him; she will fall apart. Porter stops and pulls the paddle in the boat. They drift. They are inside a cloud.

"Say what you need to say, Molly."

His face is stony. She breathes, closes her eyes. "I cannot be your wife."

A splash in the water—a leaping fish. Her head jerks to find it. She watches the water; she cannot look at him, she feels his pain.

The boat moves. There are ripples and little waves. She feels the paddle pulling strongly through the water. She turns and looks: his body sits straight, his eyes look across the water.

"I wanted very much to be your wife. I wanted to be the wife you want. I'm not. I know I'm not. That person isn't me." Tears well like pools in her eyes, staying there, not running down her cheeks but making a prism of the world.

Molly feels the boat bump and scrape. She turns around. They have landed on an island. Porter is rolling up his pants and stepping in the water. The water looks like ink. Porter pulls the bow and reaches for her hand. She kicks off her shoes and steps into the water, up to her calves, beside him. His hand is strong and keeps her steady. His arms move around her, holding her. She lays her head against his shoulder and wraps her arms around his back. The mist is there, the rocking boat, the flitting birds. Her tears are on his shirt.

"I hate this," she says. "I hate hurting you."

They move like two sandcrabs and inch from the water to the beach. His hand stays on her back, smoothing her hair, kneading her shoulder blade. The sand has pebbles and hurts her feet. She turns again and wraps her arms around him. His cheek is on her cheek. She feels wetness. She looks into his eyes. The gray is pale and does not smile. She puts her lips on his and kisses. She means to comfort—a wave of passion rises in her chest. His arms tighten; his tongue is in her mouth. The flush from her chest races down her body. Her sadness is now lust. He has it, too. She feels it in his hands, his mouth, the hardness that presses against her belly.

His hand goes under her shirt. Her hand is on his fly, reaching for him, pulling him through the zipper opening. She's on the ground, the sand and grass and pebbles on her back; he's pulling at her shorts. She aches to feel him, to connect. The aches turn into ripples of release, pleasure running through her legs. He falls against her. She holds him against her chest. She wants to whisper words of love, of comfort. She wants to stay connected with him, let the final parting be slow and careful and sweet.

She hears the birds, the lapping water. The boat bangs against a rock. Her body feels like ointment soothing him.

He squirms, pulls away, and stands. "Get dressed," he says.

His body had been warm; the air is cool, the ground is hard. She wants to run into the water and be warm and feel protected. She finds her shorts and pulls them on. She'd love a glass of water.

"Let's go," he says.

"Let's stay and talk."

"I think you've said it all."

She follows him. He holds the line and waits for her to get into the boat. He pushes off. She sits and stares ahead. The mist is gone. the houses all are back along the lake.

"I'm sorry, Molly."

His words stab her heart. The ripples on the water look like tiny eels.

"I don't know what else to say," he continues. "I don't understand you but you know what you want. I think we could have a good life together." The paddle clunks against the fiberglass. "We must tell my folks right away."

Annette stands at the dock. "The lovebirds out canoeing. Did he take you to his special island? Where he and Anne played endlessly as children."

Annette wraps the painter around a cleat. "I made cornbread muffins with blueberries—your favorite, Portie."

Molly races for the bedroom, peels away her sandy shorts, and rummages through the clothes inside her suitcase. She hears Richard's voice through the door. "Porter, your office called. They said it's very urgent."

Molly quickly takes a shower and joins Grace and Porter's parents on the porch for breakfast. Porter stands in the doorway. "I have to go to New York right away. Molly, please call the airline while I get dressed."

"What's wrong?" Molly asks.

"I'm taking the rental car."

"When will you be back?" Annette asks.

"I don't know."

"Shall I come with you?" Molly says.

"You and Grace stay. You have things to arrange here."

Molly calls the airline and goes into the room where Porter dresses. "Is it bad?"

"You'll tell my folks right away."

"Don't worry. What's going on?"

"It's Harlan. He didn't do what I said. Damn him. Some of the partners think I'm part of it. It could be bad. I could be disbarred."

"You? Disbarred?"

"He stole money. I covered for him. He promised to put it back. Obviously, he didn't."

"Harlan—stole money?"

"He could go to jail. I could, too. Damn it. I only did this because of you and Grace."

"Should I tell Grace?" Molly leans against the bed.

"If you want to. She's got to face it sometime."

"Grace is in love with you."

"What?" He puts quarters from the dresser in his pocket. "What did you say?"

"Grace is in love with you. She told me."

He swings out to the porch, stuffs a muffin in his mouth, and swallows coffee. "Mother, Dad, take care of these girls while I'm gone." He kisses Annette on the forehead. Molly and Grace follow him through the living room, to the front door.

He kisses both on the cheek. "You two have fun."

Molly whispers to Grace. "Go with him to the car."

Molly stays by the door and waits. Porter and Grace stand and talk. He bends and holds her face in both his hands and kisses her. She reaches around his neck.

Molly goes back to the porch. She pours coffee and breaks a muffin into pieces, which she eats with her fingers.

"He'll be back before the weekend, I hope," Annette says.

"I hope. It's not good. Harlan's caused some problems."

"Grace's husband?"

"I don't understand it." She looks out at the water. Thinks about the island and telling Porter's parents.

Grace storms onto the porch and to the glider. "I hate Harlan."

"Grace, things will be all right," Annette says.

"I hope he burns in Hell," Grace says.

"Have some coffee." Annette collects the dishes and puts them on a tray.

Molly follows her into the kitchen. "Show me your garden, Annette. I'd like to talk in private."

They push through the screen door and go out onto the grass and into the air which is on the edge of being hot. The sun is alone in a blue sky with no clouds. Molly's bare feet make footprints on the lawn. Annette points out bushes she has planted, flower beds, a new apple tree. Molly thinks about her promise: never to hurt her son.

"Would you like to sit?" Annette uses a paper towel to wipe the dew from the wooden bench. She brushes off a leaf and picks off a caterpillar. They sit. "I know there's something on your mind." Annette says. "Have things changed between you and Porter?"

Molly stretches out her arms. "We're not getting married."

"I've sensed it." Annette gets up and pinches off a dead daylily. "I'm sorry . . . are you all right?"

"I'm fine. I promised you this wouldn't happen." She turns and puts her arm across the back of the bench. "I don't know what to say."

"Some things happen for the best. Don't you agree?"

"I guess. I feel so bad. I just decided I couldn't . . ."

Annette sits on the bench. "It's Grace, isn't it?"

"Grace?" Molly says.

"I shouldn't have said that."

"No, Grace didn't break it up. I did. I only told Porter this morning."

"This is terrible. He had to leave."

"He'll be all right. I know."

"What will you do?"

"What I'm doing now. I love my job. I want to paint again. I'm not what Porter needs. I wish I were sometimes."

"I do too. You know yourself. You sound very wise."

"I hope I am."

"I don't like seeing my son in love with a married woman."

Molly turns to the daylily bed and snaps off a dead flower. "Love just happens, don't you think?"

"Oh, Molly." Annette pats her knee. "I like you."

"I like you, too. I wanted you to be my mother-in-law."

"Let's pretend I am."

Molly and Grace spend the week swimming and canoeing and lying on the chaises on the dock. They talk about their childhood. They shop with Annette and crowd inside the kitchen, cooking trout and corn and stuffed baked potatoes. At night the four play Scrabble on the porch with popcorn and crickets and fireflies outside the screens. On Friday, when the moon is almost full, when Richard and Annette have gone to bed, Grace talks about her marriage. She and Molly lie on the bed in the dark. They can hear the water lapping at the dock. Molly lies looking at the ceiling and listening. Grace rambles and cries and swears.

"I don't like divorce. It's like defeat."

"It's like admitting you made a mistake," Molly says.

"Harlan seemed perfect. He had everything I wanted."

"Except . . . ?"

"Passion. That's what you want me to say."

"You said it yourself, you feel different with Porter than you ever felt with Harlan."

"I feel connected to Porter in a special way . . ."

"That's why you were pushing me to marry him."

"Why wouldn't you want what I want?"

Molly laughs. "It would be boring. We would hate each other."

Grace giggles. "And we would fight over Porter."

Molly looks at the moon. The curtain and the breeze play at the window. Porter is like family. He's coming back tomorrow. Today there was a meeting at the firm; he called and said it went okay. The partners rallied for him. Next week Harlan will be indicted. Molly thinks about her mother and how she felt Harlan couldn't be trusted. It's good her mother never knew that she was right.

Molly wakes to Grace's tugging hand. "Let's go canoeing."

"Let's stay in bed."

"What time is the plane?"

"Late morning."

Molly rolls over, sleeps, and wakes mid morning to the smell of baking pies. She finds Annette and Grace with coffee at the kitchen table. "What's happening?"

"Grace decided to bake."

"Doesn't sound like you, Grace."

"Of course it does. I'm practicing for motherhood. Those boys I'm going to have are going to need home-baked pies. Annette is giving me a lesson."

"It's too bad we can't announce the engagement at the party on Sunday," Annette says, laughing.

"Might be a little weird before the divorce and before Porter knows he is going to marry Grace," Molly says.

"How shall we tell him?" Grace asks.

"If I were you," Annette says, "I'd suggest a canoe ride . . . maybe to the island that he loves."

"What do you think Molly?"

"The moon is full tonight. I think you should go out into the middle of the lake and drift."

Twenty-six

Molly is in a taxi on the Triboro Bridge. The traffic's like a school of stagnant fish. She rubs her thumb across her palm. Let's move—let's get going—the plane trip took too long. She resets the oblong watch on her wrist. It's afternoon; they left Minneapolis-St. Paul at eight this morning.

She sat alone next to the window and flew beside the plane in and out of clouds. She's free. She felt it in the tunnel, going through the airport. Grace and Porter walked behind. It was a surge—a burst of joy—one moment. It was a spotlight from within. Existence of herself apart from all the others, highlighted in the crowd like a single yellow mark across a page of black.

She opens her filofax to the orange page that has the list: move downtown, tell no one. She holds an ad from *New York Magazine:* "Must sublet my SoHo loft 6 mos/longer—Call Coco." The stagnant fish begin to move. She grabs the strap above the window. The taxi jerks and backs around and takes the exit off the bridge. Harlan really blew it. What a jerk. Grace will be the perfect wife for Porter. Wait until she sees Ten Gracie Square.

The city streets look good. The taxi turns; the large white building standing on the corner is like a giant welcome mat. She hauls her bag and pays the driver, dashes for the elevator. Inside her apartment, she lifts the phone and dials the numbers she has memorized. Coco answers. A man is interested—come quickly—bring a check.

No time to change her clothes. She's back inside a taxi, watching as the streets go by, the city whirls. the pulse is in her veins, people, buildings, buzzing in the buildings. The taxi crosses Houston Street, the mood changes to stillness. SoHo has a bleakness, strong and full of quiet energy. The taxi leaves her off. She stands before a metal-fronted building, once a factory. She finds the buzzer and presses. It buzzes back. The lobby's painted pink and red, the elevator, big enough to hold an elephant. She presses number six.

The loft takes up the whole sixth floor. It stretches out forever, the windows overlooking tops of roofs. Coco shakes her hand and leads her to an L-shaped couch.

"I'm going to Budapest. Doing a film, darling. I prefer a woman to stay here. What do you think? The man, he was a creep. If you take it, I leave right away. Maybe tomorrow, no Thursday. I leave everything with you. I can trust you, yes?"

Molly watches Coco's blue-green eyes peer through her white-blond fringe.

"You need nothing. I'll call you from time to time. Who knows when I'll be back. Come visit me. Budapest is Paris."

Coco leads a tour. Everything is perfect: a wall of brick, a wall of kitchen, a skylight, a bathroom big enough for dances with a tub on legs and a shower full of shower heads, a drafting table and an easel and a large brass bed with silks drifting from the ceiling encircling it. Molly writes a check.

She leaves and walks around the streets of SoHo. She goes up and down and back and forth. She hugs her arms around herself. This is home. She crosses Houston. She isn't far from Saunders and Associates. She could go there, to Jed's office and display her empty finger. Her plan is not to tell him until she moves, gets settled. Breaking up with Porter wasn't done for Jed. She did it for herself. She'll wait; she'll know the moment. She ducks down in the subway. She'll move and have him over. The bed was big, the silken drapes were sexy. She swallows. Her life is just beginning.

At eight-thirty, Tuesday morning, Molly is back in her office. A vase of long-stemmed flowers sits in the middle of the oak table with a card like a tent on the table in front of it: Best Wishes on Your Engagement. Names are sprawled in different-colored ink—Jed's is in the corner at the bottom, in black, a stick figure carrying a sign saying "Jed." Molly lifts a daisy from the bunch, snaps off the stem, and puts it in her buttonhole.

The door opens. "How did it go?" Amy walks in.

"Great. Thanks for the flowers."

"Was there a boat? Did you sail?"

"Canoed. I even rocked the boat. What do I need to know?"

Amy hands Molly a stack of papers, a list of phone calls, a schedule. "We've been flying around here. We need you back."

"How's Jed?"

"Working night and day. He's hired some new people—some through Candace. She's here a lot."

"Let him know I'm back."

Molly wades through the papers on her desk. She calls and gets an update from Ellen, interviews an art student for an internship, and works with Angelo. At three o'clock, she wanders to the center room. "Jed in?"

"He's at Keith's. Something on Amtrak. Go on over," Amy says.

Molly walks three blocks and climbs the stairs holding her nose against the smell of subway tunnels in the rain. She opens the door and feels blasted by the yellow color on the walls. The man behind the desk waves, points down the hall. The door is closed. She opens it partway. The room is semidark; there's a crowd. She feels the heads of all the people turn, look at the door, and turn back to the screens in front.

She tiptoes in and takes a seat behind the other chairs. Keith stands in front and talks. The monitors are on. Molly notices the back of Jed's head in the chair in front of her; her stomach quivers. She listens, glancing from the screens to Jed, following his arm and hand that run fingers through his hair. She moves forward on her chair and leans her mouth close to his ear. "Hello, I'm back."

He turns, looks at her, and nods. His arm extends

and hands her papers. She sees him switch his leg, from knee to floor and back to knee again. He pulls his ear. He could have smiled; he could have said hello. He works a lot with Candace, Amy said. That's okay. She looks around the room for coffee. She didn't break up with Porter to have Jed—she works with Jed, that's all.

Keith finishes the talk. People mill about, stand in twos and threes, drink Cokes and coffee, eat donuts, Oreos. Jed's in the corner with a man who works with Keith. She hears the talking: virtual reality, high-definition television.

She moves around the chairs to Keith, who's talking to a man wearing glasses with round wire rims and a sweater full of holes. They talk of CD ROM, fiber optics, multimedia. She listens and watches Jed. He joins the group.

"You have to catch me up on this," Molly says.

"The papers should do it. This stuff is down the line for us. How was Minneapolis?"

"Full of lakes."

"Glad you're back. I've got to run. We'll get together soon."

The week becomes a blur—a frantic blur. On Saturday she moves. By two o'clock it's done; the movers leave. She looks around the loft, steps around the furniture, touches the walls, climbs into the bathtub, then the shower, rolls on the bed. She runs from window to window counting the wooden water towers, peering between the buildings down the alleyways.

Grace arrives at three. "This place is wild. How did you find it? I hate it."

"I love it. It's my artist loft."

"I guess it suits my artist sister." Grace puts her arm around Molly and squeezes. "Porter wants to come and bring champagne and take us out to dinner."

"Perfect. Perfect Porter." She grins.

"He is, Molly."

"For you he is. Let's bombard the boxes. We'll have it done before he comes."

They work all afternoon, tossing wrappings on the floor and stacking dishes and glasses and changing where the glasses go and drinking water and laughing and singing songs from high school.

"Thanks for coming, Grace. I'm glad you're here," Molly says, balancing on a chair, hanging her portrait on an empty nail on a wall between two windows.

"Me too. Molly, I am bursting I'm so happy. You have come to the rescue once again."

"I'm not sure about that. We need to rescue each other."

"What can I do for you?" Grace asks.

"Be there if I fall apart."

"What's wrong?"

"Nothing. My job is great. That's what I want. I wish I didn't . . ."

Grace comes from the kitchen area into the living room. "Something isn't right with you?"

"When I get settled I'll feel better."

"We'll have it done by six o'clock."

"That's not it. It's Jed. I'm jealous."

"Are you in love with him?"

Molly climbs down from the chair. "This place is dusty."

"Are you in love with Jed?"

"No." She screams across the room. "I hate it when I see him with Candace. She was there all day on Friday, in his office. I hate it. I can't work when she is there. It is stupid."

"You are in love with Jed."

"I'm not. I just can't stand her. I can't stand the way she looks, the way she speaks to me. He should find another woman—then I wouldn't be jealous—someone I like."

"Is he in love with you?"

"Of course not. We have a business relationship. At times that can get intense. It doesn't mean—"

"Have you slept with him?"

"Let's finish the refrigerator."

"When did you sleep with him?"

"Where's the garbage? Where do we dump the garbage?"

"Did you do it in Florida?"

"No. We didn't do it in Florida."

"In Connecticut?"

Molly looks at Grace who holds up her pink rubber-gloved hands. "In Connecticut. I wish I never had. I didn't mean to—now it hurts and I am happy and I hurt and it doesn't make sense. Damn, damn."

"You have to tell him how you feel," Grace says.

"It could ruin our relationship. He would feel pressure that has nothing to do with work."

"He slept with you, too. What did he feel?"

"I don't know. Amy saw him afterward and said he looked sad and hurt. I was with Porter and he knew it."

"Does he know about you and Porter?"

"Not yet. It isn't time. I don't want him to think I did it for him. I didn't. I did it for me. He's my business partner, not my boyfriend."

"Are you sure?"

"I don't know, Grace. I don't know."

At seven, Porter rings the buzzer. Molly gives him a tour, they drink champagne and go down to the Green Street Cafe for dinner. They talk about Harlan going to prison.

"It will be good for him. Help him break his addiction."

"Addiction?" Molly asks.

"Cocaine."

"I never knew. Did you?"

"Grace suspected and so did I. I thought I could talk him out of it."

"Does he know about you and Grace?"

"He knows and approves. He wants to come to the wedding."

"He's relieved." Grace says. "He doesn't have to do the divorce and I don't want money. We were never right for each other."

"Like me and Porter."

Porter lifts his wineglass. "I do love you, Molly. I want you to be happy."

"I love you too, Porter, like a brother, like a very good friend, or maybe like an old boyfriend if Grace doesn't mind."

After dinner, they listen to a jazz trio. Porter orders champagne. Molly watches him; his face is lit with smiles. "He lost his smile," his mother said. Molly feels the liquid in her heart. He has it back again.

Molly climbs into the large brass bed and listens: a honk, a voice, the ghosts of old New York, memories seeping through the bricks. She slips out of the bed, and, like a dancer on a stage, she twirls across the floor and stands in patches of the moonlight. The easel's like a mannequin; she covers it. She smells the paint and climbs up on a stool before a slanting sketching table. She draws the moon, balloons, and firecrackers, one single boat with waves and waves and waves. She bends her head and sees the moon, the shadows on the roofs. It could be Paris or Vienna, Budapest. It's not. It's New York, her New York.

On Monday morning at nine o'clock Molly walks into Jed's office. "I guess I better make an appointment if I want to see you. When can we meet?"

"You name it," Jed says.

"Tuesday or Wednesday, late afternoon."

"Wednesday."

"I need a long meeting. Any objections?"

"Whatever it takes."

Tuesday night Molly wanders through Dean and DeLuca picking up crusty bread, a torte of marscapone and blue cheese, imported prosciutto, a container of olives, chewy salami. On the way home, she stops for a bottle of Barolo. Wednesday morning drags; she cannot concentrate. She loses a file, misses an appointment with a client. She tries to walk, to eat. At four-thirty, she takes her files and walks across the center room to Jed. He's on the phone. She stacks the papers on his desk, the drawings on the table. He finishes the call and turns to her.

"What's first?"

"Amtrak."

He hands her pictures. She spreads them across the desk. "What are these?" she says.

"They're from the Smithsonian, train interiors, 1885, 1890."

"Pretty somber people. Where's the fun?"

"They're having fun. They just don't look like it."

"I don't believe you," Molly says.

"They're entrained on the bouncing wheels, the motion across the tracks."

"Sitting there with the clickety-clack?"

"Like a rock concert." He laughs.

"Get real, Jed. What do you want to do with this? Look at these two people. What are they doing?"

"Looking out the window."

"At what?"

"At the passing scene. The passing of reality."

She pushes the pictures at him. "The passing of dreams?"

"The passing of life."

He stands and goes to the window and leans

against the sill. "I've got a new woman, part-time. I'd like you to work with her on this."

"I thought our strength was our ideas together."

"It is but it's a luxury. We don't have time, either you or me."

"Let's talk over dinner. I'm hungry."

He glances at his watch, drums his fingers on the desk.

"It's early, Jed. No excuse. You'll love this place. I promise."

She moves to the door and waits for him. He moves the papers on the desk into a stack. "I thought we were going to work. I'm not hungry. I had a big lunch."

"With Candace?"

"We were discussing her new article and some other things."

"I have other things to discuss, too. I would like to do it over dinner."

"I would rather not . . ."

"If you can eat with Candace, you can eat with me. This is important to me."

"You're insistent. Where are we going?"

"I have a surprise. Trust me. You'll like it."

He reaches for the light and follows her down the stairs. They walk south on Fifth Avenue. The night is warm. The street is like a party: people everywhere, on rollerblades, ambling together with arms around each other, halter tops and cutoff shirts, guys and guys, girls and girls, girls and guys. Jed and Molly walk in silence, dodging in and out around the people, laughing now and then as they bump into each other.

"This is like Epcot except there is no music," Molly says.

"This is real. That wasn't."

Molly digs her hands in her pockets. "Some of it was real."

"Pure fantasy."

"You think all of it was fantasy?"

"Every bit, don't you?"

"I guess so." Molly feels hurt, the way she did when a teacher once made fun of a poem she wrote.

They walk under the Washington Square Arch and into the park and dodge the splashers running and jumping and leaping from the fountain. Jed grabs Molly's hand and steers her from two bathing-suited children throwing water out of plastic cups.

"How are my flowers in Connecticut?" she asks.

"I don't know. I haven't been there."

"They're probably covered with weeds or dead from no water."

"Probably," he says. "How much farther to your secret restaurant?"

"Six blocks. It's below Houston. The food is so-so but the atmosphere is dynamite." Her palms are moist.

"I'm beginning to feel hungry."

"Good." She laughs. "I'd like to come and weed. I owe you, remember?"

"The garden's fine. Thanks for the offer."

They walk across the cobbled streets and past the

stores with mannequins in silky fabrics. She stops before her door and gets the key.

"Where are we going?" he says, backing into the street.

"You'll see."

"I don't want to meet what's-his-name. We are not talking partnership and that kind of thing, I hope."

"He's not here. He doesn't live here." They stand together in the elevator. Her panic rises with each floor; her heart is hammering. She steps inside. Jed is right behind. The loft feels eerie, lit only by the purple-banded sky. She goes into the middle of the room and lights a lamp that puts a white round circle on the floor and high up on the ceiling. Jed stays back, a foot from where they entered.

"Where are we?" he asks.

"This is my new apartment."

"I thought you said . . . This is where you plan to live when . . . Why did you bring me here?" He pushes the elevator button and the door glides opens. "Let's go. We'll talk another day."

"Wait, Jed, please don't go. I have to tell you something. I have to explain. Will you sit down?"

"Tell me."

"I broke my engagement. I am not getting married."

Jed runs his hand across the back of his neck. He looks at the spot on the ceiling. "You brought me here to tell me that?"

"I thought you should know."

"I'm sorry. I don't know what to say."

"I made a commitment to myself like you said. I'm moving my own digits. Don't you see?"

Jed walks into the kitchen area and back. He turns around and stares at Molly.

"Do you like my new apartment? Isn't it great?"

"When did you move here?"

"Saturday."

"It's nice. Congratulations. Let's go eat."

"I've got some things in the refrigerator. Would you like some wine . . . or beer?"

"Let's go out. There's a pub on the corner."

"Look around first. I've got great cheeses and stuff. I'll get them out."

"Show me around if you want—then we'll go."

She leads him to the back to the easel, the painting area. "It's a sublet. The woman left all this stuff for me to use. Look out the window—the city is fabulous."

"Yep."

She takes him to the bedroom and laughs at the bed. "Isn't it perfect—brass and all?"

"Everything's nice, Molly. Let's get out of here. I think you made a good move."

On the street his pace is fast. Molly walks beside him. She feels like throwing up. She wants to scream. In the pub they sit across the green Formica table from each other. He drinks beer and eats steak fries and chicken. She picks at the ham and turkey in her salad.

"What's the matter, Jed?"

"I was hungry."

"I didn't ask you to my apartment to seduce you.

I didn't split with Porter because of you." She laughs. "I love my new apartment. I wanted you to see it. I want you to know I'm committed only to you and Saunders and Associates. I'm going to start painting again and I may take some classes and—"

"Stop." He wipes his mouth. "The agency is growing—sometimes I think too fast. Your commitment makes me happy. Let me think about it and we'll talk again about your role. Everything you've done is first-class. You are my kind of woman. I want you to know that—the kind of person I like to work with." He picks up the check.

"I meant it when I said I'd like to weed the garden."

He fumbles in his wallet, takes out bills and smooths them on the tabletop. "I haven't been there. The place should be checked. Maybe Saturday, just for the day."

"This Saturday is fine."

He nods. He hands the money to the waitress. "I'll walk you home."

When she opens the downstairs door, he takes her hand and kisses her cheek. "Thanks for dinner and the tour."

Twenty-seven

At ten o'clock Saturday morning Molly sits beside Jed in the little red car. They drive across the Third Avenue Bridge and head north on the Major Deegan Expressway. Molly stretches her legs. "I've missed this car. I missed the smell."

"The smell?"

"The leather smell. The tack room smell, like horses."

"Wash your mouth. This car is not a horse."

"It's a nice smell, a special smell." She fingers the radio knobs, turns, and looks at Jed. His shoulders push back and his neck stretches.

"I haven't been to the house in weeks," he says. "Thanks for pushing me."

"Thanks for going. I haven't been out of the city in weeks. You go all the time."

"I do?"

"To your friends on Long Island." She crosses her leg.

Jed nods and bounces his hand on the gearshift. She stares at it. The movement aggravates her. Pictures roar through her mind of Jed on the beach, gazing from a porch into a sunset with his arm around Candace, holding a bottle of beer and laughing around a table and leaning close to Candace and kissing her mouth. Her breasts ache. She adjusts her legs, uncrossing them, recrossing them. His hand moves to the dashboard, where he drums his thumb. She watches it. His arm is bare. She rubs her hand along her arm. "It's hot," she says.

"And it will get hotter. This isn't a good car for heat."

"It's a good car for driving. I loved driving it."

"You hate sitting there, right?"

"Why do you say that?"

"You seem itchy."

"So do you and you're driving." She slouches into the seat and puts her foot on her knee.

"Maybe we'll come back after dark when the sun is down."

She pictures being in the house at dusk, seeing the sun descend through the trees. She reaches under her sandal and scratches her foot. "How do you suppose those trains in the pictures smelled?"

"Like cigars."

"Cigars?"

"Sure, everybody who rode Pullman smoked cigars."

"Were there no smoking cars?"

"Of course not."

"How about the women and children?"

"They liked it."

"Cigar smell?"

"Why not? It's manly, rugged, a power smell."

"Have you smoked one?"

"Of course."

"Liked it?"

"So-so."

She feels his glance. Her arms stretch toward the windshield. "I'll have to try it sometime," she says.

She watches the road. Perspiration gathers on her neck. The car moves from the middle lane to the left lane and back again. She should have stayed in the city and gone to an air-conditioned movie and bought popcorn. Her stomach feels uneasy. Jed rolls the window down, then rolls it up again.

"What time will we come back?" she asks.

"Depends on when we leave. You need to be back by—"

"Anytime. I have no plans. Do you?"

"No." He bangs the horn. A car cuts in front of him. "They don't see me, stupid drivers."

"Busy tomorrow?" she asks.

"I've got plans."

"I want to explore SoHo. I really like living there. Did you like my loft?"

"It's nice. You can walk to the office. That's nice."

"I like that, too."

Molly riffles through her bag. There are loose coins on the bottom. She hunts around and pulls them out and drops them in a tiny purse. "Going to Long Island?" she asks.

"When?"

"Tomorrow."

"Maybe."

"Candace has a house?"

"She rents."

"The Hamptons?"

"Orient."

"How long does it take?"

"Three hours. I'll leave early."

Molly leans her head against the seat. Her eyes close. She squeezes them. She laces her fingers and presses them back until they hurt and lifts her foot onto the seat and wraps her arm around her knee. She doesn't want to weed. She wants to go back to the city.

"My sister is marrying Porter."

"I thought she was married."

"She's getting a divorce."

"I'm sorry, Molly. It must be hard for you."

"No, it isn't. I'm glad."

"Glad? Your sister steals your husband and you're glad?"

"What's wrong with that? He's her type, not mine. I broke the engagement. I don't want to be married." She digs inside her pocketbook. "Want a Tic Tac, green or orange?"

"Ever?"

"I like working. Marriage interferes."

"It doesn't have to. It doesn't with Bill and Ellen, Keith and Pamela."

"It would for me. Husbands make demands."

"That's true. They do and you're the independent type. You do what you want. Porter is well out of it. Is your sister like that?"

"No. Besides, she's in love. That makes a difference."

"Weren't you in love?"

"With Porter?" Molly twists her hair behind her ear. "Not really. He's a nice guy."

"Why were you marrying him?"

"I don't know. I had feelings for him. I wasn't numb or anything."

"Marriage is something I think you can't help doing."

"What do you mean?"

"It just happens between two people because they can't help themselves. Don't you believe that?"

Molly pulls at her short cotton shirt. She rubs her bare skin where the shirt meets her shorts. "I don't know." She gnaws along her finger edge. "Is the house nice?" she asks.

"What house?"

"The beach house in Orient. Candace's rental." She sits up and faces him.

"It's just a beach house."

"You go there every weekend? Did she expect you today?"

"What are you asking?"

"I don't know. I've changed my mind. I don't want to weed. I feel sick. Maybe we should go back to the city. You can go to Long Island. It's too hot to weed."

"It's too hot in the car. I'm sorry there is no air conditioner."

"I don't think going to Connecticut was a good idea."

"I thought you wanted to see your handiwork—all those flowers needing your care. There are bushes of them crying out."

"How do you know? You haven't been there."

"I saw them a few weeks ago. If you are hot, take a swim."

"I don't have a bathing suit."

"I'll lend you mine." He laughs.

Molly scratches her knee. "You are not funny. What would I do for a top?"

"We'll find a scarf, a handkerchief."

"A scarf? You are making fun of me."

"I'm not really. The pool is nice."

"I could wear nothing. Seeing me naked is nothing new for you . . . another female body to add to the bunch . . ."

"I'll stay in the house."

"Don't do that. We could have sex after we swim. Isn't that what you do with girls who visit your house?"

"I don't know what you're saying. I'll take you back if you like. Better yet, I'll put you on the bus and you can ride alone."

"You don't like what I'm saying? It's true, isn't it?"

"Do you want to return to the city?"

"Tell me it's true. Amy said it was."

"What did Amy tell you?"

"Never mind."

Jed swerves into a rest area. He parks at the end away from the one other car.

Molly swings open the door and tramps through the grass to the shade of a tree. She listens to the roar of the traffic on the highway. She puts her hands on her ears and looks through the trees, around the parking area for a place to run. She wants to scream.

Jed follows her and yells over the traffic noise. "What did Amy say?"

"That you can't keep your pants on."

Jed bangs his fist in his hand. "I don't believe you." He wipes his forehead and starts back to the car, kicks the grass, and turns around. "Get in the car, I'll drop you at the bus station."

Molly walks away from him, back into the trees. She walks in circles, her eyes sting, her fists burn to punch.

Jed follows her. "Who are you to accuse me? You got in your car and drove away—calmly drove to the bed of another man . . . after—"

"I did not." She takes a step toward him.

"Of course you did, and when you came back you proudly carried a big trophy ring on your finger. What did you do to get that?"

"I hate you, Jed. I hate you." She bangs her head with her hands. "I don't even like your blasted job and all that." She walks around the back side of the tree. "I'm going to leave New York and go to graduate school in Vermont."

"Good. Good for you. Before you leave let me tell you that the most pain I have ever had in my life was on that day." Jed puts his hand against the tree.

"What day? Your two women day? Pain where? How did I feel when I called you, when all I wanted was . . ." Molly turns her back. Sobs wrack her.

"Molly?" Jed leaves the tree and takes her arm. "Are you okay?"

"I'm not sure."

"What's the matter?"

"Jed. I didn't leave. I couldn't leave. I called to come back . . ." The sobs are back.

He puts his arms around her back and rubs between her shoulder blades. "You called my house? When?"

"I called and Amy answered. I hung up."

"You thought—"

"I thought wrong but it was awful. I lived all weekend with thoughts of you with her. I felt like a fool again—a stupid fool misinterpreting what I thought was happening—"

"Wait." He unfolds a handkerchief from his pocket and dabs her cheek. "You misinterpreted . . . ?"

Molly pulls away. "I don't know. I thought that afternoon was something special."

"Molly, it was." He walks in front of her and grabs her upper arms. "My God, Molly it was the most special day in my life . . . until you left . . ." His finger smears a tear on her cheek.

"I hurt you didn't I?" she says.

"You broke my heart."

"No, Jed. I didn't." She finds his hand and holds it to her lips and kisses the front and the back and smooths the hair along his wrist. She runs the back of his hand across her eyes. "I didn't mean to hurt you. I think we hurt each other."

"I thought you didn't care."

"I care so much my heart has been in traction like a wounded lump."

His hand cups her head the way a doctor would a newborn baby and holds it to his cheek. She feels the trembling through his body and his warm lips on the wetness on her face and she turns and meets his lips with hers and she melts and his arms envelope her and his mouth is moist. "Do you forgive me?" she asks.

"And do you forgive me?"

She tangles her finger in his hair. "For what?"

"For loving you. For wanting you. For yearning for you since the day I met you and trying to pretend I didn't."

Molly's legs have turned to cooked spaghetti. "Hold me, Jed. I'm trembling." She swoons into the kisses that are covering her cheeks and eyes. "My mouth, Jed, kiss my mouth and I'll forgive you."

Her eyes close. She's inside all the dreams that plagued her. His tongue and lips are love inside her mouth, inside her being. "Oh Jed," she says, pulling him against her body. "Jed, tell me again."

"Which part?"

"The part about love. Tell me about love."

"I thought I knew about love. Right now I'm not sure. This is . . ." The back of his hand runs across her lips. "I can't tell you. I feel like I've walked into another world."

"Call it paradise."

"The sailboat. Gasparilla. I was afraid." He pulls her tight inside his arms.

She kisses his ear and neck. "We found our secret there. It was love but it felt like pain."

"I was angry. I felt we were destined forever to be apart."

"No, no. Don't say that. Destiny has put us together."

"Shall we go home?"

"Home?"

"Lucy's house. You made it feel like home again for me. It's been waiting for you, asking for you, craving for you. I couldn't go there alone without you."

Molly puts her fingers on his lips. "I've been like that house, waiting and craving."

"Let's go."

He pulls her to the car. She wants to stay and kiss some more. She climbs into her seat and watches as he walks around the other side. The seconds he is out of reach seem endless. He starts the car, she rubs his cheek, his arm, his hand. "How long?"

"Forever."

"No." She wallows for a second in the warmth that floods her. "How long till we are there . . . we are home?"

"Thirty minutes, maybe forty."

"That's too long."

"Too long for what?" He turns and grins at her.

"To wait."

"For what?"

He guns the car into the traffic and over to the left-hand lane. She rests her hand along his thigh.

His fingers touch her fingers and sparks run up her arm.

"For kissing and tasting and feeling my tongue on yours," she says.

He lifts her hand to his mouth, nuzzles his lips inside her palm, and runs his tongue down her open hand to the end of her middle finger. "How's that?"

"You are making my blood . . ." She sighs. "I can't explain."

"Turn red-hot."

She grabs his thumb and drags it to her lips and puts it in her mouth and sucks it and strokes his palm with her thumb while running his inside her mouth and out again and in again.

"I'm finding it hard to drive with one hand."

"I think you can leave off half that sentence." She laughs and pulls his hand across her breasts.

"You're right. If there were another rest nearby . . ."

"Are you going to Orient tomorrow?"

"Where's that?"

"It doesn't exist."

"It never existed."

"I want to make love to you," she says.

"No kidding. I hope the house is empty?"

"Who would be there?"

"Amy."

"Amy?"

"She has a habit of dropping in."

"She hasn't—"

"No, she hasn't. I'm kidding you."

The car exits the highway and they drive on curving country roads. She puts her finger in his mouth and rubs it on his tongue, then sucks the wetness from it. "I have no bathing suit."

"I know."

"Can I borrow yours?"

"No. Besides, I've already seen you naked. It's nothing special."

She pulls her shirt up to her chin and relaxes back against the seat.

"What are you doing?"

"Nothing special."

"Are you showing the whole world."

"What else can I do in a car without air-conditioning?"

She watches him drive, both hands on the wheel, his head facing forward on the road. She glances down his body to his jeans. Her bare breasts, her legs, her whole body jolts at the spot she finds and watches and thinks about. "Do you wear a bathing suit?"

"Sometimes."

"Is the water warm?"

"If it isn't, it will be. My body will make it boil." He reaches and runs his hand on her bare nipples. "It will be like silk and honey." He smiles at her. "Like you."

"Jed, I can't wait."

"For what?"

"To swim in the pool."

She hears the car hit the gravel driveway. "Who's that?" She sees a truck and pulls down her shirt.

"I don't know." He laughs.

"You do too. Tell me."

"Looks like pool maintenance."

He leaves the car and comes around to her side. He reaches down and lifts her out and bites her breast. "What are you doing?"

"Getting back at you." She pushes herself against him and feels his buckle dig into her skin. The truck door opens; a man emerges. Jed moves away, flips the keys to her, and walks toward him . She watches the two shake hands and walk together behind the house.

She takes her bag and picks her way across the path to the front door. Inside, it smells of must and heat. She stands in the hallway, gazing into the living room, smiling at it as though greeting an old friend. She runs her hand across the sofa back, pats the chair and the banister of the stairs. She walks through the kitchen and out the door and down between the flower beds. The flowers smell of pepper and soft dirt. The air is hot. She picks and hums and watches down the grass for Jed. She sees him from the corner of her eye, come up behind her. She backs until she feels his arms around her, his lips along the creases of her neck, his fingers moving on her breasts. She hears the truck make crunches on the gravel.

"I'll get towels and meet you at the pool," Jed says.

Through the grass she goes, inside the picket fence and to the pool, carved in among the rocks, dark and looking like a tiny lake. She sees him walking toward her and her yearning screams and makes her stand immobile.

"What do you think?"

"I think you're wonderful."

Her breasts feel round and beautiful beneath his touching fingers.

"These nothing-special breasts are wonderful." She watches the softness of the hair along his arms and looks at him and smiles.

Her fingernail traces the smoothness of his hand, and runs up and through the hair that meets his wrist. She runs her nail around the hand that has the fingers on her breast, and the fingers that move below her breast, undo her shorts, and round the skin below her waist. She holds her breath. She runs her hand along his arm, the taut muscle of his arm that reaches with his hand to push away her shorts and find the place where skin is covered with dark hair and his fingers in that hair and her fingers in the hair that lies across his arm. She watches his hand and his fingers and the place below her belly and she gasps.

Her gasp is covered by his lips, his taste—a taste she craves. She moves her tongue to taste and feel the moisture in his mouth. She leans into the kiss and grasps the muscles on his arms and tastes the inside of the lips, and tongue. Her hands seek his body, his clothes. Taste his tongue and push away the clothes. Taste and touch the hair below his waist—the hair that matches hers—the hair she wants to feel against her own.

"I'm drowning in your mouth," she says.

"Come drown with me inside the pool and let me drown in you." He lifts her and carries her and nuzzles into her belly with his face. She nips his arm and smells him. She is a virgin being carried to the altar for a ritual, a sacrifice. She is spread across his arms and he takes her down the wide pool steps and through the water and lets her go. She floats. The water's warm, like cream. He dives below and up between her legs and kisses places that she cannot see, places that throb and glow and glisten. She is lying on the water dying, hoping they will drown together. She wants to drown with him. To become the water and explode together with him in the water, with the mermaids. She swoops under and holds her breath and finds the part of him she craves and takes it in her mouth to make it part of her.

She surfaces and finds his mouth and wraps her legs around his waist and listens to his moans and listens to his heartbeats and plays her tongue along his cheek and in his mouth. She floats with him. She pulls him with her legs and leads him to the steps and rolls on top of him and runs her hands across him and her tongue and mouth and hears his words of love. She spreads the towel on the grass, lies face up on it. He stands above her, dripping water.

"Hurry," she says.

"There is no hurry. This is our life. You are my love. Call it paradise."

"You are paradise."

She feels his lips start at her toes and move by

inches up her legs. She feels the blood drain from her arms. She feels his mouth in places that put blushes on her face. No moisture in her mouth; wild beats pounding in her breast. She feels his mouth close to her own, warm breath, his eyes, falling in her eyes, falling as his body slips, his body joins. One—locked as one—no boundaries. Heartbeats, thumping, thumping, hers, his, one heart, one beat, her breath, his breath, breathing, gasping, gasps, one flight, eyes locked, the thunderclap, lightning flash, bursts, booming, soaring, one sun, one sky, one joy.

Paradise.

WATCH AS THESE WOMEN LEARN
TO LOVE AGAIN

HELLO LOVE   (4094, $4.50/$5.50)
by Joan Shapiro

Family tragedy leaves Barbara Sinclair alone with her success. The fight to gain custody of her young granddaughter brings a confrontation with the determined rancher Sam Douglass. Also widowed, Sam has been caring for Emily alone, guided by his own ideas of childrearing. Barbara challenges his ideas. And that's not all she challenges . . . Long-buried desires surface, then gentle affection. Sam and Barbara cannot ignore the chance to love again.

THE BEST MEDICINE   (4220, $4.50/$5.50)
by Janet Lane Walters

Her late husband's expenses push Maggie Carr back to nursing, the career she left almost thirty years ago. The night shift is difficult, but it's harder still to ignore the way handsome Dr. Jason Knight soothes his patients. When she lends a hand to help his daughter, Jason and Maggie grow closer than simply doctor and nurse. Obstacles to romance seem insurmountable, but Maggie knows that love is always the best medicine.

AND BE MY LOVE   (4291, $4.50/$5.50)
by Joyce C. Ware

Selflessly catering first to husband, then children, grandchildren, and her aging, though imperious mother, leaves Beth Volmar little time for her own adventures or passions. Then, the handsome archaeologist Karim Donovan arrives and campaigns to widen the boundaries of her narrow life. Beth finds new freedom when Karim insists that she accompany him to Turkey on an archaeological dig . . . and a journey towards loving again.

OVER THE RAINBOW   (4032, $4.50/$5.50)
by Marjorie Eatock

Fifty-something, divorced for years, courted by more than one attractive man, and thoroughly enjoying her job with a large insurance company, Marian's sudden restlessness confuses her. She welcomes the chance to travel on business to a small Mississippi town. Full of good humor and words of love, Don Worth makes her feel needed, and not just to assess property damage. Marian takes the risk.

A KISS AT SUNRISE   (4260, $4.50/$5.50)
by Charlotte Sherman

Beginning widowhood and retirement, Ruth Nichols has her first taste of freedom. Against the advice of her mother and daughter, Ruth heads for an adventure in the motor home that has sat unused since her husband's death. Long days and lonely campgrounds start to dampen the excitement of traveling alone. That is, until a dapper widower named Jack parks next door and invites her for dinner. On the road, Ruth and Jack find the chance to love again.